She'd waited a

Trey Henry!

Nessa moved to the center of the alley and rubbed palms that were suddenly wet and sticky on her thighs. She could feel her heart pounding clear up between her eyes. She relaxed her shoulders and thought: Well, all right.

"Trey Henry!"

Henry stopped and shook himself like a hound rising from a nap. "Me?" When she nodded, he retraced his steps and his spurs—the kind with spiked rowels that scar—jingled like bells.

She pointed at him. "Hold it right there." He did. "Now." She parted the air with her hand. "Go on an' draw."

He glanced behind him and then steepled his fingers on his chest. "Me?"

"Yes, you. Trey Henry! You . . . you murderer! Horsethief!" Rage shook her. "Child despoiler . . . an' cold-blooded . . . godless fiend." She licked her lips and tasted spit. She took a steading breath. "Draw or I'll shoot you like a snake!" She could see the beginning of fear in his eyes. Then he made a slight move and she shot him three times before she could stop herself.

It happened that fast. I sort of remember walking to him and looking down. I must've stepped over him then but I don't remember. Not getting on my horse. Not riding out of town.

Had he gone for his gun?

Don't know. Can't remember. Don't care.

WHILE THE RIVERS RUN

Wynema McGowan

Pinnacle Books
Kensington Publishing Corp.

PINNACLE BOOKS are published by

Kensington Publishing Corp.
850 Third Avenue
New York, NY 10022

Pinnacle and the P logo Reg. U.S. Pat. & TM Off.

First Printing: October, 1996

Printed in the United States of America
10 9 8 7 6 5 4 3 2 1

To my agent,
Elizabeth Cavanaugh

Prologue

Texas Hill Country, 1923

The rooster came first, like always, then the clink of metal on glass, the sound of soft-soled shoes on wood. The old woman moaned and pulled in her neck. But then soon from the kitchen there came the low murmur of voices and the creak of a floorboard in the hall and she whispered, "Balls!" Why couldn't she do it? Damn near everybody else could. Indians. Animals. Even her own mother.

She hadn't understood about her mother back then. But she sure did now. Oh, yeah. Had ever since the day Tom died. Only nothing happened. She just kept right on losing . . . memory, vision, hearing, teeth, the predictability of her bowels. She was eighty-seven. "For pity's sake . . ." she muttered and opened one eye. Dust motes danced in a shaft of sunlight beneath the window. A haunting breeze swirled the curtains, and the smell of cut grass mingled with the fragrance of the climber twining on the trellis. Honeysuckle and horse manure. The Hellangone.

The screen door slammed. Two bodiless heads bobbed by belonging to her great grandson Kyle and Tom A. Hawk. They paused for a minute while Kyle squared his hat and pulled on his work gloves. Then a third head appeared, grizzled and gray, and there came a sudden burst of laughter.

The old woman smiled along. Crazy ol' . . . ol' . . . Why, she couldn't remember the third fella's name! The foreman of The Hellangone for over forty years, Tom A. Hawk's grandfather and a man whose name she knew as well as her own. *Damnit if that's what I don't do all the time now.*

That's just about enough. It's time. Way past time, as a matter of fact. Well? What about the river? It's handy. Bloodless. She saw herself, sprawled on the bank, limp and sodden, a pathetic little kitten, and she rolled her lip. No.

Well, all right then. A stiff rope and a short drop? She shook her head. Even less appealing. She'd been an unwilling witness to a hanging once. Better a sodden kitten than a human fruit with dirty drawers.

What about . . .

A workman walked passed the window, a small man with an air of importance and his pants screwed up to his armpits. *Who the hell is that?* She struggled to place him and finally did. The stump remover. That's right. She'd been warned lest the explosion alarm her.

Well, now. Is this a well-timed opportunity? She considered the petit point leaves in the wallpaper and the questions. Should she scurry out there and snitch a stick?

The thought of her offspring on ladders with spatulas brought a smothered cackle. Followed by spine-stiffening words.

Let's see. A knife? No. God, no! She'd been faced with the prospect of cutting her own throat once. Believe-you-me, that's a task much easier said than done.

All right then. A gun. That'd be the easiest. The ranch house was full of firepower. Racks of rifles and shotguns lined the walls in the office. Often times a carbine was carelessly propped in the corner nearest the back door. She held up one pincerlike hand, good only for making duck shadows on a wall. Well, she might handle a pistol. Maybe. "I can sure give it a shot." She chuckled and then shook her head. *You are crazy as a bedbug.*

All right, a revolver then. But not just any ol' gun. My own gun.

God, that's mushy! an inner voice declared.

It's my death, she argued, *I guess I can use any gun I damned well please.*

She hadn't seen her pistol for fifty years. Was it in that old trunk? Probably. Yeah, that's where it is all right. In with all that other old stuff, Tom's guns, her mother's things, the journal and the . . .

She jerked like she'd been shot. Her heart hammered against her ribs and the ever-present ache in her chest sharpened.

Dear God! The journal!

For a long time she lay perfectly still, taking in air through her teeth. Soon as the room quit spinning, she sat up and threw off the quilt and swung her legs over and picked up the bell on her bedside table. She rang it shoulder to elbow like a schoolteacher. The door flew open and Rebecca skidded in.

"Gran'ma! You all right?" Becky had the O'Connor coloring. Crow black hair. Blue, almost translucent eyes.

"Don't worry. I could scarcely be croaking and ring the bell like that."

"You like t' scare me to death," Becky pressed one hand dramatically to her breast.

She stood, aided by her cane and the sure knowledge that she could forget her purpose in a heartbeat. "Help me get dressed, sugar."

"Sure, I will! I'll be right back . . ."

"Please help me now, Becky. I'm in a terrible hurry."

"Why? You haven't even eaten your breakfast yet."

Her great-granddaughter was an engaging child but a mite pushy. She might yet outgrow it, as she had other things. She used to whine like a cross-bred hound. "I'm not hungry, Becky. I want you to run catch Tom for me before he leaves."

"Tom, Gran'ma?" Becky asked kindly.

She bent her head. "Oh, Becky, there I go again. Kyle. I meant to say Kyle."

Becky smiled winningly. "Won't I do, Gran'ma?"

"Not this time, sugar. Please ask Kyle to come in. Soon as I get presentable."

"Well, all right. I best hurry then."

"Oh, sugar?"

"Yes?"

She pointed to a vase of yellow jonquils. "Thank you for the flowers."

"You're welcome, Gran'ma."

A few minutes later she was dressed and seated in her rocker next to the window. It was a bright May day but she was seeing stars.

Some time ago—she never noticed exactly when—the simple ability to take a seat had left her. From force of habit she'd confidently point her rear at a chair. Descending fast, she'd remember. *Too late.* Her body would topple backward, her feet would fly skyward and she'd land as if she'd been dropped from a ten-story building.

Kyle strolled in, cock of the walk. "Hey, good-lookin'!"

Kyle took after his great-grandfather. Same lean physique. Same way of carrying himself.

He had that same side-eyed here-comes-trouble look as well. She smiled. Oh, she remembered that look. Oh, yeah. He bent to kiss her cheek and favored her with the smell of horses, leather and sun-struck air.

"Want me for somethin', Gran'ma?"

"Yes, please, Kyle. What's it like outside?"

"Warm, but not hot. Little breeze. Nice. Why?"

"Would you take my rocker outside for me? I want to sit down by the river."

"Sit by the river?" His brows converged. "Did Doc Lockert say that was all right?"

"Lockert doesn't know his butthole from a knothole. Three years ago he said I had less than a week to live. Three years!" She jabbed a crooked finger at him. "I ask you . . . just . . . just look at me!"

"Why, I am lookin' at you, Gran'ma. You look all right to me."

"You know what I mean!"

"Yeah, well, I don't know, Gran'ma. What if you catch a chill or . . . you know?"

She threw him a disgusted look. He gave her a narrow-eyed one back then he laughed. "All right."

"One other thing. You know that old trunk of mine?"

"Old trunk?"

"The one that belonged to my mother."

"Yeah, I guess so."

"Fetch it down from the attic, will you?" He was giving her another measuring look. "I just want to go through some of my things . . ."

He held up a hand. "Hey, you're the boss. Where's it at?"

"Somewhere up there. I haven't seen it . . . *since the day Tom died* . . . for years."

"You want me to put it out yonder. Under the oak?"

"Yes. Please."

"All right. What goes first."

"The rocker."

She watched from the window as, under Becky's direction, the rocker was placed in the sun just so and then the trunk positioned next to it. "There," she whispered and turned.

She was waiting, cane planted and legs spraddled for balance, when her eye fell on a slightly askew tintype. She shuffled to it and bent and plumbed it. Then she looked at it, something she hadn't done in a while.

The picture had been taken as she handed Teddy Roosevelt the reins of a prize Hellangone quarter horse. They were standing on a banner-strewn platform. Roosevelt's train was in the background. The space between the platform and the train was crowded with people, shouting and waving. The wind had glued a swath of hair over her lips. Saying it was a toss up as to whose 'stache had the most dash, Tom had had the picture framed. She always swore she'd get rid of it first chance she got, but she could never bring herself to touch that picture after Tom died. Because he had.

Kyle appeared in the doorway, brushing cobwebs off his denims. "Well, you ready?"

"Yes."

"Here you go then."

Funny how she would remember little things that happened years back and yet couldn't recall what she'd had for breakfast. Or even if she'd had it yet!

When Kyle picked her up she flashed on the first time she'd been carried over the threshhold. Then a day eight months later popped into her mind with sudden clarity. Splay-footed in order to accommodate a hundred-pound stomach, she had been sitting in the kitchen husking corn. She heard one of the hands ask after her. Then she heard Tom tell the man she was bigger'n a bull but not as congenial. She tossed an ear of corn out the window and beaned him square on the back of the head.

Kyle strode down the hallway, passed the familiar etchings of prize quarter horses, passed an oval portrait of Etta Cutter above a three-sided table, passed a very poorly tatted runner . . . "Lordy, I can see my mistakes from here."

"What, Gran'ma?"

"I said, doesn't anything ever get thrown out around here?"

"Oh, no, ma'am. Not unless you say so."

She made a mental note . . .

Kyle paused in the kitchen where Prairie Wind was rolling out pie dough. A young girl sat on a high stool at the sink destringing green beans.

Prairie Wind was full blood Cherokee, Tom A. Hawk's grandmother, the Hellangone cook, her dearest friend. She knew all that, cold. *But who in the sam hill is that girl?* The girl flashed a smile that it hurt to look at without squinting and said, "Buenos días, Señora."

Balls! "Buenos días to you too, ah mm . . ."

"Rita," Kyle supplied while staring at the girl steady. "Cómo está, Rita?"

Wind's niece! That's right. *How could you forget?*

"Buenos días, Rita." My but she's lovely! Black hair. Black eyes. Skin the color of a brand-new penny. Appears to be fidgety though. Maybe she's high-strung. Yes. Must be. Too bad.

Wind pointed a flour-covered finger at her. "Where do you think you're goin'?"

Everybody's a boss. "Well, I'm gonna go get some fresh air. If that's all right with you." She smiled to soften her sarcasm—which was sometimes sharp enough to shave with—and changed the topic. "That sure looks good. What's for supper?"

"Chicken-fried steak, garden beans and mashed potatoes. Dessert's gonna be rhubarb pie."

"Mm, good."

Wind pointed again. "Don't tell me 'Mm, good' when you ain't got the appetite of a pissant . . ."

"Say?" Kyle shifted his feet. "Hawk's waitin' on me."

"Well, go on! Ya ain't nailed down, are ya?"

He laughed. "No, ma'am. I guess I ain't." Before he backed out the door he paused long enough to say, "See you tonight, Rita."

"Well!" she said, as Kyle clomped across the gallery.

"Well, what?" he countered, descending the worn wood steps.

"Nothing. Just . . . well."

They passed the old well and the paddock—two men stopped forking hay and touched their hats—then they crossed the long expanse of bermuda grass. Like a ring bearer at a fancy wedding, Becky brought up the rear, carrying her shawl and a lap quilt folded on a small pillow.

"What's that pillow for?"

"For your back," Becky replied. "Yesterday you said your back was troublin' you somethin' awful."

"I did? Huh!"

Once seated she proclaimed herself warm enough and comfortable enough and lacking only youth. Still they stayed. Kyle cocking and uncocking his hip. Becky eyeing her like she was a snake egg. "Well? What?" Trying to be cordial, but so impatient to have at it!

"Are you sure you'll be all right?" Becky asked.

"Fine. Just fine. Y'all go on about your day."

"I'll bring you some iced tea in a bit. How'd you like that?"

"Fine. That'd be fine."

"Maybe you'd rather lemonade. Would you rather lemonade?"

"Either'd be . . . fine. Now, please!" She waved. "Scat!"

She watched them walk back to the house. My, but they're good lookin'! Tall. Straight. Long-legged. Kyle peeled off toward the barn. Becky shot a calculating look over her shoulder at her but she smiled and waved and at last Becky closed the screen door behind her.

Well. She took a deep breath and glanced around. Sunlight was reflecting off the river like fool's gold. Cows were lowing over the rise. She leaned her head back. The live oak was immense, casting shadows yards from its trunk. What a fine place to die!

A soft wind stirred the old oak's leaves. A mockingbird was up there somewhere. Faded blue eyes searched and searched and then . . . they closed. Her mouth dropped open and . . .

Dynamite rocked the ground beneath her feet.

Lord, she looked around. She'd almost dozed off! That

would not do. Not at all. She sat up, patted her hair and wiped her mouth. Well, all right. She extended a shaky hand and opened the trunk. Oh, God! It was *his* smell. Just a whiff. Just for a second. Her throat closed. She tugged on a scratched and worn cowhide vest and held it to her face and rocked. Her vision shimmered and a sob broke. She laid the vest on her lap—Lordy, it's so heavy!—and fumbled up her sleeve for her handkerchief.

After a while she took a steadying breath and tucked the handkerchief away. This will be the hard part. She'd known that. It was exactly why she had packed up all these things to begin with. She smoothed the vest's side seam, touched a curled edge, and whispered, "Tom."

Everything and everybody had tried to best them. Floods, blizzards, tornados, brush fires, droughts, Comanches, Kiowas, Comancheros, garden-variety cattle rustlers, horse thieves and bushwackers. Hell, they'd stood them all off, she and Tom.

And here she was, about to set herself off again!

She watched a red-tailed hawk circling idly overhead and after a bit, she was able to go on. She removed her mother's patchwork quilt and set it in the lid of the trunk. A fold slipped to the grass, skirting the lid with vivid color. Leaning slowly forward, she peered inside.

Everything was there. Pa's stemwinder. Ma's button box with the mother-of-pearl top. Tom's pocket knife and his bowie. Squashed saddle bags. A Colt Peacemaker. Etta Cutter's Bible. A lace mantilla. She fingered a braided riata and then touched it to her cheek. It smelled faintly of sweat.

"Yes, we have no bananaaaas." The senseless words came floating across the yard at her. Somebody in the kitchen was singing along with that little Atwater Kent radio. "We have no bananas todaaaay."

She wasn't sure what to do. A part of her wanted to call those two kids back outside and grill them like steaks. Do you know whose Bible that is? Do you know who smoked that soapstone pipe? What about that dog collar? Surely you recall the story behind those two lances! *And whose fault is it if they don't remember?*

"Mine," she whispered, "all mine."

All right. I can fix that. I will fix that. Soon as I fix the journal.

Learning about their forebearers' physical appetites wouldn't be so terrible. After all, dead is dead. But that their great-grandmother was personally responsible for the death of three men? That she'd shot the only man she'd ever loved? No, that wouldn't do at all.

There was a packet of ribbon-tied letters—mostly from herself—which she set aside for later. She moved a box of carbine shells and finally there it was, clear at the bottom in a mass of lint and dust. She lifted it out and blew dust off the black pebbled cover and then she simply held it for a while, the sun warm on thin and bloodless hands.

Well, all right. I'm ready. Opening the journal, she began to read the words she'd written seventy eight years before. *My naim is Vanessa Cutter. This is my Jernal. It is jenuwine cowhyde. My father's naim is Nate and my mother's Naim is Alma. I am nine. To day is Christmas Day 1845.*

From the beginning she read a line here and there. Amazing what she'd thought momentous! A six-toed kitten, a trip to San Antone. My, the simplicity of life back then. Quilting, canning, cleaning and cooking with her mother. Tracking, hunting, trapping and shooting with her father.

12th of February 1848—Last nite Ma asked Pa Can she shoot? Nessa recalled that she had been in the bedroom, all ears.

"About as good as me," her father had replied.

Then her mother said, "I wish you wouldn't curse in front of her. You know she tries to do everything like you."

"Curse? I didn't realize I had."

"You must've. I had to get on her for saying *balls.*" Her father chuckled and then her mother added, "She asked me 'How come *balls* is bad and *ball* isn't?'"

There was another deep chuckle and her father said, "She'll figure it out. She's sharp as mustard, that girl."

11th of March 1848—My father was Buryed yesterday. I felt Like I wood die my Self from the hurt But it is ma Who is reel sik now. She just sits. Staring. Staring. Won't spek. Won't sleep. Won't do nothing.

Her mother was dead within the week. People said because she'd lost her only reason to live. Nessa had felt forsaken. *Didn't she love me, her onle daughter? Cood not she live For me?*

20th of April 1848. (She remembered that time like it was yesterday.) *It's just me and Aunt Etta now.* A little while later she wrote—*I figure I will strik Out on my own soon. No sence in me staying here and being a berden on Aunt Etta. I figure I will Take a job Trailing catle to Kansas or may Be get work As a scout for the arme.* She recalled that she gave serious thought to buffalo hunting but *only if presst into it.* She'd always hated to kill any living thing unless it was for food.

Yet not too much later she had killed a human being.

More than one. Tracked them down and executed them in cold blood and with no regret.

Some might find that hard to figure. Hell, there was a time when she'd had difficulty with it herself.

She touched an ivoried lace mantilla which had belonged to her father's half-sister, Etta Cutter and smiled. Etta Cutter. Now there was a woman of uncut grit.

Along with unconditional love Etta Cutter gave her niece an opinion on about every subject imaginable. She also taught her to hate liars or unkindness or cruelty in any form. "It is possible," Etta once said, "for a person to be hard without being mean. Strive for that."

Pages of tranquil years passed. Then when she was seventeen there was a brief reference about a new hired hand named Bob Fane. Within weeks the words *Bob Fane Kist me!* were written big and underlined. After a six-month courtship—of sorts—they were married.

Her wedding night was less than idyllic, Bob being as inexperienced as she was. He must've sensed her disappointment. (Or maybe he was disappointed himself.) "It'll get better," he'd promised, "I'll get the hang of it."

With Etta's wedding gift of two thousand acres—and over her protestation about their living so far apart—she and Bob built a cabin nine miles upriver from the big house.

10th of May 1855 . . . We took Sunrise over To Aunt Etta's to Day. She acts fit but I feel better noing that Aunt Etta and Sanchez are Keeping an eye on her.

Nessa closed her eyes, unable to turn the next page. Some things might dim with age. Obviously clawing hatred did not. Why, here it was practically seventy years later and she was trembling hard enough to hear her tiny double-hoop earrings.

Nothing that went before prepared her for what happened that day. In a heartbeat her home and hope for happiness was destroyed, her destiny irreversibly altered. Bound by every rule of conduct she'd ever learned she became obsessed with one thing only: exacting retribution. Although she had little chance of succeeding, it was a responsibility willingly shouldered.

Oddly enough, it was one that she almost seemed to have been waiting for.

One

11th of May 1855—Summer's here. It is onle noon but All ready it is hot as Hades and bone dry. It rayned over nite–finalle–but it did Not amount to much. The wild grass around This place is still as brown as a Butter milk biskit. Bob is working on The well.

Nessa was making soap, a chore she hated. She set aside the basin of wood-ash lye and coarse lard and, wiping her hands on her apron, walked over to the edge of the well. The sky was overcast. She could barely see Bob. "What do you think? About twenty feet?" she asked.

He passed his arm across his brow. "Yeah. Won't be long now. I'm starting to get mud."

"That's encouraging." Something warm and wet pushed into her palm. Leaning close to the chunky little calf, she whispered "Shoo! Go on, now, git! Oh, all right." She licked her fingers and stuck them into the salt in her pocket and let the calf lap it off. Wanting more, the calf bawled once. She muzzled it but not quick enough.

"Nessa!"

"What?"

"Are you hand-feedin' that calf again?"

"Nuh-uh."

"Are you?"

"No."

"I tole you about makin' a pet outa that calf."

"I know. I said I'm not. C'mon up now and we'll have dinner."

"All right," he said and she heard the sound of his pickax hitting shale. "Shit!" he said.

She giggled and herded the calf toward the barn before she hurried into the cabin. There she sliced two apples, buttered two pieces of bread and put three pieces of cold fried chicken on a plate. Slinging a sacking towel over her shoulder and holding the plate of food in one hand and a jar of cool water in the other, she walked to the door just as Bob's old hound dog, Dot, let out a sharp bark that ended abruptly.

Curious but not alarmed, she stepped outside. A hand grabbed the front of her shirt. The plate of food and the jar flew as she was spun around. Bob was on the ground. His lip was bloody. A man with a high-crowned feathered hat had his knee on his chest. She saw the downward sweep of a knife. Heard a horrible sound like water over rocks. The man jumped back. Blood spurted. Bob grabbed his throat with both hands and looked at her in amazement—and died.

She ran but one of the men stuck out his foot and tripped her. She fell and rolled onto her back and looked up. Time stopped. Everything got still.

The breed leaned over and wiped his knife on Bob's denims. The bearded one looked at her with glarey eyes like a wild horse. She crabwalked backward until she met with wet sticky fur.

The bearded man threw his hat on the ground—he was bald as a skinned onion above the ears—and untied the rope holding his pants. The breed spoke gutturally. The bearded man grunted and laughed and dropped his pants.

She came into a crouch then. Blocked from the house and the carbine, she thought to try for the shed where there must be something . . .

A slight man/boy came out of the barn leading Bob's Morgan. "Hey, will ya look at this danged horse? A danged sodbuster!"

"You look at his horse. I'm lookin' at his woman."

"Damn!" The young one noticed her then and started over, pulling the dancing horse behind him. "I tole ya! Didn't I tell ya?"

The bearded man held up his hand. "Now jes' hold on there, kid. Is it gonna be the horse or first go at the poon? Ya got t'call it." He talked slow, as if the other one was mentally lacking.

While the young one considered the question, she thought: Now! and tensed to run.

The breed stepped on her hand. He smiled at her and wagged his knife. Then he put his weight behind his foot and ground down. A stone split her palm.

"Both!" the young one said and smiled as if he'd achieved something. A teardrop of drool glistened on his bottom lip.

The bearded man shook his head. "Nuh-uh. They ain't good fer nothin' after yer done. If you get first go, Ladino gets the horse."

"The hell ya say!"

"We done already talked about this. Jes' the other day."

"I ain't agreed t'nothin'."

"Well, you did." The bearded man showed his teeth. They were corn yellow and square as dice. "Lookit. Why not keep the horse 'n' take seconds? Hell, I'm jes' gonna git her good 'n' oiled for ya." He looked at her. "Lookit how she's a-eyein' me. She's jes' beggin' fer it. Ain't ya?"

She fought. Punched, kicked and scratched. But the other two held her for the bald man. He was kneeling between her legs polishing his thing with spit when somehow she jerked loose and hit him square in the nose. Blood spurted and he put a hand to his face and swore. She kicked and connected and she was up and running. She tripped, tried to regain her balance and somersaulted into the well. There was blinding pain and a big sunburst and then nothing.

She came to slowly. A knife twisted in her shoulder but some instinct kept her from crying out. She looked up through mud-snarled hair and saw three silhouettes above her. One of them held a rag to his nose. "Thnit!" he said and then stared into the rag.

The young one said, "How'd she get away like that?"

"Suppose you tell me how she got away? Right when I'm fixin' to poke her? I'll tell you how. Because ya let her loose! Didn't ya? Ya jealous little whore!"

Two of the three heads disappeared but one remained. The half-breed judging from the feather in his hat. She held her breath but her teeth were clacking like knitting needles. He straightened then abruptly he leaned over her again . . . *Oh God! Oh God!* . . . but then he spat and was gone, too.

An undetermined period of time passed. She heard sounds of destruction, dishes breaking, wood splintering. She smelled smoke. Once she heard the kid say, "Keep yore dirty paws offa that horse, Ladino." Drowsy and feverish, she lost all awareness again.

When she woke it was quiet as a grave—which was exactly what the well would be if she couldn't get out. How, though? The knotted rope Bob had used to climb in and out lay tangled on top of her. She could move her legs all right but when she tried to move her arms a sharp pain shot across her back. She rolled to her side and heaved dryly. Afterward she lay dazed and it was a long time before she could bear to move again. She took off her shoes and found the pickaxe. One-handed, she notched a ledge at knee height. Opposite she made another ledge a foot higher. She put her bare foot in one, then in the other, and stood spread-eagled until she could make another ledge. In that manner she worked her way up the wall of the well. Every so often she stopped and listened but she heard nothing. Hours passed. Better than halfway up, she slipped and left two fingernails embedded in the dirt. She landed hard and passed out again.

It must've been nearing midnight when she finally crawled out. She attempted to stand but the earth pinwheeled so bad she stayed where she fell, face down with her toes hooked on the lip of the well.

She woke at dawn. In those first seconds of half awareness, she thought—she hoped—she'd been dreaming. She lifted her head slightly and then screamed—at the turkey buzzard on Bob's face and then at the red pain that came when she tried to pitch a clod of dirt. Wobbling to her feet, she circled the yard in search of something she could use for a cover. She staggered to the cabin and the shambles stopped her cold in the doorway. Everything of value was rent, busted, shot or burned. She found a quilt spared by the fire and pulled it over Bob. But not before she'd seen the noose of crusted blood, his one remaining eye. Fixed. Fly-specked.

Oh God! Bending double, she got sick again.

She kept moving after that, afraid to sit for fear she'd sleep that strange sleep again. What should she do? Her mind was in as much disorder as the farm. Her garden was trampled. The hay was burned, oats scattered to the wind. They'd tried to fire the buildings but were foiled by the previous night's rain. Wandering around, dazed, she found the calf beside the barn. Part of its haunch was hacked off, the bloody ax still embedded in its neck. She pulled the ax out and laid her hand on the calf's nose and started crying, great racking sobs that hurt her back so bad she had to stop or die.

She couldn't manage a sling one-handed so she tucked her hand into her torn shirt and prepared to walk to her aunt's place. They'd taken Bob's horse but at least they did not get hers. Lord, had it only been the day before that she and Bob had taken Sunrise over to her aunt's?

She was ready to leave when the cow appeared, spraddle-legged from a swollen bag and expecting to be milked. "You're lucky you were out roaming around, Judy." She looped a rope around the cow's horns. "Quit your bawling and come along. . . . oh God, don't do that . . . Slow an' easy now. Slow an' easy."

Two

12th of May—Girding my self, I started out. I kept my mind Free and thought only of puting one foot in front of The other. Not of The devastashun I had left behind. It was nine miles To Aunt Etta's. Nine bone jaring miles.

Clothes cut off her, Nessa was cocooned in a blanket except for her arm—which was twisted back behind her like a bird's broken wing. She could hear her aunt moving around, getting ready and didn't want to think about what was coming. "If that cow moo'ed one more time I'd've taken a rock to her."

"I 'magine. Gawd, girl! Ya ought t'see these here colors. Rust 'n' blueberry. That part there's likely t'turn a right purty cornflower yalla."

"Aunt Etta!"

"Awright. Well, Sanchez?" Etta braced her foot on the chair.

"Sí. Sí." The Mexican segundo did likewise.

"Git a good grip 'n' hold 'er steady."

"Sí. Sí. Yo tengo."

Nessa concentrated on the big river-rock hearth, the way the steam snaked out of the black bean kettle, up and up, until it curled around the smoke-blackened rafters.

Seemed like she was concentrating a long time. "Heck fire! Aunt Etta!"

"Well, I got to get it just so. They like't tore it plumb off ya."

"You don't have to tell me!"

Etta Cutter was eighty pounds with her boots on. With her tiny bird bones and stature of a ten-year-old, she appeared as delicate as a pansy. In reality she was tougher'n boiled owl.

"This'll hurt."

Nessa got out "It can't hurt much worse'n . . ." before she found out she was wrong.

Later Etta said, "Ya know the odds are ag'in ya." She was rubbing her special linament into Nessa's shoulder, a foul cure-all used on everything from piles to lumbago to screw worms. "This here's a job for a man. An' the bigger the boots the better."

Nessa turned her face but it was seeping in everywhere, coating her teeth and twanging her nose hairs. "I can shoot," she said clench-jawed. "When I find them, that's all I've got to do."

"Hold still! Ya know, it is possible fer a person to be too full of hisself. There's been lots of 'em throughout history. They're often famous but short-lived. Will ya quit fidgetin'! Aw, dern! Now ya made me fergit what I was sayin'. What was I sayin' anyway?"

Nessa sighed. Some things will never change. "People who are too full of themselves."

"Yeah. Some might say they was heroes, but their mamas knowed 'em for what they really were: harebrained idjets." Etta folded her cloth and covered the tin of linament. "Ever' last one of 'em."

"What's your point?"

"My point is: I'm thinkin' maybe ya best let sleepin' dogs lie. Jus' go on. Bury yer dead an' git on with yer life."

Nessa waved a hand in front of her face. "Pa'd turn over in his grave."

"I expect he would at that."

They were silent as each pictured Nate Cutter in her mind. He'd been a big rawboned man who looked plenty rough. And was.

There was unconcealed pride in Etta's voice when she said, "Yer Pa forked a horse better'n any white man I ever saw."

That was a mouthful for Etta Cutter. She was fond of saying that a person who understands horses is a person who understands the meaning of life. "There's somethin' very elemental about a horse," she often said. "I ain't sure what exactly, but I am sure of its existence."

"I wish . . ." Nessa lost control of her lower lip right then and bit it till she could finish, "I sure do wish Pa was here right now."

"They coulda ripped his arms out by the roots. Long as he had breath in his body he'da kept acomin'."

"And God help those fellas when he caught 'em."

Etta snorted. "Nothin' else would. He'da showed 'em what it meant t'get crosswise of a Cutter."

"A lesson they'd've never forgot."

"An' taken with 'em t'hell."

They both felt better after that odd exchange.

Etta loaded and lit her favorite pipe. It was carved out of Cherokee soapstone and given to her by a grateful member of that tribe before the Cutters left Tennessee. "I assume ya've given some thought to Injens? The Comanch' ain't the same as those bead buyers that hang around the fort."

Nessa bridled. As if she didn't know about the Comanch'!

Etta pointed a finger that hooked a hard right. "Don't give me that sassy look a'yourn."

Nessa lowered her eyes, chastened. "Sorry."

Etta returned her doctorin' paraphernalia to its proper place. The tin of cure-all to the mantel. Her knives and scissors to a small wooden cabinet in the pantry. Her aunt was fastidious about her house, her person and her horses but most definitely not in that order. Nessa watched her. She'd have to ask her aunt which horse she should take. If there was one thing Etta Cutter had it was a knowledge of horseflesh. "What makes a good human bein'," she once said, "are the same things that makes a fine horse: Spirit an' endurance an' bones an' o'course ya got t'have keen eyes an' quick responses an' . . ." As a child Nessa had been worried half to death about her surefootedness.

"I never agreed with the way yer Pa did ya. Teachin' ya to handle yerself like he did. It weren't natural fer a girl."

"You were taught how to ride and shoot."

"Not like that. Day after day, poundin' it into ya afore all else. tried to tell him onct." Etta shook her head. "Lordy, I thought yer mama was gonna have a purple hissy. That scar on her forehead got so red it looked like it was fixin' t'bleed."

Nessa said nothing. They both knew why her mother would take on like that. For pretty much the same reason, neither one of them wanted to think about it right then.

"Well," Etta continued, "I cannot tie ya up 'n' keep

ya from it. So, I'll say this: when ya catch up with one of 'em fellas, 'member one thing."

"What?"

"Facin' men like that idn't the same as no Nawleans duel."

"I know."

"Be sure you don't make the mistake of treatin' it like one. When ya see 'em, nail 'em. Backshoot 'em if ya hafta."

"Yes, ma'am."

"Then git."

"Yes, ma'am."

"You'll have t'outguess, outride 'n' outshoot 'em."

"Yes, ma'am."

"Lordy, girl, I'm likely t'worry myself t'death."

"I know you will. I'm sorry."

Their hands met across the table, Etta's cool and paper dry with purple veins the size of garter snakes; Nessa's long and narrow. Except for two tips which had been bandaged into miniature beehives.

"Yer a young girl, ya know. Ya can get yerself another man."

"Like you, Aunt Etta?" Nessa spoke without thinking and as always, she was immediately sorry she had. Etta Cutter had never married but she'd had a beau once. He'd been killed while felling a tree. The accident occurred only days before their wedding. They said she never recovered from it.

"I'll be back before you have a chance to miss me, Aunt Etta."

"I doubt that. I've missed ya ever since ya moved off over there. I tole Bob there weren't no reason for y'all to live clear off over yonder."

No sense rehashing that again. "How's Sunrise?" Nessa asked, craftily changing the subject.

Etta visibly perked up, as she always did when discussing horses. "Big as a horse." Nessa waited while Etta cackled at her own joke. "She's got to be carryin' double. I bet Sanchez a nickel on it."

"Soon do you think?"

Etta nodded. "Sometime this week."

"I had hoped to help."

"Ya can. Ya still can."

Nessa adjusted her arm in the sling Etta had fashioned and shook her head.

Etta sighed and gave up. "Well, I'll have Sanchez fetch ya a good horse. Provided he's done milkin' that cow. He probably ain't. He's gettin' slow as molasses." She hobbled to the door and hollered, "Sanchez!" To Nessa she said, "Ol' coot's deaf as a door, you know."

Nessa thought: He'd have to be, for her aunt had a set of lungs that allowed her to be heard in Via Acuna.

Etta waited at the door, grumbling about Sanchez, ". . . gettin' so derned old he ain't hardly no use a'tall. I'm fixin' t'tell him he's got t'leave his duties t'others."

Nessa had heard such talk before but her aunt was all wind and no weather. Besides being her oldest friend, Hector Sanchez was her aunt's right-hand man. What Sanchez didn't know about horses had not yet been discovered. He shuffled in a minute later.

"Sanchez, we got to go over an' bury Bob."

"Sí, sí!" He turned his watery eyes on Nessa "Qué lástima, señora!"

"Gracias, Sanchez."

"Ain't no use cryin' over split milk," Etta said as she

propelled Sanchez onto the porch. "Jus' bring the buck-board 'round an' let's get at it."

Nessa closed her eyes. Without the powerful pain in her shoulder she now felt all her other hurts. Worst of all was where her nails used to be. She rubbed her eyes, trying to stay awake. She felt all used up, but she could not give in to it. She had to think. First about weapons. "They got all our guns, Aunt Etta."

"Well, hell. We got guns."

She must've dozed because a loud clatter roused her. She sat up and looked over the items on the table. A small-bore 5-shot Colt revolver and a gun belt with the loops loaded, an Adams .40 calibre breech-loading Maynard with two boxes of shells and a .41 caliber single-shot Phila-delphia derringer. The derringer, aptly called a "boot gun," was the shape and size of a large man's big toe.

"Here's your daddy's bowie," said Etta. "Give t'him by the great Jim Bowie hisself."

"I know." Reverently, Nessa removed the knife from its beaded and fringed scabbard. It was sixteen inches long, single-edged and not curved except for the point. It had a buckhorn handle and weighed a pound and a half. "Good. What about that other one, Aunt Etta?"

"That l'il ol' sneak knife of yer daddy's?"

"Yes. Where's it at?"

"It was in yer mama's trunk. Last time I saw it." Over her shoulder, she added, "Good thing we didn't haul that trunk over to yer place yet. All yer mama's stuff'd be ruint as well."

She brought the knife then and helped Nessa into the specially designed cross-draw rig. One piece of rawhide spanned her chest like a bandaleer. Another went around her middle and under her breasts. Tied that way, the snakeskin scabbard was snugged under her left arm and made the small flat-handled knife within it virtually invisible. Nessa touched her thumb to the thin blade. "Still plenty sharp."

"Nobody's messed with it. Want me t'slit yer shirt?"

"Yes, please." That accomplished, Nessa tried drawing the knife a few times but her fingers were stiff and clumsy.

"Yer back'll loosen up by tomorrow," Etta said.

"I hope so. Feels like I'm humpbacked."

"Ya know, the boys ought to be back from Abilene purt near any day now. Ya could take a couple of 'em with ya."

"The boys," vaqueros with an average age of sixty, had gone to deliver some horses. Etta Cutter bred mounts for the U.S. Cavalry. Made a good living at it, too. Nessa shook her head. "No. I'll be less noticeable alone and can make better time as well."

"I ain't worried about yer makin' time," grumbled Etta. "I'm worried about yer time bein' up! Texas is changin', girl. An' it ain't for the better neither. Seems like every cussed, low-down snake in the Union has gone to Texas." *Gone to Texas* was the phrase used to describe hiding out from the law with little danger of being arrested and extradited.

"Want me t' braid yer hair for ya?"

"Yes, please." Her hair was no easy chore with two hands, for it was slippery and straight as an Indian's. She laid her head on her knees. Etta brushed her hair to the top of her head, tied it with a strip of rawhide and then braided it and coiled it like a snake. When she was a kid her aunt would leave the bristly end sticking up out of the coil. Told her it made her look snake mean. It used to be her favorite hairdo.

They waited in silence, hands once again clasped across the table. Nessa looked around, wondering how long it would be before she'd see this room again. How long before she'd see her aunt again? She almost said something but her aunt had her head bowed like she might be praying.

It shamed her, but she couldn't pray yet. Not yet. Not until she'd done what she had to do.

The mantel clock ticked loudly and a log settled on the grate and finally, the buckboard rattled up in front. "There's Sanchez."

"I expect. About time, too."

Nessa stood and waited while Etta swung on a lace mantilla that was ivoried with age, and then picked up her Bible. They walked outside together. Tied behind the wagon was a pearl gray mare with white fetlocks and a prideful lift to her tail. Nessa looked at Etta, shocked. "That's Duchess!"

"Well, I guess I know my own stock."

"Oh, Aunt Etta, I can't take Duchess."

"Yes, you can."

"No, I can't."

"Don't argue with me. You can and will. She's the fastest horse we got. An' I got a powerful feelin' yer gonna need speed." Etta pushed her gently. "Let's jus' go, girl. We got t'git poor Bob in the ground."

"You're gonna make me?"

"I am."

"Well, all right." Nessa slid the rifle into the boot and then hung the gunbelt on the saddle horn. "You know I'll take good care of her."

"I know. That's why I give her t'ya. Ya sure ya feel up t'ridin'?" Etta asked as she climbed in the wagon.

"Oh, yeah. Be a lot more comfortable than bouncing around on that buckboard." Despite those brave words, she mounted like she was balancing a glass of water on her head.

It didn't take long. Nessa wrapped the dog in a sacking towel while Etta washed Bob and tied a clean bandana around his neck.

Graveside, Nessa and Sanchez stood bowed and silent while Etta read from the Bible. A last mumbled prayer in Spanish from Sanchez and it was done. Bob and his dog had been buried together Indian style.

"Well, when do ya plan on leavin'?" Etta asked.

"Soon as I pack."

"Today yet?"

"Yes, ma'am."

"Yer sure?"

"Yes, ma'am."

"Well, I see yer mind is made."

"Yes, Aunt Etta. It is."

Sanchez shooed the rooster and handful of setting hens into the barn where they might survive in the rafters if they were wary. Meanwhile Etta helped Nessa pack, collecting items and putting them in a morral, the fiber bag that would swing from her saddle horn. When finished, Nessa went through the list in her mind—a wool blanket and a brush coat. Chaparejos. A skillet, a tin cup and a tin plate. Food that Sanchez had brought in the wagon— flour, beans, bacon, coffee. Her journal. A sack of flints and—under pressure—a jar of Etta's cure-all.

"They git yer money?" Etta asked.

"Yes, ma'am, every dern dollar."

"Well, here's a couple of double eagles."

"Thanks, Aunt Etta."

"Put 'em in yer boot."

"Right."

Etta looked up at the sky. "Yer bound t'get rain, it bein' spring in Texas."

"You're right," Nessa replied and returned to the cabin. A part of the dirt floor was covered with a gerga, a heavy tightly woven cloth that was almost waterproof. She pulled it up and cut off a large square, rolled the blanket and her coat in it and then tied it behind her cantle. She looked around, hoping she hadn't forgotten anything. "Sanchez finished?"

"He's back in the barn."

Sanchez had sawed off a piece of barn board and, using a burned stick he was trying to draw the universally recognized sign for quarantine.

"Here! Gimme that, Sanchez." Etta grumbled. "About the only thin' you can draw is flies." She worked a minute. "Now, there. That's some better, ain't it?"

Nessa printed the word *Meezils* and then Sanchez nailed the board to the door. "Kinda like closin' the barn door after the horse's gone, ain't it?" Etta said. "There ain't a whole lot left t'trash."

"I just don't want some ol' . . . person in there. Pawing over my . . . our stuff," said Nessa. Finished now, Sanchez walked toward them. "Gracias, Sanchez."

"De nada." Using both hands, he removed his sombrero and bowed solemnly. "Vaya con Díos, chica."

"Y usted, el viejo."

He shuffled to the wagon, somehow suddenly a sad figure himself with his baggy pants and floppy hurachas.

Nessa turned to her aunt. "Well," she said and slapped the reins against her thigh. "I guess that's it." For want of something else to do she mounted up. "Boy, my shoulder's a hundred times better already."

"Rub some more of that linament on tonight. Far back as ya can reach."

"I will."

Etta put her hand on Nessa's knee. "Everythin' will be yours when I die. All ya got t'do is try t'outlive me."

"I'll do my best."

"See that ya do, girl."

"Don't worry, Aunt Etta." She leaned down and pressed her lips to the spiderweb of wrinkles on her aunt's cheek. "I'll be back," she said and then raised her voice for Sanchez's benefit. "Don't y'all go eatin' my cow now, y'hear?" The sun was on his face but his sombrero jiggled.

She watched until the buckboard was out of sight, then kicked the horse and rode hell-bent over the hill.

Dust settled. Silence descended. A crow pecked at a splash of dried blood. A chicken stuck its head out of the barn door then strutted out and started scratching. Another followed then another. Soft clucking swelled.

Suddenly a horse and rider were outlined against the sky. The horse blew and snifted then settled and stood stock still. The rider took a good long look then wheeled the horse and disappeared.

. . . *the house, like The mariage, was less than Two months old. Our front door had been made at the German saw Mill in Fredricks Burg. A lot of The furniture Bob had hewn by hand. He'd been nineteen.*

Three

13th of May—I will never Forget taking that last look. It was Like a curtin had drawn on every Thing I'd ever nown.

Well, nothing to do now but git on to the job at hand. The wether has held. The sky is the coler of smoke but still no rayne.

She only rode for a few hours before the rising pain in her shoulder forced her to stop. She off-saddled then started a fire using dried grass and a wad of punk. She had two ready-made meals in her saddlebags—thanks to her aunt—but the thought of eating made her queasy. So she set a pot of coffee to boil. When it was ready, she drank it to the accompaniment of the mournful wind and the eerie cries of the night birds.

Staring out at the shadowed moonscape, so desolate and still, she felt like she was the only person in the universe.

She finally unrolled her blanket and spread it. She drew her gun and laid it by her side and closed her eyes but, tired as she was she couldn't sleep.

She couldn't quit thinking about Bob. Images of him kept flashing through her mind. The first time she saw him. The day they got married. Sitting across the table from her, eating breakfast. *Yesterday! Was that only yesterday?*

He'd been a person of sunny good humor. More talkative than most men. More talkative than herself. And now he was dead! It just didn't seem possible. She tried to fix his smiling face in her mind's eye but she couldn't hold it against how he'd looked the last time she'd seen him. A clay man with a bandanna covering his open throat.

She slept very poorly. It rained in the morning.

Tracking after a hard rain is one-tenth skill and nine-tenths luck. She crisscrossed the land for three days before she got lucky and found a track in a stretch of dried mud beside a creek bed. A horse with a bent calk had stepped close to an outcropping of rock and on a small patch of ground where the rain hadn't fallen. That horse was Bob's.

The next day she came upon a dribbling stream. She was splashing a handful of water on her face when she saw a bit of color on the other side. Drawing her pistol, she waded over, into the sullen buzz of flies, into the strong stink of decay.

A man lay crumpled in a high wave of buffalo grass, shot in the back of the neck. She pulled him out of the water and rolled him over. There was no weapon on him. That wasn't normal. Not this close to Indian territory. She walked the area and found plenty of tracks—including some that had been made by Bob's horse—but no riderless mount. She returned and knelt to study the man. Dirt-peppered eyes stared at her from behind lizard-like lids. She closed his eyes and then sat back on her heels.

With his butternut skin and black hair he looked like he might've been a Mexican, and a prosperous one at that. He wore a well-cut coat and uncracked boots that were only slightly down in the heel. But if he'd been carrying any money, he sure wasn't any more.

Funny. What moved her most was seeing that one of his outturned pockets had been mended with red thread. It was, she supposed, the idea that someone, somewhere had cared about this man. Whoever it was—wife, mother or sister, she was a woman frugal enough not to waste thread. A woman who, unlike herself, could sew a straight line with tight neat little stitches.

She followed the rippling path some small animal caused as it moved through the grass along the shore. *His wife, I'll bet.* A small woman with brown hair and flashing eyes. She'd probably be plenty angry at first. "That John/Juan! Always a day late and a dollar short!" Apprehension would set in next. "Could something have happened to him? Oh, God!" she'd cry. "It just isn't like him not to write." Then doubt, sharpened by someone heartless and cruel, like an evil stepmother. "I think John/Juan got fed up with your harpin'. I think he up and headed for New Orleans . . ."

Enough! She stood and brushed off her pants. Her mother'd always said, "If imagination had wings Nessa'd be soarin' with the eagles."

She tied one end of her rope under the dead man's arms and the other around the pommel then hauled him to a shallow gully. After she rolled him into it she attempted to straighten his skewed limbs. Then with the gerga stretched between two branches like a travois she gathered enough rocks from the stream bed to cover him. It was the best she could do without a shovel.

There was no surefire way to prove who'd killed the traveler, she thought as she rode away, but every sign pointed to the men she was after.

She followed the stream south a ways before crossing and heading due west again. She kept to the brush where her tracks were less apt to be noticed and gave wide berth to the scattered homesteads she came upon. She stepped off her horse often to check for sign.

One day she passed three covered wagons which were headed, judging by their direction, for Ft. Inge. She sat with one leg snagged on the pommel and watched until the travelers pulled level. A man who was walking alongside a team of oxen spotted her and lifted his hand in a silent salute. As she returned his wave, a bonneted head popped out of the back of the wagon and the thin cry of a baby came on the wind.

She watched them until the wagons were out of sight. They were the first people she'd seen since setting out.

No, she amended as she turned her horse. They were the first live people she'd seen since setting out.

It wasn't three hours later that she flushed a man who'd been sleeping behind a clump of purple prairie clover! She almost shot the man dead when he jumped up in front of her. They looked at each other for quite a time and she'd be hard-pressed to say who was more surprised. He was the biggest human being she'd ever seen and dark as lampblack. His hair was a mass of woolly corkscrews not unlike a buffalo.

Although she'd never seen one before, she figured him for an African, probably an escaped slave. The man's red-lined eyes had the look of a hunted animal to them and he was all scratched up and dirty and barefooted. He was either catching his food barehanded or eating grass; there wasn't a weapon or snare on him.

While keeping her gun trained, she reached inside her morral. "Mexico's yonder ways." She tossed a strip of cured beef between his feet and pointed south. "And it's right far."

He looked at her a bit longer. His eyes darted down to Duchess and then back to her. Their gazes locked. There was no malice in his look that she could see, only speculation, but his massive arms were loose and his fingers slightly curled. He looked . . . ready. She shook her head slightly. "Don't even think about it, mister."

The silence lasted so long it haired over. Then suddenly he scooped up the meat and took off. Duchess almost bolted off, too. Once she had the mare under control, she just sat and watched him run. It was amazing! That man moved so fast a person could've played marbles on his shirttail!

She camped that night near an abandoned wagon that had been weather worn to the color of suet. In selecting a site for her camp she always chose an open area so that anyone trying to come up on her would have to do so without the benefit of cover. But that didn't stop someone that night.

She was wrapped in her blanket sound asleep when a rustling sound roused her. She looked around and saw two amber eyes staring at her from across the fire. She pointed her gun and waited. A lone lobo? Maybe. But it made no threatening moves during the two-hour staredown that followed. The dawn revealed a mangy old dog hunkered beneath the wagon's cracked felloe.

"You are one ugly critter," she said, pouring water in her plate then pushing it closer with a stick. "Well, c'mon. I ain't gonna hurt you."

It took a while but finally the dog crawled out to slurp the water and she saw that he was trailing a rope with a frayed end. She tossed a piece of bacon on the plate and then wrapped her arms around her legs and watched him eat.

The poor dog was half wolf, half starved and all old. His coat, if it could be called that, even showed gray where the hair ruffled wrong way in the wind. It appeared that someone had used a leaded quirt on him. His muscular flanks were crosshatched with rope-thick scars, two of which were recent and festered.

She took out the ginger jar containing Etta Cutter's cure-all. She spread some on a piece of bark and added water, keeping up a soft, one-sided conversation all the while. He offered to bite her twice but then all the fight went out of him and he just stretched out, still as death. She'd seen that happen before with other animals. Her personal opinion was that the smell of Etta Cutter's cure-all went directly to their brains and paralyzed them.

She cleaned his wounds with warm water then dabbed on the paste. After sawing through the rope around his neck she put some paste on the abraded hide beneath as well. He must've felt safe with her because he slept the whole time she packed up. It made her sad, seeing an ol' dog who'd been mistreated like that. He didn't seem bad-tempered to her.

She rode hard to make up for lost time, but whenever she came to a hill she would stop at the top and stand in the stirrups. Sure enough, there'd come that dog, limping along behind her. By midafternoon, when she didn't see him any more she figured she must've outrun him.

At dusk she followed a path the animals had made on their way to water. She soon found a small running stream and camped in a stand of alamos nearby. She baited a snare with a piece of dried apple and got a brown rabbit almost immediately. She skinned and gutted it, but full dark still found her with a handful of guts, trying to whistle up that derned old dog.

"Dumb cluck," she mumbled to herself finally and tossed the entrails in the bushes. She stoked the fire and cooked the rabbit. She was closer to hostile Indian territory now. Starting tomorrow she would cook her main meal in the morning when the smoke from a fire would be less noticeable.

She was finishing her coffee when she saw the dog. He'd apparently made short work of those rabbit entrails and was now bold enough to think he could have the remains of her dinner.

"Haw! Git away from that rabbit. That there's my breakfast!

"Well . . . just that one piece. But that's it now.

"Oh, all right, that little bite there. Hey! Cut that out. Hey you! Come back here with that!"

That dog woke her up four times that night, snapping those bones with a sound that was just like the crack of a rifle. She picked up a rock but then she couldn't bring herself to chuck it. At least that old dog was another living thing.

It was getting so she dreaded the night. The country was becoming more desolate and dangerous with each passing day, but she never gave it much thought when she was on the move. She had plenty to do—keeping her eyes skinned for Indians, looking for a sign, searching out water.

But it was a whole 'nother story after dark. The sun would drop behind the horizon like a stone down a well and there'd go her spirits, right along with it.

For some reason the night brought the certainty that she was destined for an inescapable and very tragic end. That's when an intense longing to go home would come over her.

Lately she'd even started imagining what it would be like to turn around and do just that. She'd ride into the yard and Sanchez and Aunt Etta and Suggs and everybody would be so glad to see her! But then, after things settled down a bit, somebody would say . . . well, did ya git 'em? And she would say . . . Well, no, I didn't. You see, I just got so blamed homesick that I decided to come on back.

She could just imagine everyone's face when she said that!

No. She'd stick. And she'd let the dog stay if he wanted. Revenge, she had discovered, is a mighty poor companion.

18th of May—A giant tongue Slurpt me upsid the Head this morning and I opened my eyes to a set of ten-inch fangs grouted with purple gums. It' is a dam good thing I have grown as much as I am going To.

19th of May—He kept up Pretty good today. I decided he wasn't cripled up so much as He was starved half to death. In honor of those fangs, I have Naimed him Bite.

Four

20th of May—I caim over a hill and saw a Smear of yellow below. It was a square, squat building built out Of ruff timber. A well rutted rode caim down the treeless slope from The east, widened in front then continued west. A muddy creek cut a crooked path Out back. Several horses stood in a Split rail padock but None at the hitching rail. I figured it for a stage Relay stashun.

The main room was empty but it hadn't always been. The stale smell of tobacco, whiskey and gamey armpits hung heavy in the air. A man hurried through the curtains, thumbing on frayed suspenders. "I didn't hear you ride up," he said. Keeping his sharp bright eyes on her, he moved behind the counter where she figured he probably kept his gun stashed. She removed her hat. The man was visibly taken aback by the sight of her braided top-knot.

"I see you sell supplies," she said nodding at the tiered shelves stacked with cans and bags of staples that climbed the wall behind him.

"Yes, ma'am, some," he said, recovering somewhat. "Do you need somethin'?"

"Yes, sir." He nodded again and waited. "I need bacon and salt if you have it. Some corn meal. A sack of beans."

On the counter she laid the double eagle she'd had the foresight to remove from her sock before she rode in.

"Got it all. Anythin' else?"

"Some information maybe. I am looking for three men, sir. One is dirty with bug eyes and a ginger-colored beard. I don't know his name but his sidekick's a Mexican half-breed called Ladino."

"Means outlaw," the man translated.

"Yes, sir. I know. There's a third man who has got loose lips and face sores. He's got a baby face but I'd say he's at least twenty."

"They was here two days back."

"All three?"

"All three."

"Sir, did they have a black Morgan mare with a white star?"

"They did. The first fella you described said they might be interested in selling it. It being a fine horse, I made them an offer. I couldn't afford what the horse was worth, you understand, but the bearded fella seemed interested. The younger fella was not. Not a bit. Claimed the horse was his alone to sell. They had words until the big guy got tired of jawin' and knocked the kid upside the head."

"That guy's done that before. Where was the breed?"

"Sat right there." The man pointed at a table. "Drinking. Appeared to be all he was interested in. He downed a whole bottle in about a minute and then offered to plug me when I didn't get him 'nother'n fast enough to suit him. Why are you lookin' for 'em? If I may ask?"

"They stole that Morgan and killed my husband."

He hit the counter with his palm. "I knowed they were no good the minute I laid eyes on 'em. Well, I'm sure glad I showed my firepower an' . . ." He hitched his thumb, ". . . hid my wife."

That was the first Nessa noticed the woman standing in the doorway. She was beak-faced with thin black hair that looked painted on but she had a wide, ready smile. In spite of one buck tooth, the smile improved her looks considerably. Nessa smiled back.

"Take a seat, miss." The man motioned her toward a ladderback chair with a laced cowhide seat. "Gert, get us some coffee, will you?"

The man's name was Ezra Cobb. Gert was his wife. Both of the Cobbs proved to be real hospitable. Mrs. Cobb offered their loft area for the night. "We'd be pleased to have you eat with us, too. It'll be simple fare." Nessa accepted. She accepted the bath the woman offered as well.

"Bath first or food first?" Mrs. Cobb inquired.

"Food, if you please."

The woman nodded and briskly left.

While waiting she learned that Cobb had spent twenty-one years as a United States soldier. Unfortunately he was assigned to Ft. Clark in '49 and arrived for duty only weeks before the cholera epidemic hit. It took the Cobbs' two teenage daughters within a day of each other. "I quit," he said, "and we went back to Kentucky. We tried to make a go of it but you see," he leaned closer and lowered his voice. "Gert took the girls' dying so hard I was afraid she might grieve herself to death. I don't know what I'd do without my Gert."

Nessa looked at her lap, discomposed that a man could wear his love for his wife like his beard.

"So that's how come I took this job. I figured we could both do with a change of scene, you know?"

Changing the subject, Nessa asked him whether he'd ever had a problem with Indians.

"Some Lipans tried to steal a horse last month but I got off a lucky shot. They let go of the horse and lit out."

"And you have had no trouble since?"

"No."

"You're lucky."

"I ain't worried none. This place is solid as a fort."

Nessa was going to say that the Indians could just walk in, like she had but in the end she decided not to. It was not her place to tell a man his business. Instead she told him about coming on that dead man. When she had finished describing him, he said, "No, I don't know no one like that. Dry-gulched, you say?"

"Yes, sir."

"Well, those fellas were trailing two horses." He sucked his tooth. "Damn them! There ain't nothin' I hate worse'n a horsethief."

It was the way most Texans felt. Because of the harshness of the terrain and hostility of its natives, stealing a man's horse was about equal to taking his life.

They made some small talk then—which was a disappointment to Ezra Cobb. He would've liked some details about the husband's death. The girl turned out to be mighty tight-lipped for a female.

"I'll have something heated up in a jiffy," Mrs. Cobb said as she sat down. "You know, there was a Mexican family come by here two or three days before those men. A man and his wife and a girl eleven, maybe twelve years old. Said they were headed for Monterrey."

"They best keep a move on it," Nessa said. "Those men are mean for meanness' sake."

While Ezra cautioned her about riding in the direction she intended to ride—"They say the redskins're actin' up ag'in, especially south of the Nueces."—she ate spicy venison stew loaded with potatoes and carrots. When unobserved she stuck two hunks of meat in her pocket and then said, "Well, I guess I'd best go check on my horse."

She was thinking that the dog had probably run off but then there he was lying next to the corral. He made a flying leap to catch the meat, something she was certain he couldn't have done two days ago. She thought he might start hunting for himself soon. If she didn't ruin him for it first.

She soaked until her fingertips looked like dough then knelt by the tub and washed her shirt, socks and undergarments—every stitch except her britches which were "foxed."

Sewing soft deerskin in the crotch and inner thighs was an old ranger practice used to prevent galling. The major disadvantage, particularly to a person with one pair of britches—was that they took a minimum of two days to dry. Her father said that was the reason why a lot of men strip naked when crossing deep water. It was a practice that had been known to cause some hoohaw among the uninitiated. Her father told her once about a company of rangers who crossed the Red and ran smack into a wagon train of Methodists immigrating from Louisiana. One of the rangers—just teasing of course—told the shocked pilgrims that riding naked was the custom in Texas. Before anyone could stop them, three wagons had peeled off and headed home.

She laid some clothes on the sill and some over the

back of a chair that she'd pulled close to the open window. After iron-hard ground, that feather bed felt wonderful. She slept like the dead.

She woke to the smell of sorghum, yeast and fresh-ground chicory snaking up through the wood floor. It was late. Birds were going at it and the eastern horizon was already shot with the first rays of light when she walked into the kitchen.

Gert turned. "Oh, my, look at you with your hair down! Why, you are prettier'n the nigh side of a peach!" She noticed what Nessa was carrying. "Is there somethin' wrong with your pillow?"

"I got it damp. I hung my head off the bed but I must've rolled in my sleep."

"I'll just pin it outside," Gert said, pouring coffee. "It'll be dry in no time. Sit right down. Please."

"Thank you. Say, Mrs. Cobb, do you suppose I could borrow a pair of scissors from you?"

"Why, sure. But I'll be glad to help you mend something."

"No. It's my hair, Mrs. Cobb. I need to cut it."

"Oh no! Why, it's clear to your waist."

"But it's too hot and too hard to keep clean. It'll be safer, too."

"Cutting your hair will not fool anyone, you know. Any fool can see that your face has never known a razor."

"Yes, ma'am, but if they get that close, the next face they see'll be their Maker."

The older woman considered that and the matter of fact way the girl said it. "I . . . see. Well, then. If you insist, I'll do it for you after breakfast. How much are you gonna want off."

"I'd like to leave enough to keep the sun off my neck is all."

"Oh, my. That much? Well, I suppose you know what's best."

Nessa watched Gert set the pot back on the stove, select a brown egg out of a basket and crack it on the side of a large clay bowl. Gert kept her eggs in a basket filled with sawdust, same as her ma. It made her throat tight, which surprised her. She was not generally sentimental by nature.

"You'll think I'm a nosey ol' biddy . . ."

"No, I won't. What?"

"Well, Ezra and me was wonderin' how old you are." She glanced over her shoulder. "You mind my askin'?"

"No, ma'am. I'm nineteen. Well, almost."

"Nineteen!" Gert shook her head. "My stars! I'd never believe it."

"Why? Do I look older?"

"Heavens, no. It's just that you act so . . . sure of yourself. You've got a presence that a person don't ordinarily see in one so young." She smiled over her shoulder. "Why, you're only a year older than my Amity would've have been. Had she lived." She looked out the small window at the trees beyond the corral and then down at her hands. "Amity was nothing like you. That girl was such a scaredy cat. Mm-mm. Scart of her own shadow. Why, she'd scarcely go to the necessary by herself. Even in Lexington."

The woman's voice had turned tinny and her chin wobbily. Nessa quick said, "My ma was like that, too. Why, I recall one time when she thought she heard somebody coming and got spooked and hid in a little space between the wall." Nessa held up her hands. "It wasn't any big-ger'n this."

"My stars! How did she get in there?"

"I don't know. Pa and I hollered and searched. We never thought to look in that little place. I could tell that Pa was beginning to believe she'd been carried off when we finally found her."

"Couldn't she answer you?"

"No, ma'am. She was so scared she'd lost her speech."

"Oh, the poor thing! How on earth did you ever find her?"

Nessa stopped short of saying. "She'd . . . well, we just did."

"That something should scare her so!"

Nessa looked at her hands. "Well, it didn't take much. You see, my ma had had a . . . run-in . . . with the In-dians that she never did get over. Just about any little thing could set her off. Why, I remember a time when she spotted an ol' Indian sitting outside of the drygood store and she went off right there." She snapped her fin-gers. "Just like that."

She hadn't thought of that day in a long time. The way her mother had grabbed her arm, screaming, "Kill him, kill him, hurry, kill him." She wasn't sure who she was supposed to kill but she was trying to get at the derringer in the special pocket sewn in the lining of her pinafore. She did—finally—but by then her mother had a death grip on her arm. They both went down amid a welter of dust and dancing hooves as they rolled near some hitched horses.

Suddenly her mother scrambled up and took off down the road, screaming at the top of her lungs. Nessa sprawled there frozen with shock as her father tore out of the blacksmith's after her. He caught up with her at the edge of town, but she turned on him, crazy like a shot animal.

Abruptly her mother's screams ceased and her father swung her up into his arms. He headed for the buckboard. "Get in the wagon," he ordered as he passed Nessa. It was only when she was sitting with her feet dangling off the back of the wagon that she noticed the whole town was standing outside or at their doors.

"I remember looking at the place where the Indian had been sitting but he was long gone."

Mrs. Cobb had put her hand over Nessa's. "That poor, poor thing! Had she known him? The Indian?"

"No. One day much later I asked Pa that same question and he said no, that she'd never seen him before. He guessed that there was just something about him. That's when my father decided he better tell me all of it." She looked up into Mrs. Cobb's soft eyes. "You see, my ma'd been an Indian captive."

"Oh, no!"

"Yes. Her name was Alma O'Connor Jackson. In 18 and 25 she was captured by one of the last fighting bands of the Tonkawas. She was eighteen, and seven months . . ."

. . . pregnant. The 'Kawas, her father explained, allowed Alma to have her baby and then tied her on a horse and left the baby mewling among the offal of a three-month camp. Nate Cutter was one of four men who ransomed her in '27.

Like many hostages Nate Cutter had seen, the girl they thought was Alma Jackson was close to broken and had only a fragile hold on sanity. She would lift her eyes no higher than a man's spurs and was unable—or unwilling—to speak. Even after being freed she refused food for so long her rescuers feared she would starve herself to death.

Then one day Cutter held out a piece of bacon and kept holding it out until she took it. Every day after that he did the same thing. She got so she would accept that little bit of food, but only from Nate Cutter. Why, he wondered, a man closer to fifty than forty and ugly as a tote sack to boot?

They finally arrived at Alma's home only to find that it was no longer her home. Her husband, figuring her to be either dead or ruined for a white man, had remarried.

Nate Cutter stood threading his reins through his fingers, an unwilling witness to what should have been a joyous reunion. He felt like he'd been horse-kicked himself. He couldn't begin to imagine how Alma Jackson felt.

Alma's husband's new wife was young, freckled and redheaded as a woodpecker. Cutter couldn't tell if the baby she held was a boy or a girl. It had ugly pink fuzz on its head, big ears and scarcely any nose at all. Both mother and child were bawling while the husband, who was little more than a kid himself, seemed only able to shuffle his feet with embarrassment.

Alma swayed and faltered and Cutter took a step toward her but somehow she drew herself up. A long last look at the girl and her baby and Alma turned and looked straight at Cutter for the first time. Her eyes were clear sky blue and filled with such anguish . . .

". . . that Pa said they went through him like a lance. That's how come he took her to live with him at the place he and my aunt had together. Still it was five years before she spoke a single word. I was born three years later." Nessa glanced at Mrs. Cobb and then at her hands. She laughed nervously. "I don't know what's come over me. Telling you all this." Mrs. Cobb covered her hands with her own.

"People need to talk about such things. I did. You know, when Amity and Hannah died I hurt worse'n a person can and still live. Ezra, too. But neither of us let on to the other. We sleep walked through almost a year, protecting each other—or so we thought. One day I said, 'Remember when Amity swallowed a peach pit and Hannah laughed so hard that milk came out her nose?' That was all it took. The floodgates opened. We sat and cried and talked for hours. 'Remember this. Remember that.' We needed to do that. I believe if we hadn't the hurt would've killed us. Sooner or later."

She didn't get Mrs. Cobb's point. What had happened to her mother hadn't hurt her personally. It had hurt her mother, of course, but that was because her mother had possessed no true strength of spirit. A sad failing and one that would have been fatal if it weren't for the constant protection of Nate Cutter.

She decided she better change the subject. Mrs. Cobb was starting to get sort of mushy. "Do you ever miss Lexington? All the people and things to do?"

Gert Cobb sighed and then selected another egg. "I'll admit I do, yes, sometimes I do. But then I'll see a sunrise like that one coming right now and I'll think: the sun just doesn't rise anywhere like it does over Texas."

"I've heard that's true but then I've never been anywhere else but Texas."

"Well," she continued but in a different tone, "after

what you've told me it's obvious which parent you take after. Except for your looks."

"Yes, ma'am. I guess."

Nessa ate a breakfast of flannel cakes and bacon and then Gert cut off about two feet of hair, moaning the entire time she was at it. When she finished Nessa said that it was past time for her to leave.

"Wait a minute." She picked up an oilskin package. "Take this along."

"What is it?"

"Some head cheese and baked chicken and corn dodgers. For later."

"Why, thank you. Can I . . ."

Gert waved away Nessa's hand. "Heaven's sakes, I don't want your money. Why, I ought to pay you for your fine company. There's so few white women come this way nowadays, what with the Indians and all." She looked at her hard. "Now you be very very careful, hear?"

"I will. I'm real wary. You all be on the look out, too. Way off like you are."

"Ezra says we're safe enough."

Nessa wasn't sure about that but no sense saying so. They were pioneer people and were not likely to give up because it was chancy.

Gert's looks grew on you, Nessa thought as she rode away. Within no time you were wondering how you'd missed noticing her big amber eyes or that her skin was as smooth as fresh churned butter.

Nessa rode hard all day, not even stopping to eat. Not so for Bite. He had to stop to eat the scraps she tossed and then run like hell to catch up. But catch up he did.

* * *

21st of May—I had cut Indian sine twice before but today Is the first Time I actualy spotted some. I am hiding behind some rocks rite now While they cross a mesa about a mile off. I dare not move for fear of raising dust so I am catching up on my riting. I may Well stay rite here tonite.

She figured she was pretty close now and expected to catch up with those men either on the morrow or at the latest, on the following day. Would she kill them? Or would they kill her? Well, whatever happened, she reasoned, it will all soon be over.

One thing bothered her. That kid had definitely slacked his hold on her arm. Right when the bearded one was getting set to poke her. Intentional or unintentional, it had probably saved her life.

It made her wonder. Her father always said that someone who sees a wrong done and does nothing to stop it is just as guilty as the one who actually committed the wrong. But she wasn't so sure about that in this instance. That young one was obviously dimwitted. Maybe he was along with the others against his will. Maybe he didn't know any better. Then again, maybe he did and that's why he'd deliberately helped her. Maybe he hadn't wanted to see her hurt.

It sure muddied things up in her mind.

Five

Trey Henry killed for fun. He had started very young by burying small animals alive. He could sit for hours staring down at the mound of dirt, speculating about the kitten or puppy down there. How long did they struggle, he wondered?

His body grew but his mind did not. Except for his maudlin curiosity. That's why he stopped burying his victims. He discovered something he liked much better: Playing with them while he watched them die.

There was no plotting associated with his killing and no malice aforethought. If an opportunity arose, he seized it. Although he was incredibly cruel, his actions were totally instinctual. Like a predator, he was simply hunting.

His uncle buggered him when he was five. It hurt like hell. But later he remembered his uncle's reaction and he wondered if maybe it would feel good if he did what his uncle did. He tried it with a goat and it did! He became consumed with that region just below his abdomen, and took to inspecting and fondling it constantly.

People who used to be kind to him started avoiding him. They shut their gates against him or walked the other way. Some kicked at him, like they did old lady

Steel's dog when it tried to hump their leg. He became angry and grew lonely. He looked homeward.

His mother was very upset when he killed his ten-year-old sister. She couldn't believe he'd done it. Even when he told her that he did.

The preacher and the sheriff came. There was talk about having to send him away but his mother hid him until her brother—that same uncle but he seemed nicer now—could come for him and now . . .

And now here he was, having the time of his life, going down to ol' Mexico with his uncle, going to have some fun, going where there were a lot of people younger and littler than himself.

His horse recoiled and jumped. Without thinking, he had raked his stolen Spanish spurs against his mount's flanks. He fought the dancing horse, cursing. His struggles caused the other three horses to snort and shy as well.

"Goddamn!" his uncle said. "You gonna handle that damned horse or what?"

The old Indian gave his horse a good whack with the butt of his knife. Right between the ears and his horse instantly settled down. Yeah! Henry thought and drew his gun. His uncle took it away.

"C'mon!"

"No."

"Lemme jus' nick it shy."

"No!"

"Why?" he whined as he dodged a roundhouse swipe from his uncle.

"Because we're gonna sell it to Ruiz. I done tole you that ten times already."

The kid was finally bringing the mare back into line

when Ladino said, "Mira abajo!" and handed an old brass telescope to Flatt.

Flatt took a long look then handed it to Trey Henry.

"Take a look at that down there, kid." Flatt smiled as he watched the kid's mouth drop.

"Can I? Huh? Can I, Uncle Caleb? Huh?"

"Yeah. Go on down. I guess you've earned yoreself some fun. But remember this the next time we get a likely buyer for that horse."

Henry hooo-haaa'ed and spurring his mount hard, he headed down the hill.

Emiliano Gomez did not see the three men on the hill. Nor did he hear the exuberant yell nor the horse's pounding hooves. Emiliano only heard a pitiful lament. *Fool. Fool. Fool. . . .* in concert with the twitch of the ox's tail. *Fool. Fool. Fool. . . .* in harmony with the creak of the wagon. The same dull chant had been running through his head ever since he'd left San Antonio with his tail between his legs.

He was completely penniless.

How could he have been so trusting? Estúpido! At the very least he should have held back some of their funds. *Fool. Fool. Fool.* He should not have sold their belongings to begin with. *Fool. Fool. Fool.* He should have left Inez and Luz in Monterrey until he'd checked the situation out in person. *Fool. Fool. Fool.* He'd taken no precautions whatsoever. *Fool. Fool. Fool.*

He looked dolefully at a clump of scrub brush. It looked familiar. Dios! It probably was. Why not? It had only been four weeks since they passed this way before.

Four weeks! Surely it had taken him longer than that to lose their life savings.

It all began only three months ago. With a letter. His brother Rufino wanted him as a partner in his shoe store. "Delay no longer," Rufino's letter had urged. "Come to San Antonio now!" At first Emiliano had been scared to death! San Antonio. So far! Why, the burgeoning city was not even a part of Mexico any more.

To his credit he had not done as his brother urged until the third letter. "My shop is close to the mission of San Antonio de Valero, the place the Texans call The Alamo. Already people come to see where the heroes died. And after they pay their respects, they spend their money. Lots of money, mi hermano."

The letters were written by Rufino's abogado, Señor Lolly, a fact that did not surprise Emiliano. Emiliano had always been bookish but his devil-may-care brother was just the opposite. Even the brown robes, who were patient to a fault, had despaired of ever teaching Rufino Gomez to write.

His brother's last letter contained the promise of immediate wealth beyond their wildest dreams. "Send all the money you can get your hands on so that I can buy more leather and better tools—then pack up and come immediately."

Emiliano acquiesced—finally—and sold everything they owned except what could be transported in the little wooden-wheeled carreta next to which he now trudged.

En el nombre de Dios! What had he been thinking?

Emiliano wiped his brow. He could feel his wife's gaze but was determined to avoid it. He knew what he would see. Several clumps of brush later and he could still feel her looking at him. Reluctantly he met her gaze. Exactly as he expected, Inez's face was clear and utterly serene. She smiled at him and nodded encouragingly and then returned her eyes to the horizon.

Emiliano looked at the horizon too, fuming. So perfect. So peaceful. So forgiving. So . . . holy. Mira, even now the hand she had hidden in the folds of her dress held her rosary! If only she would berate him. If only she would scream and rage at him. But no. Never. His wife Inez had a disposition that bordered on fatalistic. It was her opinion that God intended that they go to San Antonio and lose all their money. Only this morning she'd said, "In His good time He will show us His true purpose. Trust Him. You will then see His wisdom and rejoice." Emiliano's thought had been: I hope it happens before we starve to death.

Emiliano realized that he must've made some slight sound for his daughter was squeezing his hand and looking up at him with concern. *"Bien, Papá?"* she asked.

"Sí, muy bien, chica." he said. Ah, little Luz. Always gay, always bright and smiling. What a beauty she'd be someday with her full soft mouth and soulful bottomless eyes. A last smile at the child and Emiliano returned his sombrero to his head and his thoughts to San Antonio.

Bien? Hah! If only it were so!

Upon arrival in San Antonio they found nothing was as they expected. His brother, it turned out, did not own the shoe shop but only rented it—from a very unpleasant man who informed Emiliano that they had two days to pay the rent or all his brother's meagre belongings would be placed in the street. But where is Rufino? Emiliano had asked. The unpleasant man did not know for certain but were he to hazard a guess, he'd say: right where he always was. And where, Emiliano asked, is that? Lolly's

Cantina, the man replied. Drunk as a skunk and stinking like one as well.

Lolly? What a fluke! Lolly was the name of his brother's abogado!

Emiliano did not embarrass his brother further by asking the landlord about that strange coincidence. Using the last coins he had, Emiliano paid the rent and then went searching for his brother. He found "Señor Lolly" instead—a two-hundred pound whore with a big gold tooth in the center of her sneer.

Lolly refused to talk to Emiliano but with only a little encouragement a man who worked at the cantina had been delighted to enlighten Emiliano as to the unimaginable depths of degradation and depravity to which his brother had sunk.

Enamored to the point of blindness Rufino had not seen what any sane person could ascertain at a glance. Señorita Lolly cared not for Rufino—or any other man for that matter. Stone-hearted Señorita Lolly cared only for money. Evidently once she got her hands on the money Rufino culled from his muy estúpido hermano, she threw Rufino out of her bed and took up with a handsome young cowboy from Driftwood. Insane with jealousy and emboldened by a gallon of tequila, Rufino challenged the cowboy to a gunfight. The result of said gunfight, the helpful man continued, was that poor Rufino Gomez's body now contained more holes than his hurachas.

And so, with his brother resting in a pauper's grave in a foreign country and with himself owning little more than the clothes on his back—he was taking his family home to Monterrey. To begin again.

Emiliano trudged along, quietly contemplating his

woes, when it suddenly occurred to him that until this luckless chapter of his life, his existence had been remarkably untouched by the vagaries of fate. He had never been sick. Nor had he ever wanted for any of the basic necessities of life. Neither, for that matter, had his loved ones.

Inez. Luz. He looked at his beloved Inez, his lovely Luz. Suddenly, it was as if scales dropped from his eyes.

Dios, but he was still blessed! Very much so. The only thing about which he had been correct was that he was a fool! Why, he had everything that was truly important in life. Health. Family. Faith.

Sí, eso es! This devastating experience was God's way of showing him how fortunate he was. He saw it all now. The result of this terrible tragedy was the opening of his eyes. Many have suffered far worse and prevailed. He had a loving wife, a beautiful daughter and his God. And unlike poor Rufino, he was alive. *Por Dios! Instead of wallowing in despair, I should be saying a fervid prayer of thanks.*

"Mira, Papacita!" Luz said and pointed at a man riding toward them fast.

" 'Liano?" Inez shaded her eyes with her hand. *"Quién es?"*

"Está bien," he said soothingly and patted the air. It was then that he saw the other two men on the hill and he experienced a small twinge of concern. Which he immediately suppressed. He was being unduly distrustful. His experience in San Antonio had soured him against his fellow man. Now that the man was closer Emiliano could see that he was merely a boy. A gringo by the looks of him.

Emiliano jumped back and pulled Luz to safety. El loco! He'd almost ridden them down!

The gringo sawed on the reins and the horse discharged a mist of blood-flecked froth. Emiliano brushed off his serape and thought: this person does not deserve to own such a fine horse. Nonetheless, he recaptured his charitable outlook and said, *"Buenos días!"*

Laughing, the kid replied, "Nuh-uh, greaser. I feature it's more like *buenos noches* for you!"

The bullet that killed Emiliano Gomez was fired at such point blank range that it set his beard on fire.

Six

22nd of May—The sky to The west was turning red and purple. I was riding up a rise, thinking the other side might be a likely Spot to stop for the nite when I Heard the lowd Roar of exploding gun powder. Too shots, a paws Then another shot. I dismounted and ran up to a place Where I cood look over.

The same men who killed Bob were in the small box canyon below. She guessed the Mexican family the Cobbs had told her about were there as well. Staked to the ground were a woman and a girl, their naked bodies heat swollen into beached fish. A man, equally lifeless, was curled nearby.

Moving from tree to rock brought her closer and then she could see the breed, Ladino, laying against a saddle with his mouth glued to a clay jug. The bearded man was on his knees going through the Mexicans' wagon. Pans clanged and colorful clothing fluttered onto the ground as he tossed things over his shoulder. The gunfire was the kid who was practicing his draw by firing at some cans and bottles lined up on a flat rock. Nessa watched him for a full minute and saw that he could not have hit an outhouse if he was inside it.

Abruptly the breed stood up. Maintaining a strangle

grip on his bottle he staggered over and fired some pretty wild shots himself. Suddenly he whirled and fired three times, a bullet for each of the bodies on the ground. The kid bent double, laughing as if it was the funniest thing he'd ever seen.

Choking anger welled inside her—the kind that blots out sane thought and turns an ordinary human being into a raging animal. It was all she could do to keep from opening fire right then and there. She set her teeth and tried to do the same to her mind. Hard though it was, she had to stay calm, be sensible and plan.

Well, all right. She would circle around to the north where there was better cover and then wait until it was totally dark. The breed was, she guessed, one of those men who couldn't drink and once started, couldn't stop. He was already staggering. All right. She would give him time to do some more drinking. Then she would kill the bearded man first, the kid second and save the easiest for last.

She worked her way into a better position. Finally total dark descended and it was time. Her palms were damp and her heart was going like crazy but she figured she couldn't miss. Not at this range. Not with her rifle. She was lining up her shells when she heard clinking metal and creaking leather. She peered over the rock and saw seven men ride in. With her feeling like a guttered lamp, she slowly lowered her gun.

The riders were welcomed by the three renegades like they all carried cold cash and couldn't wait to part with it. That was exactly the case. Items and money started changing hands almost immediately. The kid led out a fine gray gelding that was saddled and ready to ride. The stirrups, she noticed, were high, the way that dry-gulched man might have set his. There was some haggling and then apparently a bargain was struck because a small man wearing a sombrero and twin bandoleers led the horse off.

A brass moon rose and although the trading appeared to be finished, nobody was in any hurry to leave. More bottles made the rounds. Some men knelt around a serape and started rolling dice. Others joined in. When it was fully night someone pulled the ticking out of the Mexican's wagon and set it afire. The smoke made it a ghostly scene, like something from a horrible nightmare.

She didn't see much of a chance for her original plan—unless the others rode off as abruptly as they rode in—so she crawled closer, hoping to hear which way the three renegades were headed.

The kid was now so drunk he couldn't find his ass in a muleyard. He tossed his empty bottle into the rocks and stood with difficulty. Wiping his mouth on his sleeve, he staggered around until he was within twenty yards of her hiding spot. She hunkered but needn't have. His intent was to see how loudly he could pee on his boot while imitating grass in a heavy wind. She looked away when he spent more time than necessary on the job. He must've fallen because there was some laughter and when she looked back, he was struggling to his feet. Laughing good-naturedly, he tottered to where the girl lay and knelt between her legs and dropped his pants.

It was a moment before she realized what he was doing. Someone yelled something in Mexican about wadding in a rifle and then the kid's rear started to flex and bunch.

She ducked behind a rock, shocked and queasy. How could any human being be so . . . twisted? She heard more laughter and stuck her fingers in her ears and covered her eyes. *I'll just go on an' open fire. Kill as many as I can. I know I can get three maybe four . . . At least I can kill that . . . that animal!*

She sat stoppered and blinded for a long time. Long enough, at least, for reasonable thinking to return. There were too many. She'd be a fool. She could do nothing for those dead people now except join them. She should be patient. Pull back. Pick her time.

Without looking into the canyon—she wasn't sure she could make herself leave if she did—she hurried to where Duchess was tied. Moving as quietly as possible, she led the horse down the rocky hill.

A loud crack and she ducked, thinking that she'd been fired upon. But it was Duchess who stumbled and went down and then struggled to stand three-legged.

She knew then but still she checked, carefully running her hand down the horse's right foreleg until she felt the break in the cannon bone.

She was heartsick as she removed the saddle and blanket. The horse was making a soft whuffling noise and shivering all over. She pulled her pistol and cocked it then lowered it. She looked back behind her. She put her cheek against the horse's neck and whispered, "Oh, please God! Don't make me do this."

But she had no choice in the matter. With the bridle in her left hand, she pulled the bowie knife from its deerskin sheath.

The smell of fear was thick in The air. Mine and the horse's both. Moonlite showed Duches was watching me with her big trustful eyes. I kist her and talked To her. I cood tell she was hurting pretty bad. Then I did it.

   God! I no there will be dificult tasks in my life but I hope there are not many more like that one.

Seven

23rd of May—A sad day all a round but I must put it behind me and go on. I hid the saddle, bridle and rifle boot in a nest of high rocks. I tyed my gere in the gerga Then I pitched a rope over a madrone limb and hauled it high Enough to be out of inny predator's reech. It was well hidden unless some One goes looking for it.

She covered her tracks by brushing a leafy branch behind her. Finished, she stuck the branch into the dirt and jumped onto a rock then another and another. Gaining flat ground again, she slung her rifle and set out at a fast wolf trot.

Winded after only a couple of miles she searched the ground until she found a small round pebble. She spit on it, rolled it on her pants and then popped it in her mouth. She confidently took off again, encouraged by her father's words. "For some reason nobody can figure a pebble will give a runner wings on his feet and iron in his heart."

Less than three miles and she stumbled to a stop. She spat the pebble. Way she was sucking air that pebble was liable to end up in her drawers! After that she alternated between a fast walk and a slow shuffle.

It was very hot and very still. For as far as the eye

could see the only movement was wavy ripples of heat rising from the ground. And, of course Bite. The dog always ranged ahead of her now, occasionally making a foray into the tangled warrens of brush that bordered the trail.

Suddenly there was a lot of thrashing and crashing and the dog streaked out of the brasada going like the dickens. A pack of mean-looking javelinas were right behind him.

She searched for something tall enough to climb but there was nothing. She drew her gun and her knife. She could tell Bite was ready to fight them now so she jacked one leg in front of him. It's hard to speak strong and not raise your voice above a whisper but she tried.

For seemingly endless minutes they stood, stiff-legged and with every hair on end while the javelinas snorted and pawed the earth and slung slobber off their terrible tusks.

There must've been some silent signal because at last the big boar turned and led the pack back into the brush. With trembling fingers she returned her knife to its sheath and leathered her gun. She leaned down. The dog's head lifted, tail wagging and tongue lolling. "You know," she said, "I had a pet horned toad once. Never barked and ate next to nothing. Think about it."

Midafternoon she scooped out a little wallow on the south side of a fallen log but she couldn't sleep for worrying. What if those men backtracked and found Duchess? Would they come looking for the horse's owner? Or would the knowledge they may have been observed set them on a faster pace in the opposite direction? And what about the Comanche? Suppose the Comanche decided to investigate all that smoke and gunfire and found her tracks instead! *God help me then!*

None of her thoughts were conducive to sweet dreams yet it was rain that woke her, fat drops that threatened to drown her if she didn't stand up.

It never slacked. Great windblown sheets of water came at her head on for two days straight. She slogged along, mud sucking at her boots and water channeling off her hat, and it was hard to imagine a bleaker time in her life.

Finally, leg-weary and wobbily, she saw the Cobbs' relay station squatting solidly below her. Pale tendrils of smoke spiraled out of the stone chimney and amber seeped from its shuttered windows. She'd never seen a more welcome sight.

When she was close enough to be heard, she cupped her mouth and called out, "Hey! Y'all in the station." A flash of lightening lit the sky followed by rumbling thunder. The door opened a crack and a voice called, "Who's there?"

"Vanessa Cutter Fane, Mr. Cobb."

The door opened wider. Cobb stepped out on the porch and peered into the night. "Come into the light." She did. "Well, I'll be. Is that you? Or a drowned rat?"

"It's me, all right."

"Afoot in this gulley washer?"

"Yes, sir. I lost my mount."

"Aw, no! Not that beautiful horse?"

"Yes, sir."

Sounds like the poor girl's gargling, Cobb thought. He stood aside and waved her in. "Why, you look all stove up. Did you get throwed?"

The half-hinged sole of her boot slapped the wood

floor with a peculiar rhythm. "No, but I've been walking for so long I can't even feel my feet."

Gert came in swinging on a shawl over a flannel nightgown. "My stars! Look at you! Wet to the bone. You'll catch your death."

"Is them yore toes?" Ezra pointed at her boot. She sat and cocked her leg. There was a hole the size of a playing card in the bottom of her boot.

Ezra said, "Worn clear through."

"Balls!" she muttered. The boot made a sucking noise coming off.

"Looks like mice've been at that sock," Gert exclaimed.

She pulled off her sodden sock. "Every red cent I had was in my boot!"

"Not any more it ain't," said Cobb as he sat down across from her.

"Shoot! Well," She sat a minute, silent and dejected. "I guess it could be a lot worse."

Her voice had gone flat. Cobb looked at the girl and then his wife. He had a strong feeling of foreboding. "Those men caught up with that Mexican family?"

"Yes, sir. Yonderways, about a day's hard ride."

"Are they dead?"

"Yes, sir," she whispered. "They are."

"Even that sweet little girl?" Gert asked the top of Nessa's head.

"Yes." She would not say more.

"Why would they do such a awful thing?" Gert asked, sitting heavily. "Why, those poor people didn't even have a horse."

"They had an ox but that wasn't why they were killed. It was still hitched when those men set fire to the wagon.

It likely ran itself to death unless . . ." She looked up, suddenly hopeful. "Say, you know, it took off south. Same way the storm came in. You don't suppose the rain . . . ?" Her words hung in the air until her girlish concern embarrassed her. She looked between the two people then made a production of taking off her other sock. She imitated a chuckle. "My skin looks like chicken fat."

"Why, yes," Gert agreed. "It sort of does at that."

"Well," Cobb scratched his beard. ". . . you were sure right about them ol' boys."

"What?"

"About them bein' mean for meanness sake."

She looked up, honest puzzlement clear on her face. "Do you know why, Mr. Cobb?"

"Why?"

"Why a person gets like that?"

"Here, child," Gert said. "Dry your hair with this towel."

Cobb gnawed his mustache and welcomed the interruption. Explaining evil was more than he cared to take on. "I can't rightly say. Maybe someone was mean to them onct and they don't know no better."

"I'll never understand that." Muffled by the towel. "Not if I live to be a hundred years old."

A fair warmth came from the fire. Mrs. Cobb hung her coat on a chair back and set it close to the hearth, and the air soon filled with the smell of wet cloth.

"Mr. Cobb, did that Mexican family say they were going to Monterrey?"

"Yes."

"Did they ever give their name?"

"I don't believe I heard it. Did you, Mother?"

"If I did I don't recall now.

Nessa thought of the traveler she'd buried. "More people never showing up somewhere," she said glumly. "More people sittin' around, waitin' and wonderin'."

The Cobbs exchanged a look. Gert left and then returned with a mug of coffee and a plate of meat. "Have at this hunk of ham. It'll tide you over until I can get some hot supper in you." Walking to the door, she said, "I suppose you still got that mangy mutt?"

She held a ham bone that was stringy with meat, perfect for red beans. "Yes, ma'am. He's attached himself to me like a tick."

Gert opened the door and peered out. "Yes, there he is." She slapped her thigh. "Git on in here, dog. C'mon now!" Bite slunk in belly down and Gert slammed the door and dropped the bone on the floor.

"Thank you very much, ma'am."

"Gert."

Gert's kindness hit her hard. A huge sodden lump lodged in her throat and she found herself on an edge, damn close to crying. She chewed a long time and passed her sleeve across her mouth before she felt sure enough of her voice to speak again. "Gert, then. Thank you."

"I'll lay out some dry clothes for you," Gert said and left again.

Ezra considered the dog a minute. "There was a man I heard come through Ft. Clark. Had two fightin' dogs. He'd put 'em up ag'in another man's dog for a dollar."

Nessa looked at the dog.

"Ever been to a dogfight?" Ezra asked.

"No, and I believe I can live out the rest of my life just so." She turned back in the twisted rawhide seat.

"Mr. Cobb, I'd be most grateful if you would sell me a horse."

"I'll be glad to. But a word to the wise . . ." He paused until she looked up. "Did you know that you ain't the only one follerin' those men?"

"I'm not?"

"Nope. Somebody come along right after you. Askin' after them same fellas."

"Huh!"

"Showed up the day after you left. He had 'em pegged all right. Said the Mescan bandito goes by the name of El Ladino. Called the other'n Caleb Flatt 'n' said the kid's name was . . . let's see . . . Henry. Yeah, Trey Henry."

"Was he the law?"

"I don't know for sure but he had a look about him."

"What kinda look?"

"The kind that says 'I walk through trouble,' " Gert supplied as she set down a plate of scrambled eggs with chili peppers and chopped ham. "Here. Step behind the curtain there and put on this dry shirt."

"Thank you."

Cobb raised his voice to be heard. "The man said his name was Doubletree."

Nessa returned, rolling sleeves. "No!"

"Yep. That's what he said. Wasn't it, Mother?"

"Yes. Doubletree. I recall thinking—what an unusual name."

Nessa looked into the fire. "Well, I'll be."

"You've heard of him?"

"Yes. Haven't y'all?"

"No," they said together.

"Huh. Must be because you haven't lived in Texas that long. He's real famous around these parts."

In between bites she told them about how her father's friends occasionally stopped by their place. How after dinner they would settle themselves down at the river for a bit of what Nessa's mother termed "sittin' an' spittin'." Unbeknownst to them they had a rapt audience of one taking it all in.

"That's when I heard about Rio Jones who survived being scalped by Comanches only to die of a bee sting at a barn raising. And about Gus Tabor who'd lost his mount and been afoot for days. Crazed from lack of water he shot hisself within ten feet of a seep hole. And about Lane Wells who had a run-in with the Kiowa he rode twenty miles through the hot sun with his nose shot off.

"That's when I first heard stories about the man named Doubletree. He was the one with 'chain lightning hands.' The man who has 'no weakness or softness in body or mind.' Then there was also that part about he-hair on his huevos. She still didn't know what that meant.

"They said he could track a bird you know," She took a swig of buttermilk that left its mark on her lip. "Stuff like that."

Gert looked at the girl—milk mustache, wool-ragged hair—and thought she looked about eight years old.

"Well, they was right about his trackin'," Cobb said. "He said whoever was trailin' those men was leaving a track like a kid."

"Huh!" Depth of depression was only fair reading of sign but she did not point that out to Cobb. He'd been a cavalry man. Everybody knows cavalry men depend on their scouts for tracking. "What does he look like?"

Cobb studied a cross beam. "Tall and lean. Dark. Hard lookin'. Almost like he could have some Apache in him.

Got a bad scar right here." He touched his cheek. "He was no spring chicken, was he, Mother?"

"No . . ." Gert winked at Nessa as she set down another platter loaded with food. ". . . but I'd say he's quite a bit younger'n you, dear."

"Aw, no way. He's got a good ten years on me!"

"Dream on, dear."

While Gert and Ezra went back and forth, Nessa dined on hot cornbread with mustang grape preserves and venison steak and sliced potatoes fried crisp on the outside. Midway through, she said, "I believe this is the best meal I've ever eaten, ma'am."

"Thank you," Gert said. "A man who came through on the stage showed me how to make spuds like that. He called 'em fried potato chips."

Ezra snorted. "Hell, a person'd eat fried cow chips after a walk like that."

"Ezra!" Gert swatted his arm. "Shame on you!"

"I ain't sayin' your cookin' ain't good, Gert. Just makin' an observation."

Nessa smeared a slice of potato around the plate sopping up as much hog-ham gravy as possible, then said, "Mr. Cobb, I don't have a cent to my name, but if you'll sell me a horse on credit, I'll write to my aunt and ask her to send the money on to you. She's good for it but you'd have my word on it to boot. Suppose you would be willing to do that?"

He glanced at his wife. She nodded and said, "Why, of course we would."

"Sure 'nough," he said. "We'll pick something out for you in the morning."

"If you have paper and pen, I'll write my aunt right now."

Gert brought over the lantern and then the Cobbs left her alone.

Encircled in a corona of light, Nessa uncorked the ink-pot and aligned the yellowed foolscap and curved her forearm around it and dipped the sharpened goose quill and sat chewing her lip. The right words escaped her. There was so much she could not say. The lantern hissed and the fire popped and whistled from an occasional raindrop that slipped past the chimney shield.

Finally she just wrote what happened, omitting, of course, any mention of the Mexican family and omitting also the method with which she'd had to put Duchess down.

> . . . *I cood Not see for the dark but it must've bin a dog hole. I guess I don't need to tell you how terible I feel.*
>
> *I'll leave Here tomorow but having lost three days, I am prakticaly starting over. About the onle thing I've akomplished is finding out their naims. In kase They get me, they are Caleb Flat, El Ladino and Trey Henry. These men are even Worse than we suspishuned but I will not go into detale About that here.* (Or ever, Nessa added to herself.)
>
> *A old dog has joyned up with me. He is pretty pityfull and will eat inny thing—even burnt beans scraped off the bottom of the pot—but as long as he keeps Up all rite I'll let him come with me. I value the Kompany, especialy now that Duches is gone. I know you will shed a few tears as I have done all ready.*
>
> > *Yer loving neece,*
> > *Vanessa Cutter Fane*

She almost stoppered the ink before she realized she'd forgotten to ask for the money! She added a postscript requesting that Etta send twenty dollars to Mr. Ezra Cobb, care of the stage station between the Sabinal and Frio Rivers.

The Cobbs were being patient as well as generous. Her letter would be picked up by the next stage and routed to the nearest fort where it would lay until someone happened to be going in the right direction. It could be a year before they got paid. Actually their best hope of prompt payment was if she beat the letter home and tended to the matter herself. It was her devout wish as well.

Seeing as how the Cobbs didn't know her from Adam's off ox, she showed Ezra the letter before she sealed it. "I don't want you to think I'm trying to pull something funny."

He stared at the letter real solemn-like and then offered it to her . . . upside down. "Right purty, miss." Face flaming, Nessa took it and quickly sealed it up.

The next morning she was up before the dew dried. She'd dressed in her new britches—which were way too large but which, after all, had been purchased solely with her good looks—and was carrying her grip outside when Ezra Cobb intercepted her.

"I'd like to go along and help bury those people," he said apologetically, "but my contract calls for me to be here when the stage comes through. Barring Indian trouble, it is due tomorrow." Gert joined them. She carried a gunny sack tied off with rope.

"It's all right, Mr. Cobb. I can manage. Well, thank you for everything, Gert."

"T'weren't nothin'." Gert said and handed her the

sack. "This here's potatos and a wedge of suet. So you can make some potato chips in your skillet."

"Why, thank you. I will."

"Now you be sure to stop on your way back."

"You bet I will." The two women looked at each other and then stepped together and hugged.

"What's your favorite pie?" Gert asked, as they walked arm and arm to the door.

"Dried apple with raisins," replied Nessa promptly.

Gert nodded and patted her arm. "All right then. Soon as I see you comin', I'm gonna start a'bakin'."

"I'll look forward to it. Well, bye!"

She'd selected a lively, grulla mustang earlier, a mare about thirteen hands with sharp eyes, small ears and a strong straight back. About the mare, Cobb said, "She might be short on looks but she's long on endurance. She's cavalry," he added with pride, "so she's broke to gunfire."

"I like her fine," Nessa replied and took a run at the horse and jumped on.

"You sure you don't want to borry a saddle?"

"Heck, no. I started out ridin' bareback when I was three. My pa said it's the only way to get the feel of a horse." She waved, "Well, bye."

The Cobbs lifted their hands as she rode out. Ezra turned to his wife. "Jehosephat! Did she say three?"

"I believe she did at that."

He looked back at the settling dust. "I don't believe I've ever met anyone quite like that girl."

"I don't believe it's likely that you ever will, Ezra."

She figured she must look a sight. Her damp denims were draped over the horse's neck, a short-handled shovel was tied to her belt and she was using a piece of rope as a bridle. Seeing as how there are not many self-respecting cow ponies who would stand for such shenanigans, she started calling the horse Easy.

She rode west until she was safely out of sight of the station then doubled back to the stream where she'd buried that Mexican-looking stranger. Cobb had a limited selection of boots. Two pair, too large—even after Gert had stuffed rags in the toes. Nessa had put some cowhide in the bottom of her old boots and tied the soles shut with rope. She'd told the Cobbs they felt fine but the truth was it felt like she was walking on rock-covered porcupine.

She studied the grave to recall which end was which then started rolling back the rocks. A horrific stench rose but she tied her neck hanky over her mouth and nose and doggedly kept at it.

The boots came off with a hollow mud-sucking sound. She flung them a ways off and then kicked and pushed the rocks back then scooted close enough to put her foot against one of the boots. As she'd thought, they'd fit just fine . . . provided she could stand to wear them! She tied the boots together and hung them over the horse's neck. Amazingly, Easy still wasn't objecting.

At the next clump of sagebrush she stopped and whacked off several branches with her bowie. That night she crushed the flowers and stuck them in the boots and then buried them. It worked. Well, only sort of but there are, she reminded herself, a lot worse things than smelly feet. Not being shod was one of them.

The next day was clear and hot. She swung wide to avoid the area where Duchess lay. Bite had no such sensitivity and soon there were buzzards wheeling in that direction.

When she arrived at the place where the Mexican family had been murdered she found three rough crosses—alamo branches bound with strips of rawhide. A sombrero was stuck on one cross. A broken rosary draped another. A rag doll stuffed with corn husks was propped against the last. She had her suspicions about who'd buried them.

I cood Not keep from remembering what had hapened To that family, especialy what had be Fallen that little girl. I finished my Prayer by making those poor ded people The same promise I had made Bob. While the rivers run, I will go on until I find those men.

Eight

28th of May—I went from dead asleep to bug eyed, awaken by pure animal instinkt I guess because I cood not hear inny Thing but The horse eating a few feet away and the sound of The wind running threw the grass.

Then the dog lifted his head. So. Someone was out there! I cocked my gun and waited and It seemed like for ever before the man stepped out of the shadows.

"That next step'll be your last, mister."

The cant of the man's hat shadowed all but his jaw which was slurred by a close-cropped black beard. But it wasn't his face that she was looking at. It was the way his dust-streaked brush coat was eared back behind the handles of twin Walker Colts. And the fact that both holsters were worn smooth and tied down like a draw fighter.

"I'm a friend," he said and held up one gloved hand, the one that didn't hold a Winchester carbine with its bore pointed at the ground.

"You're pretty pussy-footed for a friend."

"Pure habit, ma'am. I was hopin' to borrow a coffee pot. My own pot rusted clean through."

She almost shot him dead when he abruptly dropped to one knee to rub the dog's head!

"Say, what is this ol' hound's name?"

"Bite. I'd hoped it would be inspirational." Bite's tail was whomping dust.

"He's been sniffin' 'round my camp for two nights runnin'."

"Is that so?" No wonder the dog had been so scarce lately.

"Yeah. Makin' friends has cost me a lota grub."

She should have named the dog Easy. He was on his back now, showing a total lack of dignity and a bright red tallywhacker. "I'm standin' up, mister," she warned.

"Have at it," he said. He rubbed Bite's stomach a minute more, then stood, too. Now they both had a gun pointed at the ground. His rifle. Her pistol. Hard eyes met hers with a steady, inscrutable gaze. Finally he asked, "We gonna jus' stand here eyeballin' each other?"

"Who are you, mister?"

"My name's Doubletree." He slowly raised his left hand to his hat brim and gave it a polite tug. "Texas Rangers."

It was him all right, right down to the scar that furrowed under his cheekbone but she said, "I heard the man called Doubletree was dead." She'd heard no such thing but didn't care for the way he held himself. He dropped about ten years when he grinned.

"Did he go painful?"

"Natural causes."

"God, that's music t'my ears, ma'am." He tugged his hat again.

"Yeah, well, he was older'n those hills yonder." She got him there, judging by what happened to his grin. The dog was leaping at his knee, giving little attention-getting barks. Maybe it was the easy way he brushed the dog aside that decided her. Or it could have been all that hat tugging. Whichever, she heard herself say, "I guess I can share my pot."

"Mighty white of you, ma'am."

He set his rifle against a rock and reached for something. In a flash she had her hammer thumbed back and had dropped into a firing stance. He held up a drawstring pouch.

"Need some java?"

She took a deep breath and straightened and leathered her gun. Then she shook her head.

Doubletree pocketed the pouch and making sure he moved slow and easy and kept his hands in sight, hunkered down by the fire. He watched her add coffee to water already warmed and then start to break camp. After a bit, he said, "Is it all right if I bring my horse up to the water?"

"Suit yourself, mister. I'm fixin' to leave."

"Got a ways to go?"

"Right fair."

There was no more conversation until she offered him the steaming cup of coffee.

"I don't believe I caught your name," he said.

"I don't believe I gave it." There was a tiny battle of the eyes before he accepted the cup. He nodded his thanks and took a sip. It was a vicious brew, strong as lye. "Perfect," he said.

She looked at how his horny hands wrapped loosely around the cup until she realized what she was doing. She turned on her heel and started knocking down the brush shelter she'd made.

"Give you a hand?"

"I don't know why. Seein' as how I got two of my own."

Mouthy, he thought but he was hard-put not to stare when she bent to pick up her bedroll. The girl was pretty well filled out.

She looked over at him. "Somethin' wrong, mister?"

"No. I was just admirin' the way you made that wickiup. Looks like one I saw onct." His eyes tracked her, striding around tall and leggy in her man's britches. She was something all right.

"Wickiup?"

"Ah . . . yeah. If I recollect correctly, it was up in Ft. Worth." He used his teeth on his tobacco pouch string. "Yeah, that's right. It was Ft. Worth. A bunch of old rangers had come in to witness the hangin' of a back shooter feller who'd killed one of their compadres." She continued scattering branches. "That fella—the one that made the wickiup—was sure an interestin' ol' coot. Preferred a knife over a gun, he said. Had a flat-handled side knife that he wore up under his left arm. Got at it through a slit in his shirt." He shook his head slowly. "He could draw that thing so blamed fast it was impossible for the human eye to follow."

She shot him a look but he was staring into his coffee.

"Yeah, I remember now. His name was Cutter. Nate Cutter." While she was aligning the hair pad and then smoothing on her saddle blanket, he noticed that the girl never turned her back on him. After a minute, he went on, "They say he was cunnin' as a coyot', ol' Cutter. 'Course he'da had to be. To survive out here in the old days." She tossed on her saddle and cinched up then she walked over and stood in front of him. Her legs were locked and wide spread, like a cocky kid about to deliver a double dare.

He was inclined to take her up on it. He stood. She pointed. "I'd like to take my cup with me."

"Oh, yeah." He drained the last of the coffee and she took the cup—sort of abruptly, he thought—and stuffed it in a morral that she had tied to her pommel. Then she swung into the saddle and wheeled her horse.

"So long, mister." His words . . . whatever they were . . . were drowned out by drumming hooves.

He was about a haf mile be Hind me that hole morning. I tryed to ignore him but I cood not keep from sneaking a quik look now and then. One time he was cleaning his Finger nails with a pocket knife. Another time he was slouched in the saddle with his hat pulled low. Snozing I thought but I had no sooner turned back when he road up a long side.

She found a lot to admire on the horizon. It was a pretty sky. Bright and china blue. She found a lot to admire about his horse as well, a powerful dapple gray that he sat in the relaxed manner of a veteran horseman. They rode a mile or so, the only sound the creak of saddle leather and the chink of metal.

"Excuse me, ma'am, but see those 'dobe ruins over yonder?"

She looked. "Yeah, I see 'em. What about it?"

"Well, when I holler, we best both ride for 'em like the very devil."

"Why?"

He hitched a thumb over his shoulder. She twisted in the saddle. On a flat-topped ridge to the east was a string of Indians, keeping pace with them. "Balls!" she hissed and felt her skin clabber. Narrowing her eyes, she studied the feathered lances and the long black hair that fluttered in the wind. "Comanche!"

"Uh-huh."

She'd been so blamed busy admirin' . . . Right then the lead Indian turned his horse and Doubletree hollered, "Go!" She spared a quick look for Bite and saw him disappearing into some rocks, but then all she thought of was the Indians. Bullets and arrows were starting to kick up the dust around them and she could hear their hair-raising yells now. She stuck her nose in Easy's mane and rode flat out.

Doubletree was keeping pace with her. The adobe ruins sat straight ahead and she had the crazy thought they were going to cork themselves in the opening until he dropped back slightly.

She ducked under the low opening and had to pull up hard to keep from crashing into the back wall. Clods of dirt flew as the mare stood on her back legs. She lost her seat and landing hard, lost her wind as well. She rolled over, ripped her shirt open and pulled the journal out of her belt. Arrows and bullets were flying all over the place but all she could do was stare up at the sky and work her mouth like a beached fish.

Doubletree knelt at the window, firing. He paused and eyed her. Bared to her undershirt. Legs wide spread. "Normally I would," he said, as he squibbed off another shot. "But I just don't believe I could do the job justice right now. Thank you though, for the offer." She crossed her eyes at him. Which was about the only thing she could move at the time. He was squeezing off another shot. And talking.

"It ain't that I ain't interested. I am. Yes, indeed. If it weren't for being under a full-scale Indian attack . . ."

Breath sawing, she thought: *What a jackass!*

He squeezed off another shot then another, waited a minute and then holstered his gun. "Well, it appears they're goin' to talk it over." He gave her a long look and then knuckled both sides of his mustache. "I will say this: If those Comanch' are set on cuttin' off my dinghus they sure ain't gonna have no trouble findin' it."

She rolled up and put her head between her knees. She had progressed to panting. "I believe," she managed finally, "that you could be the biggest ass-head I have ever met!"

He chuckled. "Always try to be the best at whatever you do. That's my mot-to." He gathered the horses' reins and staked them behind the highest standing wall, then piled up some rocks to make it even higher. She noticed he had placed Easy where the mare would be the least vulnerable to flying arrows and bullets.

She coughed and wished it were cooler. The dry earth and settling dust was stifling. She glanced around. The little home had originally consisted of only two rooms. The pole and earth roof had already rejoined the dirt from which it came. It wouldn't be long now before the walls did likewise. She crawled to the crumbled opening and knelt beside him. "How many, do you figure?"

"Coupla dozen. Give or take," he replied and noticed that that took care of her high color.

"Where do you want me?"

He flashed on her laying flat on her back and thought: A damn poor choice of words, lady. "Take that side. I hope Nate Cutter taught you how to shoot."

"My aim's as good as my name, mister."

"By God you don't lack for confidence, do you? Well, you'll have a chance to prove yourself." He pointed. " 'Cause here they come."

The air was rent with Comanche war cries and the sound of horses running flat out. Nessa's scalp crawled. There was a whish and a thud and an arrow embedded itself six inches from her nose. She fired but rushed her shot, muttered "Balls" and squeezed off another and an Indian flung his arms wide and fell backward. Doubletree fired twice and two Indians dropped off their mounts. That's three, she thought and fired again. Four. And again. Five. She lost count of how many Doubletree dusted.

The Indians fell back, circling out of range. She looked at him and grinned nervously and clamped down on a fierce urge to pee.

He pointed with his chin, calm as could be. "Look for 'em t'come thataway now." She shifted into position and he was right. They soon came again, screaming like banshees or yelping like crazed dogs. A sorrel and white paint pony rode straight at her. She had drawn a bead square on the Indian's chest when suddenly the rider disappeared.

She'd heard about that trick but had never seen it. The brave had braided a loop of horsehair so he could ride against the horse's side. The only part of him showing was one heel low on the horse's back. The Indian fired his rifle from beneath the horse's neck and a chunk of adobe hit her cheek. She shot that fine horse although it about killed her to do it.

Another bullet narrowly missed her, causing her to think that things had sure changed since her father's day. He used to say that most Indians cannot hit anything with a gun unless they got up close and used the butt!

There was a clicking sound and she whirled, gun ready, but it was only Bite, limping in after his hard run. When she turned back she found that the Indians had disappeared. A long moment passed while she strained to find a target. "They're gone."

"Not gone. Not yet. They can melt outa sight like butter on flapjacks."

The sudden silence was deafening. She whispered, "Why are they . . " She cleared her throat and started again. "Why are they waiting, do you think?" She was feeling oddly deflated.

"Talkin' it over. I don't think they expected two good shooters," Doubletree replied. He spun the cylinder of his side gun, checking the load. "Your pa done all right by you. You're a fine shot."

"I ought to be. I've been practicing since I was six."

"Six? You sure about that?"

"Positive. The first time I handled a firearm was January of '42. I even remember the very afternoon." She knew she was chattering, but she couldn't seem to stop herself. "A blue norther had howled down that morning . . ."

With only that little said, she was reliving that winter and as she told it, she saw it. The frosty sleet that sheathed the branches of the trees. The barn roof, iced like a cake. She could almost feel the gusts of frigid wind that goosed her up the slippery path from the barn.

She tugged on the door and the wind caught her and sailed her inside. She latched the door against the chill blast and ran to her mother who sat by the fire mending a shirt. "Ma! Guess what? One of those kittens has six toes."

"Was that what you were doing?" her mother asked.

"Uh-huh. Wanna come see?"

"Not tonight," her mother said. "Tomorrow maybe. If this weather will ever quit. Take off your coat now, Vanessa. Your Pa's been waitin' on you all this time."

She turned questioning. Her father stood at the hearth. He stopped knocking the dottle out of his pipe long enough to point with it. "Sit down there at the table, Nessa."

Nessa hung her coat on a peg on the wall and took her usual place at the long table. Guns and knives of all shapes and sizes had been laid out on the table. Every item was something she'd been instructed never to touch before. She clasped her hands in her lap and waited for her father to gather the pouch that contained his tobacco.

"Yore ma thinks it's time for you to learn how to defend yoreself."

Nessa shot a look to her mother who was sewing and causing the rocker to yield its measured creak. To all appearances, her only concern was the busted elbow of her husband's shirt. Nessa then looked to her aunt who sniffed and quit the room.

Learn how to defend myself! Nessa tried to control her impatience as her father started performing the ritual that ultimately led to lighting his pipe. Her mother believed that her father's smoking was what caused his morning coughing fits. In deference to her wishes, Nate Cutter had taken up the pipe. He complained, however, that he spent more time fiddlin' than he did smokin'. Nessa agreed.

"There are those," he began, "in this world who are victims and there are those who are not. Yore ma would like to do everythin' possible to make certain that you are among the latter.

"Now. Just because yore a girl—an a small one at that—does not mean you have to be dominated by someone bigger and stronger'n you."

"I'm gonna grow some more, Pa."

He took the wet stem of his pipe from his mouth and frowned. "You think?"

"Uh-huh. Yes. Positive. Why, I already growed . . ."

"I've grown," her mother said.

"I've grown over two inches since my birthday."

"Well, then," he said. "it's entirely possible that you will do a bit more growin', but I doubt you'll ever be real big. An' besides, no matter how big you are, the chances are that there'll always be somebody bigger."

"What's a victim, Pa?"

She didn't miss his quick glance at her mother before he replied. "A victim is a person who has been damaged unfairly by some person or circumstance. Generally because they were unprepared to defend themselves. Which is why it is necessary for you to learn to handle a weapon."

"Because I'm small?"

"Not only that. You might be forced to defend someone who is even smaller than you." He smoked a while. Outside it sounded like it was sleeting nails.

"There's many—Christians most particularly—who

think an injured party should do no more'n pray for a person who harms them. They believe in leaving justice to God. That evil will reap what it sows and that ultimately the wrongdoer will get his just desserts. Unfortunately, I know for a fact that that is too often not the case." He paused to puff vigorously.

"One of the best examples of such injustice occurred many years ago when a man scalped and tortured five travelers in an attempt to make it look like it was Injens done the deed. I was first on the scene and I can tell you that the Apache and Comanche are generally more merciful than that murderer was. Well, I knew right off that I was after a white man but he was smart and eluded me. Years passed. Thinking himself safe, the killer opened a dry good store in a small town located clear across Texas. He prospered there and even garnered the respect and regard of his community. But he made one mistake and that was in takin' the name of one of his victims as his own. I don't know why. Maybe the murdered man had something with his name on it that the killer wanted. Or maybe the killer was arrogant and wanted to thumb his nose at the law. Which ever."

More puffing.

"Well, happenstance brought me through that town and, having never forgotten the names of those travelers, I remember being struck by the coincidence. I decided to look into it further. A search of the killer's belongings showed that he had kept everything in a trunk in the back room of his store. The least grisly of his trophies was the scalps he'd taken." He shook his head. "Children. Women. Made no never mind. Well, he finally got justice on that day. I arrested him that morning and had the pleasure of hanging him in the afternoon."

Her mother interrupted, "That wasn't what I had in mind, Nate."

"I'm comin' to what you had in mind, Alma. I wanted to point out that if it hadn't of been for the justice I personally dealt that man, he would probably still be living high on the hog."

"Yes, but I doubt if Nessa would find herself in such a . . ."

"I'm gettin' to a more apt example."

"Sorry." They smiled at each other.

Nessa was convinced her parents had a way of communicating without words. It was some kind of sign language but without hand movements. She would look at him and he'd chuckle. Or he'd look at her and she'd sigh and shake her head. Careful observation proved that her aunt did not know this language; apparently nobody did.

There'd been a lot of that silent talk lately because not too long ago her father told her that her mother'd been "carrying a baby inside her . . ." (Ptui! Disgusting! Why'd she want to carry it there?)

Sure enough, next thing Nessa knew everybody was all upset because she'd gone and ". . . lost it . . ." somewheres!

Can you imagine anybody losing a whole baby? Heck fire! You can't just lay down a little baby out in the woods or something. The durn wolves probably ate the poor thing by now!

When the time was right Nessa thought she'd suggest that Ma let Pa carry the next baby. He'd never lose it. Not in a hundred years.

"Nessa?"

"What?"

"Are you payin' attention?"

"Yes."

"As I was sayin' . . . Perhaps a more apt example is the man who had six younguns all under the age of six. He was a drinker with a hair-trigger temper and no patience. A switchin' was the least those kids took under the pretense of discipline. I heard he once maimed one of his boys by holding his hand to a hot stovepipe." He shook his head slowly. "The mother was probably the only person alive who could have helped those children, but she was so cowed she could not bring herself to raise her voice ag'in her husband—much less her hand."

Nessa looked at her mother. She didn't doubt her mother's love but she also knew that her mother didn't have the sand to stand up to her shadow. She looked back at her father. There was no question in her mind as to who she wanted to take after.

"Now." He handed her a long-barreled pistol which sunk her hand to the floor.

"Gol, it's heavy as a rock!" she exclaimed.

"I imagine it is. It's all right to use both hands. Go on an' get the feel of it. It's not loaded." He relit his pipe before he continued. "Remember that a gun is not a toy. Its sole purpose is to kill. Now it is my hope that you never have to use this gun ag'in another but should you need to, you will at least know how. Good or better than most."

She touched the cold hard barrel, the scarred and worn handle.

"When someone does you a kindness, Nessa, you must never forget it. But likewise when someone harms you or those you love you must never forget that neither. If a person truly deserves to die—and there's no one else to do the job then you must have the strength of spirit to do it yoreself. In a clear-cut case, you must have no qualms about steppin' up an' doin' your duty. Be prepared, for justice may be up to you."

Something Doubletree said brought her back. She glanced at him. "What?"

"I said, did ol' Cutter teach you anything about defending an isolated position when encircled by Indians?"

"Yes. Matter of fact, there are some things I could be doing right now." She stood and brushed her hands down her thighs. "But first I'll check the horses."

She was gone a minute. Then beneath consumptive-like coughing came the unmistakable sound of piss hitting rock. Doubletree grinned and called out, "Everythin' all right with 'em horses?"

"Yes." Strangled. "Fine." She came out with heightened color and her saddlebags.

She propped her carbine where it would be handy then opened two boxes of shells and set them next to it. She reloaded her revolver then filled any empty loops on her gunbelt. She removed her jacket and then the bowie and stuck it into the dirt a short grab away. She eased the sneak knife in and out of its scabbard. She moved her shoulders in something akin to a shudder and then turned to him and said, "Well, I'm ready."

"Good," he replied and handed her two strips of venison jerky. "Let's eat."

"Eat?"

Looked like the girl was trying to be her lips in a knot. "Yeah. Eat."

"God! I couldn't possibly eat right now." She gave the jerky to the dog then poured a handful of water on a dished out stone. She knew he was watching her and expected some comment about wasting water on an ol' dog but he didn't say anything. Just ate his piece of jerky then rolled a smoke and lit it.

They sat and silently watched crimson ribbons appear in the western sky. It was more than could be said for the Indians who were gobbling and hooting and barking at each other. Bite's ears were going crazy. So were hers. "Why don't they just holler to each other?" she complained finally. "It's not like we don't know it's them."

"It's part of their show."

"It's about to drive me crazy.

"Hell, that's what it's supposed to do. Unsettle you."

More to block out the Indians than anything, she commented, "I'd heard the Comanch' were staying south of the Nueces lately."

"Not any more. The Governor of Chihuahua's got 'em all stirred up. Declared a bounty for Comanche scalps. Hundred bucks for males, fifty bucks for females and children."

Silence descended again. Women and children! She couldn't help feeling a twinge of sympathy.

She killed time by trying to distinguish the Indians from genuine coyotes and then by trying to find Orion and his belt of three stars. If they could somehow sneak off, it would help to know which direction they were headed. Doubletree started talking again as if a long time hadn't gone by.

"A Comanche's funny."

She snorted. "I ain't seen that so far."

"By funny I mean different. We might see the day when the white man can live alongside the other Indian tribes, but I don't think we'll ever see the day when the white man can live alongside the Comanche."

"Why not? Not that I want to, but why not?"

"Because peace is ag'in their nature. A Comanche hunts to eat but he lives to make war. For a Comanche to quit warrin' would be like somebody tellin' you that you can keep on livin' but you got to quit breathin'."

"Huh."

"Add to that the fact that they don't believe they can be beat."

"And you said I didn't lack for confidence."

"Exactly. There's no Indian more confident than the Comanche. With good reason. Hell, the Comanche ran all the other tribes out of the Llano Estacado. Even the Apache." She smelled sulphur as he cupped his hands around a match. "That's sayin' somethin', you know, for I have fought those damned Apaches and they ain't women." He looked at her and added, "No offense meant."

"None taken," she replied solemnly.

At a rustling noise they both drew and cocked their guns but it was just the dog twitching in his sleep. She released the breath she had been holding and reholstered her gun.

Another long stretch of silence followed. Night draped over rocks and pooled in the flats. It was beautiful in a way, but to her it seemed that every shadow contained a skulking redman. Her eyes were starting to feel like raisins they'd been skinned so long. "Wonder what they're waiting on?" She looked up at the sliver of a moon. "They aren't going to get much more light."

"Nope. There'll be no Comanche moon tonight."

"So do you think they'll attack tonight? Or wait 'til sunrise?"

"Sunrise, I expect."

"Well, then you know what I'm thinking?"

"I wouldn't hazard a guess."

"I'm thinking that a sneak attack—right now—would probably surprise the hell outa 'em." He was looking at her with new eyes, but she was intently studying the prairie. "It's chancy . . . I know it's chancy, but it just might work." She turned to him. "What do you think? Are you up for it?"

Another loaded question, he thought. "Now, lemme see if I understand you. You wanna crawl out there and engage 'em in a fight mano a mano?" She was too intent to hear the quiet humor in his voice.

"You can use your knife if you want to. I believe I'd just as soon use my gun."

She leaned closer, like a schoolgirl sharing a secret, and he could smell her hair, the sweet scent of her skin.

"Suppose we was to catch 'em in our cross fire? We could dust a bunch of 'em and then run for all we're worth."

"Mmm," he said and took another deep breath.

"Well?"

"It ain't a bad idea." She nodded, bright-eyed and quivering like a pup. It took him a second to realize that she was waiting for him to continue. "But far as a place to make a stand I've been in lots worse'n this." He waved at the adobe walls. "They cain't burn us out."

"True."

"They got to expose themselves to our guns every time they come at us."

"True."

"We've got enough bullets 'n' water to last through tomorrow."

"True, too."

"Well then, I say: Let's hold off. Let's see how we fare tomorrow. Hellfire! We might just whip 'em out-right." He could tell she was thinking on it and the intent look on her face made him want to grin. She was a bloodthirsty little thing. "We can always pay 'em a visit tomorrow night."

"Well, all right. But we wouldn't wanna wait 'til we're too weak. You know. Lack of water or shot up."

"Um, no. We sure wouldn't want that."

She was disappointed. It was a damned good plan and like her father used to say: do the unexpected when the enemy least expects it. "Well, that's decided then."

Fireflies winked. A night owl hoo'ed and some animal screeched. She wasn't sure but she thought she could feel him looking at her. He wasn't going to get funny, was he? She purposefully kept her eyes on the plains.

She was right. He couldn't take his eyes off her. The moonlight had glazed her skin and made her pupils into black mountain pools. "Miss Vanessa Cutter," he said softly. "You sure are somethin'."

"It's Fane. Vanessa Cutter Fane. Mrs."

"What?"

"Yes. I am . . . widowed."

"Widowed!"

If mulling had a sound she was hearing it. Finally, he asked, "What happened to your husband?"

"He, ah . . . was felled by a tree."

"That's a shame. Killed right off?"

"Yes."

He scratched his head then reseated his hat. "You know, I sure had you pegged wrong."

"What do you mean?"

"I thought you were followin' the same fellas I've been after."

"Me?" She chuckled. "Oh my! Not me. Nossir." She heard her voice wobble there at the end. It was that damned flint-eyed stare of his! One of the horses stamped and blew and then it was quiet as a tomb and he was still looking at her. She needed to say something. "Who did you say you were after?"

"I didn't but there's three of 'em ridin' together. I am particularly interested in one."

"Taking him in for trial?"

He shook his head. "Takin' him to trim a tree. He's had his trial."

"Real bad, huh?"

"Real bad? Well, I'll say this on that. Out here it is possible for the line between good and bad to sometimes get a bit blurred. I myself have known some good men who were also pretty bad. Then on the other hand, I have known some bad fellas who have had some real redeemin' qualities. Some of the worst owlhoots make the best lawmen, you know, caught young enough and turned around."

Is that a fancy way of saying no? she wanted to ask, but then he went on.

"And then there are some where there ain't no blur at all. Flatt's one of 'em."

"Flatt?"

"Yeah, Caleb Flatt."

"Seems like I've heard that name somewhere."

"You might've but I doubt it. He's just one of a bunch

of blood-hungry cutthroats operatin' down along the border. Been involved in wide-spread cattle rustling into Mexico for years. Trades stolen American goods—whiskey and cartridges—for captives."

"Whiskey and cartridges! To the Indians?"

"Yeah, in the past the law's looked the other way, trying to get captives back by whatever means possible. Not any more. His go-between with the Comanche and Comancheros is a breed named Ladino. Something went haywire during the last deal. The Indians got the whiskey and the cartridges and kept the captives. They suffered bad."

There was a moment. "You said there were three men?"

"Yeah. The last one's a dimwit named Trey Henry. He's kin to Flatt I heard. Suspected of killing his own sister."

A horrible image rose that Nessa put aside. *Just find out where they're headed.* "Think they're making for the border?"

"Ladino is for sure. I imagine Flatt'll probably head off west. Toward Hermacita."

"So that's where you'll head. If we get outa here."

"I guess. Unless I catch up with them earlier. Sooner I catch Flatt the sooner I get the money."

"Money?"

"There's a thousand-dollar reward on Caleb Flatt."

"A thousand dollars!" The girl whistled through her teeth. "Why so much?"

"He made the mistake of shooting two United States soldiers. I wish he hadn't've."

"Why?"

"Because now the politicians and the lawyers are in it."

"Why is that bad?"

"Back in the old days nobody would've cared whether you brought in a man like Flatt head up or head down. Probably would've been a shoot-on-sight order and that would be that. But not any more. Not now that the politicians and lawyers have got their say in it. Nowadays a criminal gets his day in court and damned if half of 'em don't get off scot-free. I got as much use for a politician as a hog has for Sunday. Lawyers right with 'em."

"But didn't you say that Flatt's already had a trial?"

"Yeah, except that one of the soldiers killed was the younger brother of a U.S. Senator. It's worth a thousand dollars to the Senator to see Flatt hung in person. Which is why I plan to be the one who brings him in. With land goin' at five cents an acre, Flatt represents twenty thousand acres to me."

"That's a lot of money. Might be there's others after him as well."

"Mebbe. Bounty hunters, I suppose." There was a flash of white. "I'd be obliged to arrest 'em."

"Arrest them? On what charge?"

"Gettin' in the way of a Ranger in the line of duty." She frowned. "I never heard of no such law."

Another flash. "Me neither."

"Can you do that?"

"Nobody's never said I cain't."

"You mean if there ain't a law to suit you then you make up one of your own?"

"Close enough."

"I see." And she did, too. She stared out at the moon shadowed plain and thought: Good thing I came up with that tall tale about how Bob died.

Suddenly she jerked and then flopped face down. Out of the side of her mouth she whispered, "Bushes!"

"What?"

"Indians! Using the bushes to creep closer."

He barely glanced. "Naw, they're usin' 'em t'drag off their dead."

Nessa took another look, said oh, and sat up. She brushed off her chin. A minute went by. A bit sheepishly, she confessed that it was her first actual Indian fight.

"It is?"

"Yes"

"Well, I'd've never guessed."

"Really?"

"Really. You're doin' right fine. There's only one thing you need to do."

"What's that?"

"Make sure it isn't your last."

She chuckled but it came out wrong so she leaned her head back and stared up at the stars. Her last fight! God, maybe her last night! Ever. It was a sobering thought and she wondered: Is this how a person feels when they're about to die? Wistful? Intensely mindful of everything? She looked at Doubletree and the words were out before she knew she said them, "You knew who I was. Soon as you saw me."

"Yeah."

"How?"

"Because I'd seen you onct before."

She pointed at herself. "Me?" *And you remembered me?*

"Yeah. Six, maybe seven years back."

"Where?"

"A little town on the Perdnales. I forget the name."

"Twin Buttes. We live not far from there. How come you were there? Nothing ever happens in Twin Buttes."

"I'd stopped for a bath and a square most likely. There used to be an old lady who ran the boarding house there. Made the best peach pie I've ever eaten. I'd probably stopped at the store first. To buy some Lone Jack or somethin'." He paused a long time. "You were in there with your mama."

That narrowed it down. There were only two or three times that her mother ever went to town. Disastrous occasions, all of them. She'd just as soon not remember.

Saddle leather creaked as one of the horses shifted. "Here you know all about me and I don't know hardly anything about you."

He looked at her. "There somethin' you want to know about me?"

"Well . . ." She dropped her eyes and brushed some grit off her knee.

"What?"

"Well, I was sorta wonderin'. . ."

"What?"

"Are you . . ." She worked up her nerve. "Is Doubletree an Indian name?"

"No, but I could be some Indian."

"Could be? Don't you know?"

"Not for sure."

"How come?"

"Because I don't know who my folks were. Somebody left me in a pile of hay in a livery stable."

"Like baby Jesus?"

He got a laugh out of that. "Yeah, but I kinda doubt that Joseph was my father. No, I'm probably the product of some woman who was set upon by a breed. I used to wonder about it but I don't any more."

"How old were you? When you were left in the livery stable?"

"Well, ol' man Gentry—that was the name of the blacksmith who found me—he said I looked like I was five, maybe six months old. That was three days after Christmas, 1819. It was Gentry who named me Doubletree. After what he was best at making."

"Was?"

"Yeah. He's dead. Horse kicked him when I was twelve."

"Where was that?"

"A little settlement near Oatmeal Creek."

"Do you still live there?"

"No. Not for a long time now. Gentry's wife remarried. Her new husband was a preacher man. Quick with a stick as he was with a quote from Scripture. He used to tell me he had to beat my 'violent nature' outa me. Guess I was too rambunctious for him. I used to get into fights. Raise some hell. Didn't study my lessons like I was supposed to."

"That's not a good reason not to like somebody. I wasn't crazy about school myself. I'd rather be riding my horse or swimming in the river any time."

They smiled at each other—kindred souls. He was a lot nicer than she'd thought in the beginning. "When did you leave?"

He sobered. "The last time he tried to give me a whippin'. I took his stick away from him and beat the hell outa him with it and then I lit out."

"How old were you?"

"Jus' shy of fourteen."

So young! Imagine being that young and on your own. She felt she ought to say something but didn't know what. A locust filled in until he started talking again.

"I worked around. Here and there. Went clear to Denver one time, trailin' some cows. Then the war started. Joined up with Houston when I was fifteen. Started rangerin' at eighteen." He looked at her. "I never rode with your father but I remember hearin' that he'd died. I was in San Antone when someone said he'd passed. There was an ol' guy there. I forget his name but he knew your Pa well. He had plenty to say about him. All of it good."

She let some dust filter through her fingers. "You know, about the only thing I could see wrong with my Pa was he could never see the other fella's side of things. He could be stiff as stove wood about his idea of right and wrong. It was his way or no way."

"I've known lotsa men like that." He smoked. Then, "What about your ma?"

"She died right after Pa."

"So you're all alone now?"

The answer caught in her throat for a minute. "Except for my Pa's half sister. We . . . she's got a nice place on the Perdnales."

"Cows?"

"Horses."

Leather creaked and spurs chinked as he shifted to take off his hat. His hair was left crimped by the sweat band. He ran his hand through it, a long unruly thatch that shagged in ragged fantails over his collar.

She should leave it alone but found she couldn't. "How come you remembered seein' me that day in Twin Buttes?"

"How come?" He left that hang until she looked up at him. "Because I couldn't keep my eyes off you, that's how come." He ground out his smoke, but kept staring at her steady. "That crow black hair an' those blue eyes. You were the prettiest thing I'd ever seen." He looked at her bowed head. "You still are."

She tossed her hair. "You're just sayin' that."

"Lady, I don't butter burnt toast. Never have. Never will." He took a flask out of his hip pocket, removed his neckerchief and wet it and leaned toward her. She bowed her back. "I was just gonna tend that cut on your cheek." He raised his brow and waited. "All right?"

More than just a gut feeling said it was damned dangerous to let him touch her; her mouth had gone dry and her heart was like a tom-tom in her ears. Inside something was stretching out like a fiddle string pulled too tight. Yet, in spite of all those warning signs, she nodded.

He cupped the back of her head with one hand while he wiped her cheek and then their eyes met and it got awfully quiet all of a sudden. He kissed her once softly. He said some stuff to her then but words were meaningless by that time. Everything was. Even the Comanche were far away and no longer important.

It felt as natural as breathing, what happened that nite. I know I will never forget it. Not to my dying day. I never guesed it cood be like that between a man and a woman.

Nine

29th of May—I wok just before day break and There he was. What is worse was: there I was as well! I thought I wood die of shame! All the things I'd done. I do not no what caim over me—some Sort of buck fever I gess— but I do no one thing: Rite than I wood have given inny Thing in the world to be on the Other side of it.

He wanted her again but she turned away from him and picked up her shirt. She had to get her clothes on before the sun came up. There was already a rim of light to the east.

"The Comanche're gone." Hands laced behind his head, he was just lying there, watching her fight with her shirt. "They took off a long time ago. Figured they musta cornered a whole wagonload a' hog callers."

That smokey drawl! She hated it. Hated that chuckle, too. Hated him. She glared at him and then stifled a moan. There were purple teeth marks on his shoulder. He touched her leg. Soft, like stroking a kitten. "What's wrong, darlin'?"

"I'm missing two buttons."

"Buttons? Hellfire! I'm missin' a pound of flesh offa my . . . ." She stood. "Hey?" She tucked her shirt in. "What's the matter, darlin'?"

"You know what's the matter."

He sat up. "No, I don't. What?"

"Well, if you don't know I sure can't tell you."

There was a long moment then he said, "Hell, I can't explain what happened. I ain't never experienced nothin' like it before."

"I would hope not." She twisted her mouth, her face flaming. "Can't be every day that a man gets . . . gets . . . you know . . . in the middle of an Indian attack."

"Gets what?" he asked, softly teasing.

"Gets his pole greased."

His smile faded. "Where'd you hear talk like that?" She shrugged. "Who said that to you?" Silence. "Who, damnit?"

"One of the hands."

"Which one?"

"Which one? What are you gonna do? Go knock him upside the head? Just forget it! It was years ago."

"I don't care how long . . ."

"The man didn't say it to me. All right?"

"Who'd he say it to then?"

"One of the other men. I was under the bunkhouse window."

"Under the . . . Hell, you hadn't ought to be there."

"Why not? I heard a lot of interesting things about men out there. About dippin' their daubers and wielding their wangs . . ."

"Here now! Cut that kinda talk out!" He stretched for his pants, muttering.

She snapped her sock to unball it. "You didn't answer me."

"What?" He looked up at her. "You want to know

many times I've made love in the middle of a Comanche attack?"

His hand snaked around her ankle. Damn him, he was grinning again.

"Well, darlin', I got t'think a minute now."

"Don't." She moved out of his grasp and picked up her boots.

He arched one brow. "Don't?"

"Just don't . . . make anything of it, that's all."

"You talkin' about last night? You gonna try and say last night was nothing to you?"

She stamped her boots on, aware all the while of his hot eyes on her.

"All right. I know what you're feelin'. You're feelin' guilty as hell. You loved your husband. Ain't that it?" A crow's cranky caw was his only answer. "Sure it is. Well, fine, feel all the guilt you want. But I can God-damn-guarantee-ya you didn't like layin' with your husband as much as you liked it with me."

"That's not true."

"Not true? Gal, you didn't know biscuits from bull . . . hooey about what goes on between a man and a woman." Silence again. "God, how old are you, anyhow?"

"Nineteen."

"Nineteen!" He was practically shouting. "Shit! You can't be only nineteen!"

"Well, two months shy."

"Two months shy!" Now he was shouting. "Crissakes! You're scarcely out of three-cornered pants."

"You oughta know what kinda pants I wear. You tore 'em offa me."

Glaring into his randy eyes, she suddenly realized that she hadn't ought to have reminded him about last night.

Same for herself. Because she either had to leave now or lay with him again . . .now. She walked to her horse.

"Fine. Run away."

"I am *not* running away. I've never run away from anything in my life."

"Sure looks like it t'me."

She turned mad enough to kill but became paralyzed by the sight of him standing there with his shirt open over his bare hairy chest, his unbuttoned pants low slung on his hips. It seemed to take a full minute before she could gather herself.

"What about last night?"

She grabbed her saddle and slung it on and cinched up. "What about it? I thought we were gonna die. That's all."

"That's all it was to you? A last toss before kickin' the bucket?"

She shrugged. His face might've been stone except for a jerking jaw muscle.

"Well, thank you kindly, lady. I sure needed to know that."

"You asked. Now you know." She almost groaned out loud when she hit the saddle. He grabbed her bridle, forcing her to look into his eyes, which were now sizzling crazy-like.

"You know, I'm about a step away from givin' into my violent nature."

"You have no say over me, mister."

"That . . ." He pointed at his gun. ". . . is all the say I need."

She jerked the reins free and backed the horse up. He followed. They glared at each other. She slipped one stirrup and kicked at him. The horse shied. "I'm warnin'

you! Don't dog me. I swear I will shoot your damn horse
right out from under you."

He made a leap for her and pulled her from the saddle.
They tussled this way and that. She kicked him. Stomped
his bare toes. "Damnit!" he yelled and knocked her feet
out from under her and they both went down. He grabbed
her by the ears to pull her face down to his. Abruptly
all movement ceased. Very slowly he removed his hands
and held them loosely curled beside his head.

She kept the knife pressed home until she gained her
feet and captured the reins and remounted. Except for
coming up on his elbows, he stayed sprawled in the dust.
A crimson teardrop of blood hung glistening on the black
hair beneath his belly button.

She said, "Well," and held her hat aloft and danced
Easy around a couple of times. "Guess I'll see ya around,
huh? Ran-ger Dou-ble-tree."

*I slammed my hat down so far it sprung my ears! And
then I road. I stoped at the First available water, flung
off my clothes And dove in. The streem was only a Foot
deep but I had To try to get his smell off me.*

Ten

31st of May—In spyte of telling my Self I must put that nite behind me and Never think of it again, I Have relived it a hunred times.

She set a grueling pace, trying to get as many miles as possible between herself and the adobe ruins. At the top of every rise she would stop and look back the way she'd come. Although she sometimes waited a good long while, she saw no one. If Doubletree was behind her, he was doing a good job of staying out of sight.

She saw no sign of that band of Comanche either and wondered why. Maybe they'd been attacked by a hunting party and not a war party. Maybe the Indians had had to choose between killing a couple of palefaces and protecting their women and children from scalp hunters. Maybe a long fight against two deadeyes was contrary to their plans. Any guess was as good as the next.

Along about sundown she came upon a small valley within the fork of a stream and stopped, awe-struck by a waving sea of blue flowers. Here and there were towering spires of the yucca and splashes of Indian paintbrush. Amid it all was a lone lightning struck oak, home to a hundred cowbirds, all of which were singing their pea-sized hearts out.

Her spell might never have been broken if not for the covey of quail Bite spooked up. She whistled up the dog and made him heel to. "Let's not mess with heaven, Bite."

Riding around that valley took her off the beaten path. She was following a narrow animal trail when she saw the sun glinting on something on the ground. She got off her horse to investigate and found an old apothecary bottle buried neck deep. Only then did she realize that she was kneeling within a jagged border of sunken rocks. It was a grave, probably a child's. The bottle contained a once folded piece of paper but the cork shredded beneath her fingernail like tobacco. She knelt there and shook the bottle until the paper tented against the glass. It read . . . ena Kay B . . . 836.

After reburying the bottle she sat looking down at that small valley for quite a time and she was sad to the bone.

She took shelter that night in an abandoned brush and mud jacal. A storm was brewing to the north, bringing wind and lightening flashes. She pulled the blanket up and doggedly closed her eyes but every sound was magnified, the rustling of some small creature overhead, the rhythmic creaking of something loose in the wind. She thought of Bob and hated herself. She thought of Doubletree—and what she'd been doing this time last night—and hated herself a lot more.

She woke up with red eyes, a sore throat and an ugly disposition. She had no business thinking about him! Damnit she ought to be thinking about the task she'd set! And yet she couldn't help wondering . . . Was he thinking of her?

He was. And he didn't sleep much either but he did do some hard thinking. Before there was any hint of light in the eastern skies, he was in the saddle. Red-eyed. Haggard. Mad enough to chew bullets. Very determined.

A look by either into the other's thoughts would have brought amazed recognition.

It was mid-day on the fourth of June when I found The morgan's sine again. The traks led to a sun baked ranch, a well cared for and prosperous looking spread but I aproached it very wery.

A man sat on the front gallery whittling. He'd been at it a while, judging from the curls of wood that lay in a pyramid between his boots. He closed his knife, put his hands on his knees and stood. "Hoddy!" he said and then moved so the rifle propped against the rail was in plain view.

"Howdy, mister." At the sound of her voice, he stepped out of the shade and took a long look at her. She did the same. He was a barrel-built man with mouse-colored hair and a walnut-sized wen on his right temple. He pointed at a cast-iron trough. "Yore welcome to water yore horse."

"Thank you kindly." She walked the horse in and pitched some slack. Easy drank her fill, then stood patiently twitching her tail. The rancher waited, equally patient. She did not dismount. "Sir, I am trailing a horse that was stolen from me . . . oh, close to three weeks ago now."

"That a fact?"

"Yes, sir. I tracked it to right yonder." She pointed to his split rail corral. He spit an amber jet of tobacco and said nothing. "The horse is a black mare with a white star. A Morgan."

The man turned grim faced at that and said, "One horse leaves pretty much the same track as another."

"This one has a bent calk. The right front."

"Damnit!"

"There were three of 'em." She described them. "Rode onto our place, killed my husband and stole his horse."

"Damnit!" he said again and slapped the porch post. "I shoulda known."

"Known what?"

"The horse's here."

"Yes, sir. I know."

He gave a rattley sigh. "Well, light and set a while. We'll talk on it."

She dismounted and tied up her horse and then eased the cinch. Bite arrived. Paws on the trough, he slurped up a long drink then flopped in a spot of shade under the porch. She patted his head before she walked up the stairs. Once inside the house, she paused to admire the meld of furnishings. A rack of longhorns measuring six foot, tip to tip. A bent-willow rocking chair. An old grandfather clock in a blood red cabinet.

"Hunt Mallory," the man said over his shoulder.

"Vanessa Cutter Fane," she replied, following. "Pleased t'meet you."

Mallory clumped down a shotgun-style hall—he was the most bowlegged man she'd ever seen—and into a kitchen with a wide-planked wood floor and shirred ging-ham curtains. He motioned to a split-log bench beside a rough-hewn table and she sat. He offered coffee and she accepted. He set a whiskey bottle on the table and helped himself to a generous drink before he said a word. In spite of gingham curtains and a new Oberlin cook stove, she saw no sign of a woman. She eased her gun out of the holster and held it alongside her leg.

"That's a damned fine horse," he said.

She nodded. "Yes, sir, it is. A purebred."

The horse, it seemed, suffered from a sprained tendon. Nothing serious, Mallory said. "Nothing a few weeks care won't cure." Still she was sorely disappointed. She'd hoped to have a spare mount.

"A man would be a fool to pay for something twice but I'd go some to keep that horse."

She told him about how Bob had prized that horse, that the mare had been purchased specifically as a breeder, but Mallory was an insistent man and said he'd make her a good price. She told him then about Duchess and how she'd been thinking she might give Etta Cutter the Morgan to help ease the loss of her favorite mare. In the end, to get him to quit badgering, she said she'd think on it.

Mallory agreed to keep the horse until she or Etta Cutter contacted him. It was at that point that he suggested she could holster her gun. She did, a bit chagrined. "I apologize, mister, but I am real leary of strangers."

"I imagine you are. Well, one thing's for danged sure," he said, eyeballing her, "you won't be widowed for long."

She cleared her throat and worked her buttocks on the bench and cast around for something to say. "You sure keep a nice house." He picked up a rusted tin can next to the table leg, spit in it and then returned it to the floor. *Not that there isn't room for improvement.*

"My segundo's wife does for me. Cookin' an' cleanin' both. I got me thirty thousand acres here."

"Big spread."

"Yes, it is. An' I'd like to leave it to a son. But findin' a good woman is like locatin' a horse feather out here. Especially since I don't intend to settle for just anyone. I already buried two city women. Right up on that hill yonder. The next one'll have to be strong and young and tough. Someone borned to this country." He was looking at her like a duck does a bug.

She declined further hospitality but did borrow writing materials again so she could let her aunt know about finding the Morgan and explain her agreement with the rancher.

. . . *I Found out That one of those men has a big Reward on him if he Is taken alive. To bad nobody Will kollect. Ha Ha Ha*

I have a good mount. Not as good as Duches but She will do. My shoulder is all healed except for an ocasional twing.

Yer loving Neece,
Vanessa Cutter Fane

Mallory walked with her to the porch. "Which way you figure they were headed?"

"I'd say Dodge would be your best bet."

She blanched. "Dodge?! Clear up in Kansas?"

"Not Dodge City. Jes' plain Dodge. Little ol' bitty place." He pointed. "Yonderways. About a half-day ride."

"Well, I'd best get going. There's still a couple of hours of light left. Suppose I could see the horse before I go?"

He nodded. "Follow me."

Bob's pride and joy, she thought as she patted the Morgan's neck. She was glad to have regained possession of the horse even if it meant her job would be that much harder. Any kid could track a horse with a bent calk.

"What do you call her?" Mallory asked.

"Rosebud. Bob, my husband, thought that this white mark right here looked like a rosebud."

"He had a powerful imagination."

"Yes, he did," she said and weltered in guilt. "It was only one of many fine qualities."

Mallory touched a place on the horse's flank, a consequence of needle sharp Spanish spurs or plaited rawhide. "That might fester right there. I best have my segundo take look at it."

"I'd appreciate that. In the meantime I have something that may help. I'll get it out of my grip."

Mallory stepped back a pace when she opened the tin of Etta's cure-all. "Whew! That stuff'd straighten a sow's tail."

The mare reacted by rolling her eyes and stomping her feet. "Look!" Nessa cried, "It reminds her of home. Idn't that sweet?" She missed the look Mallory gave her.

"She looks sorta skinny," she said, as they walked out into the sunlight. "You suppose you could give her some extra feed?"

"I have been. I always treat my horses like kin." She dropped the tin in the morral and untied the reins.

"Say, you know, before you rode in I coulda swore I

saw a flash of sun on metal. Two, maybe three mile back. You might wanna keep an eye out."

She looked back the way she'd come. His guns and rifle had been browned to avoid glinting in the sun. Yet, as she stood staring at the endless plain, completely empty now except for a low-flying chicken hawk, she knew somehow that it was true. *He's back there somewheres. Sure as heck.* She suppressed a shiver and swung into the saddle. "Well, Mr. Mallory, I sure appreciate your understanding."

"I ain't got a lot of choice."

"That's just it. There's many who'd be looking for some choices. Well, bye now."

"Bye."

Dodge was as plain as a child's drawing with flimsy sticklike buildings so warped they looked melted by the sun. She rode down the main street which was bisected by tufts of weeds and fronted by a saloon, a mercantile, and a combination barber shop/bath house. Further on, there was a blacksmith and livery stable and five or six windscoured houses.

She tied her horse to the hitching rail in front of the Mercantile and walked up the steps. There were three customers inside, two towheaded children and a man. The man was Trey Henry.

Trey Henry! While pretending to consider the selection of goober peas, she snuck another closer look to make completely sure.

Yes, it was him all right. She paused a minute then strolled to the window. She checked the hitching posts in front of the saloon and then the road both ways. There were horses tied in front of the saloon, the mercantile and the bath house but there was no sign of either Ladino or Flatt.

Henry was standing in front of a barrel of two-penny nails watching the two kids select candy. The boy was knobby-limbed with an award-winning cowlick sticking up from the crown of his head. The freckled and pigtailed girl was skinny as a corn stalk and appeared a few years younger. They looked enough alike to be brother and sister.

The storekeeper took the children's pennies then took up a broom and went outside and started sweeping the walk. The bell over the door quit jingling and silence settled over the room. Nessa looked at Trey Henry and could only think of how she'd seen him last. A sick feeling spread in her gut.

A minute longer then the children left. Henry was right behind them and Nessa was right behind him. This bizarre human train moved off toward the outskirts of town. Halfway out of town a lad appeared across the street and called out "Hey, Willie!"

" 'Lo, Red," Willie replied and veered off to join his friend. Willie and Red gave each other a few friendly punches and then they sat with their bare feet in the dust, their legs grasshoppered by the low plank walk. Left out the little girl looked uncertain.

Nessa stood in the shadows and watched her. Henry stood smack in the middle of the road and did the same.

The girl removed a stick of licorice passay from her mouth long enough to warn, "Mama said we was t' come straight back. We-ea-eall!" But she might have been a rock for all the attention the boys gave her. At last, she shrugged and went on down the alley toward a clapboard

house with two lines of flapping laundry out back. Henry
followed.

Nessa moved to the center of the alley and rubbed
palms that were suddenly wet and sticky on her thighs.
She could feel her heart pounding clear up between her
eyes. She relaxed her shoulders and thought: Well, all
right.

"Trey Henry!"

*. . . little girl neck . . . itta bitty hairs . . . downy . . .
sweaty. Curly and soft and smelly.*

"Trey Henry!" The little girl rounded the corner and
disappeared.

Sweet milky little girl smell. Henry stopped and shook
himself like a hound rising from sleep. He turned.
"Me?"

She nodded.

He retraced his steps and his spurs—the kind with
spiked rowels that scar—jingled like sleigh bells.

She pointed at him. "Hold it right there."

He did.

"Now." She parted the air with her hand. "Go on an'
draw!"

He glanced behind him and then steepled his fingers
on his chest. "Me?"

"Yes, you. Trey Henry! You . . . you murderer!
Horsethief!" Rage shook her. "Child despoiler . . . an'
cold-blooded . . . godless fiend." She licked her lips and
tasted spit. She took a steadying breath. "Draw or I'll
shoot you like a snake!" She could see the beginning of
fear in his eyes. He made a slight move and she shot
him three times before she could stop herself.

* * *

It hapened that fast. I sort of remember walking To him and Looking down. I must've stepped over him Then but I don't remember. Not geting on my horse. Not riding out of town.

Had he Gone for his gun?

Don't know. Can't remember. Don't care.

Eleven

6th of June—I road as far as the Leona and figured On going on but When I got off to have a drink all The sand went out of me. I sat with my head on my nees and it was a long time before I moved. I had always intended to kill him but The finality of it kind of stunned me I guess.

She decided to make camp right there. One day, she reasoned, would not hurt. Besides, she needed to steady out before facing Ladino and Flatt. It might take a day. She held up her hand, assessed the tremor and thought: Might take two days.

The rest of that day she kept her mind blank and her movements slow. She turned over enough rocks until she found several slugs. Then, using a bent nail for a hook and some braided yarn for line, she went fishing. She laid on a flat rock that jutted out over the river and tied the yarn to her big toe in case she fell asleep. She woke with a purple toe and a blue channel cat. With only that little effort she caught several catfish. She kept two. After skinning and gutting them, she built a low fire under a ledge and staked the fish to cook.

She slept again and then had a long bath. She must've been bit by some bug because she was overcome with the need to wash everything in sight. Herself again, her clothes, even her horse. She stood in the river thigh deep and used the coffee pot to dip water over the mare who was tossing her head and rippling her back with appreciation. Bite paced the bank, whining. Occasionally he'd give a bark which ended up in a sort of doggie hum. She finally coaxed him in. Once wet he turned part duck and once dry, he turned the color of molten gold.

"You know, if you didn't have those hairless places you'd be right pretty." They were stretched out on the rock air drying. She sensed something the same instant that Bite went stiff. She was stretching for her gun when she heard a flurry of wings. A small tom turkey rose out of the thicket. Without thinking, she sidearmed a rock.

"I couldn't do that again in a million years," she told Bite as they splashed across the water to retrieve the bird. She poked air holes in the gerga and tented it over the fire and they had smoked turkey for supper. And breakfast. And dinner.

One day stretched to two and then to three and she still couldn't get fired up about leaving. She wondered why. She certainly hadn't changed her mind or developed an overgrown set of scruples or gotten the willies.

Or had she?

The next morning saw gray clouds scudding in from the north. By noon the sky had turned black as pitch. By sundown she and the dog were crouched under the gerga, and watching the rain pock the earth.

It was sometime during that storm that she came to grips with herself.

It wasn't that she regretted killing Trey Henry but she was genuinely sad that there was the need to kill in the first place. Did she want to go on with it? No. Honestly she would really rather not. But she would.

The rain abruptly ceased and she left—five days after killing Trey Henry. She headed south and right into trouble.

11th of June—I almost road Rite into an Indian atak. It was a War party of Kioways, nine of them. An hour earlyer and I might have been of some help but not now. Barring the burning and The looting, it was all over.

Dead oxen lay in their traces. Around the smoking wagons were the remains of six human beings porcupined by arrows. The charred body of a man was tied to a wagon wheel.

The Indians were having a high time. One brave was mincing around in a woman's dress. Another had a blue bonnet's strings tied around his neck. He kept pulling the bonnet up but it kept sliding off his greasy black head to flap between his shoulder blades. Most of the others were occupied with loading the dead travelers' belongings onto their mules.

It was then that she saw that runaway African slave. He was down on one knee going over some loot on the ground. He had his back to her but there could be no mistaking that woolly head. It surprised her to see that the African had thrown in with the Kiowa. It surprised her even more that the Kiowa had let him. Kiowas really hate the white man. 'Course, that African was about as far as from white as a person could be.

The African had found something he liked and sat

back on his heels. He held whatever it was up to the sun and turned it this way and that.

Maybe the Kiowa thought the African was some tribe of Indian. Thing was, she thought Kiowas hated other Indian tribes almost as much as they hated the white man.

Done rummaging through the trunk, the African stood abruptly and turned toward her.

That hard-sought freedom had eluded the escaped slave after all, for it was a Kiowa face beneath the African's woolly scalp. They'd skinned his whole head, ears and all.

She watched no longer but slipped quietly away.

14th of June—An uneventful cople of days. I've seen indians in The distance And have had to Veer off more than once. I've done with Out a fire for three days running. I miss my cofee sorely.

It didn't take long to outride the benefits of the rainfall. The further south she rode the hotter and drier it got. Fierce hot air sucked the moisture from her skin and gave her prickly heat on all the places where cloth met skin. Wind-driven dust got into and on everything, shrouding her and her horse until they looked like they'd been dipped in flour.

A rutted trail of sorts led to yet another scrawny settlement in the middle of nowhere. She decided to ride down. She could get some supplies. Maybe she could find out something about Ladino and Flatt.

The truth of it was, that after learning the fate of that slave, she just wanted to see some other people.

She walked her horse in with Bite, as usual, trotting at her heels. A barking mongrel tore out into the street but after it got a good look at Bite it thought better of it and slunk off.

Lame Deer consisted of a saloon, a general store, a boarding house and three other buildings, all connected by a warped plank walk. To the south there were a handful of clapboard houses.

She tied the horse to the hitching rail in front of a general store where a cobwebbed window contained an odd assortment of dust-covered wares and a sign that read "Hahn's."

The place was fusty as a tomb and empty except for a woman who stood behind the counter wearing a Mother Hubbard dress and a worried look. " 'Afternoon," Nessa said. The woman nodded. A big-holed nose separated watery eyes that were suspicious as a coyote. "I'm looking for some shells for my rifle and I'll take a box of those," Nessa said, pointing at some pistol ammunition. The lady stacked the two boxes on the counter.

"Whew! Idn't hot for May?" Nessa fanned herself with her hand and then realized she'd have to answer herself. "Yes, it's sure lucky we got that rain. Otherwise we could be working up to another drought." A cricket chirped nearby. Not in the cornmeal, she hoped. "Well, I guess I'll take some cornmeal and ah . . . let's see . . . some soap and a small bag of salt."

The woman plopped the things on the counter and then went to drywashing her chapped hands.

"Say I wonder if you could help me . . ." Nessa smiled winningly. Nothing. "I'm tryin' to locate a couple of fellas. One is a breed who calls himself Ladino and the other is a fella named Caleb Flatt." She was about to describe them when the woman opened her mouth and a river of words gushed forth.

"They was rat here! Yessir. We shore ain't likely to forgit them fellas. Nossir. Both of 'em're mean enough to bite the head off a rattler. They was here only one day . . . one day, mind you and they . . ." She counted her fingers. ". . . broke a sportin' woman's arm, stomped my husband's hand and sliced my nephew's ear off."

"Why?"

That threw her. "Why what?"

"Why'd they do that?"

"Slice off my nephew's ear?" Snort. "The Lord got His arm jiggled when He was pourin' that boy's brains." She shook her head. "Anyone who don't have enough sense not to stick his head into a knife fight . . ." She leaned close and treated Nessa to a gust of sour breath. "Must run in the family. My husband Otto hears all the hollerin' and gunfire, rat? But 'stead of hunkerin' down, like most any fool'd do, he goes out to see what in the sam hill is going on. Those fellas come aflyin' outa the saloon, jump on their horses and run rat over him."

"Huh! Do you have any law?"

"Law?" She gave a moist snort. "Ha! That's a laugh." She restacked Nessa's order. "My nephew says he's dizzy. Purt near all the time."

Once you got her going, Nessa thought. On the counter she laid down one of the coins the Cobbs had loaned her. "That so?"

"He says it's throwed him off kilter."

"I'll be."

Making change she added, "He's got it in a tobacco pouch now."

Nessa looked at her. She'd lost the thread somewhere. "Got what in a tobacco pouch?"

"His ear."

Nessa rolled her lip. "Why?"

"He says carrying it on his earless side helps to balance him out."

"I . . . see." Nothing could be further from the truth. "Say, wonder if I could talk to your nephew?"

"I guess you could. If'n you was to go on over there to the saloon."

"Suppose he's there now?"

"I expect. He works there every afternoon. Sweeps up, totes in and carts out. I'll get Otto to go over there. He can tell him to come out back."

"Well, thank you. Your nephew's name is . . . ?"

"Dewey, but I expect you'll know him when you see him." Her wide grin showed a shortage of several essential teeth. "And my name's Asia."

"Nessa Cutter Fane. Pleased to meet you. Say, uh Asia?" Asia paused. "Is there a place to stay in town?"

"There's rooms over the bath house. Bath included."

"Thanks."

Asia nodded and stepped into the back room. "Otto? AAH-TO!"

"WHUT?!"

A length of burlap sacking was all that separated Nessa from the Hahns' conversation, and something told her it might not be enough. She started filling her pockets with her purchases.

"Otto, I want you to run over to Wiley's. Tell Dewey some girl wants to speak to him. She's gonna meet him rat out back."

"Whut the hell're you talkin' about?"

"I said . . ."

"Cain't' you see how swelled up this here is?"

"Well, you ain't gonna walk over there on your hands, is you?"

"I ain't taking my hand outa this water fer no . . ."

"Otto Hahn, I tole that girl . . ."

Nessa tiptoed to the door and squeezed out. After putting the supplies in her saddlebags, she arranged for a room then stabled Easy. She ordered a meal of oats as well as hay for the horse. She told the stableboy she'd be back later to pick up her grip and then walked toward the saloon.

Well, now. She considered the building across the road with great interest as she had never seen the inside of a saloon before. She tucked her hair behind her ears and pulled her hat low. After waiting for two lean dogs to trot by she crossed the street and climbed the cupped wood steps.

The windows were painted white halfway up but she could hear the murmur of voices and the slap of cards. She sidestepped to the door and stood on her toes so she could see over the batwing doors. It was surprisingly crowded! Three patrons lined the bar like crows on a fence—boots hooked, elbows down and butts out. A poker game was in progress at one of the tables, a game of faro or monte at another. She watched for a long time but nobody got gunned down or shucked their clothes. She also didn't see anyone who could be Dewey Hahn.

Mightily disappointed, she walked around to the back of the building. The alley had an untended and untraveled look. Weeds grew as high as the third step of the rickety stairs leading to the top floor of the saloon.

She was standing there uncertainly when suddenly the

door opened and a woman stepped onto the landing. She propped one shoe back against the building, raked a match down the wall and lit a small black cheroot.

Nessa stared. Thunderstruck. Bug-eyed. Drop-jawed. Why, she didn't know what to look at first—the woman's dress, which was chartreuse and tight as sausage casing—or the purple feather, sticking Indian-fashion out of a mass of hair that was the color of fresh blood—or her face, which was painted up like a red Indian on the warpath.

She didn't notice that the woman had noticed her until the woman waved and hollered at her, "Yoo hoo! Hey there, boy!" Nessa quick took interest in the curl of her boot. "How yew, boy?"

Nessa nodded and hitched her pants and half waved back. The woman shrugged and picked tobacco off her tongue. The door opened again and a boy shot out—a scrawny kid with hair on end and a muff-like thing on the side of his head. He pedaled down the stairs and dumped a sack on the ground. Nessa did a crawdad-like scuttle and intercepted him. "Psst! Say?"

He blinked big cowpat-like eyes. "Yeah?" The ear he retained stood huge and perpendicular to his skull, just begging to be lopped off. Reluctantly she noticed that a clap to his back was likely to wing a wad of wax all the way to Waxahachie. "Dewey Hahn?"

"Mebbe." He raised his chin and lowered his lids and gave her his you're-looking-at-trouble stare. "Who wants t'know?"

"Now who do you think? Dumb cluck!"

"Ow!" he said and rubbed his arm.

It seemed to take half an hour to find out that "one of the girls said she overhead something about Magdalena."

"Magdalena?" Nessa asked with sinking heart. "That town down in old Mexico?"

"How am I supposed t'know." He talked cocky, but was careful to stay out of pinching range. "Ast LaJune why don' ya."

"LaJune?"

He pointed at the landing where the woman had her head back, blowing smoke rings. "Her right yonder." And before Nessa could stop him, he hollered, "Hey, LaJune!"

The woman looked down and perked up. "Yeah?" She smiled and tugged down her bodice until two brown half moons rose above the ruffled top of her dress.

"Say, LaJune!" Dewey clamored up the stairs. Nessa followed, much much slower. "This here . . ." He looked back at Nessa.

"Lady," she supplied.

"Lady . . ." Smirk. ". . . wants to ask you something."

"You're a girl!" exclaimed LaJune.

"Uh . . . yes . . . ma'am." Nessa overcame the urge to run a finger around her collar. The woman was even more dismaying up close.

To Nessa's question, she replied, "I didn't hear that conversation first hand. Marvella did." She opened the door and stuck her head in and called, "Marvy, honey? You awake, cupcake? C'mon out here a minute, sweetness."

Everybody shuffled and pressed close so the door could open. "This here's Marvella," LaJune said with strange pride. The new girl wore a pink ruffled floor-length duster, high heels winged with feathers and a sling that was fashioned from a paisley shawl with eight-inch fringing. She offered Nessa her good hand. It was cool and soft as a curd.

"Pleased t'meet ya," Nessa said and choked off a sneeze. The smell of lilac toilet water was staggering.

"Oh, LaJune," Marvella said and collapsed into the other woman's arms.

"Marvy's still sufferin' somethin' fierce." LaJune patted Marvy who had her head buried between LaJune's half moons. "Poor sweet thing! Are you up to answerin' a few questions about those nasty ol' men?"

Her injuries must've affected her voice for she could scarcely speak above a whisper. Probably didn't help that she had her mouth planted where it was. Nonetheless, the group closed around the girl like the petals of a flower.

Having got the information she sought—unwelcome as it was—Nessa shagged out of town. By the end LaJune had been comforting Marvella with kisses! On the lips! Nessa was shocked. She was practically nineteen years old but she had never seen the likes of that!

The wether was Bad all day with a wind that never let up, even at sundown. Sheet lightening flashed to The north but around me the nite sky was just dark and hevy feeling. I huddled under my wickiup, miserable. I'd learned where I'd Find the man called El Ladino. Magdalena! So far!

Alone as I had ever been I Found my self thinking of home and Bob and then in spite of every vow I'd made, I thought about Doubletree. I laid down, aware of myself as I'd never been before. Of my thighs, my brests. I ached for him. Sudenly I was sobing like a baby.

Twelve

El Ladino sat in the cantina and stared out at the street. He was proud of the fact that he did not yet need to close one eye in order to see the pig rooting in the burro offal or the three chickens scratching in the dust. He had been drinking since midday, two maybe three hours. By now he should be feeling pretty good.

He'd never felt worse. He was terrified, his insides a quivering mass of jelly. El Ladino had not known what fear was before. He did now.

Why? He'd been methodically searching his memory, going over everything he knew about himself in the hope that he would find the reason for his fear. It had to be something in his past.

He was born Gustavo Escovar, the product of a Comanche raid on the small Mexican village of Dos Gatos. His mother was thirteen at the time of her capture and died in childbirth nine months later. His father was one of twelve braves who participated in the raid.

Gustavo was a credible Comanche warrior, primarily because he was meaner than the other boys. He was fifteen when he participated in a raid on a Mexican estancia and killed for the first time. Thereafter, whether for pleasure or profit, he killed with ease because, quite simply, he possessed no conscience. A killing had as much meaning to him as the passage of a day. Some were exciting. Some were routine.

A fight for control of the small band of renegades was Ladino's first loss and resulted in his leaving the band. He would be *el jefe,* he declared with youthful aplomb, or nothing. Thereafter he scorned his Comanche name, which loosely translated meant Bird in Hand and started calling himself El Ladino. At eighteen he joined with some other misfits and became an equally successful bandit. They drifted into the buying and selling of Comanche and Comanchero captives. One of those other misfits was Caleb Flatt.

During the next twenty years Caleb Flatt and the half-breed called El Ladino were accused of many crimes. They were guilty of most of them. They were far from friends but many years together had bred a loyalty of sorts. Flatt was nominally the leader of the other men, but not of El Ladino. El Ladino had always been his own master. Until recently. Recently something else had become El Ladino's master. And there was his problem. Strange things were happening.

Yesterday, when he woke, he discovered that three days had passed. He recalled nothing of those days. *Nada!* He was supposed to have ridden to Hilario. He remembered stopping for some mescal. He told himself that he would not drink any, however, until he was at least halfway to Hilario. Instead he sat down in the cantina and had one drink—*solamente uno.* Time slipped like quicksilver through his hands. The next thing he knew he was in the alley. It was night. He touched his head and found it sticky with blood. *Dios!* He must've fallen! He had been injured! He moved his arms and then his legs. Well, perhaps not, but all that flailing had circulated a particularly foul smell. A mixture of vomit and sweat and something else. *Cabrone!* He had soiled himself!

He heard snickers. Fighting considerable nausea he lifted his head and found a dead chicken on his chest. He roared in anger and flung the carcass into the shadows. There was a crash and the clatter of wood on stone and then four small bare legs flashed by.

He had been enraged. That some boys had dared to make El Ladino the butt of their joke. El Ladino . . . a name synonymous with unspeakable savagery, a mutilator and murderer of many men, a brutal killer who listened to many songs of death, a man feared on both sides of the border . . .

He spat on the dirt floor of the cantina. The sour taste of humiliation was still with him. Sure he drank. He had for many, many years. He always drank and he'd always been fine. He woke, talked, walked, raped and killed and plundered and slept, all expertly.

Except lately. There were times when he drank when he should not and many occasions when he drank in spite of every vow to the contrary. Like the day when he was supposed to deliver the ransom for those five captives. That the captives lost their lives and Flatt's friends lost their money was immaterial. What mattered more was that he lost respect that day. To a man whose purpose in life was to terrorize and intimidate, it was like a death knell.

Was this the finale? The tragic conclusion of his life? Would he die a poor joke of a man?

He choked back a sob. El Ladino could not come to such an inglorious end. Not El Ladino. He looked around the cantina, which was empty except for the old man who filled his jar with mescal, and another sob welled. He loved this little cantina. He loved this pueblo. It had been his home for over ten years. He didn't want to leave. Yet, what else could he do? He had not imagined the sly looks of the village men, nor had he imagined the hushed comments of the old women. Most assuredly he had not imagined that dead chicken.

No. The news was spreading: El Ladino was now just an old drunk and he could not seem to pull himself together long enough to dispel it. Even the girl had heard.

That, for some crazy reason, was the worst.

He knew she knew! Two days ago he had caught her looking at him. She had never dared to even look at him before. Not for many years. Not since the day he removed her tongue and then tied her head down over a fence rail. He'd sat beside her that day and pared his nails and told her what would happen to her the next time she tried to escape.

He had beat the disdain out of her eyes that day, and had promised her that the next time she dared to look at him thus he would feed her eyes to the crows.

He had meant it too. El Ladino would not lose the respect of his slave. He poured another drink. Maybe he should go home and do it now, while he still remembered his purpose.

Two hours later he was in a kind of haze, drinking automatically. There was within him a persistent sense of doom. He felt weary, drained dry. He still couldn't understand what had happened to him but now there was a very important difference. Now he no longer cared.

He was pouring another drink when a man ambled into view. El Ladino felt he knew the man but could not recall from where. Of one thing El Ladino was certain: This man was looking for him. El Ladino drew his knife and laid it on his lap.

The man stepped out of the wicked heat and paused for a minute in the door's sunlit frame, blinking, trying to see into the dim interior of the tiny cantina. When he spotted El Ladino, he gave a snaggle-toothed smile and a scarecrow-like wave. "Howdy there, El Ladino!"

"Hola." El Ladino replied and motioned to a seat. "Qué pasa?"

Without preamble the man stated, "Flatt sent me. Said to tell you Trey Henry is dead."

"Quién es Trey Henry?"

"Henry. Trey Henry. Flatt's kin. You rode down with him and Flatt." The man looked longingly at Ladino's wide-mouth jar of mescal.

"Ah, sí, sí. Cómo se llama?"

"Hobb. My name's Hobb."

El Ladino could see the direction of Hobb's thoughts and pulled the jar out of the path of temptation. Ten years ago he'd killed a man from this very village for what Hobb was thinking. Tied him to a tree and practiced throwing his knife into non-vital parts of his body until he got so drunk he bungled one of his throws.

"A person's been nosing around, asking questions."

"This person killed Henry?"

"Maybe. Flatt thinks so."

"Quién es?"

"A woman."

"A mujer!" El Ladino said. This information was mildly interesting. Maybe the person was an Indian woman. Maybe she tortured Henry before she killed him. El Ladino brightened with this thought and in his benevolence, pushed his half-filled glass toward the man. He'd never tortured an idiot before. Did they feel pain the same as others? "How did he die," Ladino asked.

Hobb threw the drink against the back of his throat and then ran his sleeve across his mouth. "He was gunned down in an alley over in Dodge."

"You are certain it was not someone's father or brother?"

Hobb shook his head. "A whore over in Lame Deer tole a friend of Flatt's that a woman was asking after him. A young woman who wore a gun and dressed as a man."

El Ladino suddenly lost interest and retrieved his glass. "This does not concern me."

"Maybe not but Flatt figured you ought to know. He also wants to know how things went in Hilario."

"I . . . have not gone yet. I go tomorrow."

"But . . ."

"Crow Wing could not meet until tomorrow." He was lying. Why? El Ladino did not have to answer to anyone. Without El Ladino Flatt had no link with the Comanche. *Lo mismo los Comancheros.* Yet when he opened his mouth, another lie rolled out. "Crow Wing set the day. Not I."

"Flatt says no hostages—no carbines."

"Crow Wing will have hostages." The crafty old Indian was probably attacking some isolated ranches and farms at that very moment. El Ladino watched the man a moment then he said. "And how goes it with you, my friend?"

"Huh?" The unexpected cordiality threw Hobb.

"You have had a long trip."

"Yeah. Long 'n' dry." Hobb looked around. "Say, how's a fella get a drink around here?"

"There is an old man but he makes himself scarce when I have a visitor." El Ladino rapped on the table with his knife handle and the old man entered immediately carrying a hogskin of mescal. He looked nowhere but at the jar as he filled it and then he promptly left.

"Have a drink," El Ladino said and poured the glass full and pushed it toward Hobb. All this talk of the woman who killed Henry had reminded El Ladino of his slave. He now knew how to punish her without even breaking a sweat. As a matter of fact, he would not even have to leave the cantina. Although he did like to watch. Maybe he would watch. Then he would be able to spur the man to special cruelty, to do those things that he knew she hated. He smiled at the thought.

Hobb looked into El Ladino's close-set rat eyes and a ripple went down his spine. There was something back there, something mad and mean.

El Ladino pushed the glass closer still. "Bueno! Provecho!"

Hobb took the glass and dumped its contents down his throat.

"Sí! Eso es! Muy bueno." A moment then El Ladino asked, "You have some money, amigo?"

Hobb replied with caution, "Mebbe. Why?"

"I only consider your pleasure. Maybe you would like a woman. Eh?"

Hobb shrugged. "Mebbe." He happened to be carrying more money than normal. A few nights before, he and a one-armed man named Ladew had killed an old sheep herder and took his tiny sack of pesos. Driving off and selling his stock north of the river had brought a few more coins.

Yeah, he had money all right. And he hadn't had a

woman in a long time. But still he hesitated. He wasn't particularly enthusiastic. Not if it was the same woman El Ladino was selling the last time he was here. There was something about the way she looked at him. It was almost as eerie as looking into Ladino's eyes.

In an unconscious habit, Hobb ran his tongue around his carious mouth and felt the movement of several teeth. Damnit! It was getting so he was afraid to chew anything harder than two-day beans yet all he could think about was meat. He swallowed. He'd been smelling roast lamb for two nights straight. Ever since that asshole Ladew killed a lamb and ate it with great relish while Hobb ate pinole. Again. His stomach growled. Maybe he would take Ladino up on his offer. The woman would at least have some frijoles simmering. They all did.

"Well?" El Ladino asked. "Yes or no? One peso."

The man shrugged. It was a long ride back to Hermacita. "Why not."

El Ladino held out his hand. Hobb stretched his leg to get at his money.

"What're you gonna do about the woman who killed Henry?" he asked as he handed over the coin.

El Ladino shrugged. "Nothing. If she comes for me I will be here and I will kill her. With great pleasure. I have killed many women and improve with each." Unfortunately his boastful claim was marred by a loud and particularly fetid belch.

Thirteen

16 of June—I've entered that lawless teritory where it is said a body can run into just about inny Thing. Renegades. Bandits. Comancheros. Comanche. The only thing I have Run into is yucca, black chapparal, Katclaw and prickly pear kactus. Every Blesit thing in this country sprouts thorns!

It was a graybrown land filled with plants and animals she'd never seen before and everything was bigger. The sky. The plain. The emptiness. Even common sights were in some way exceptional, like there were the same curious prairie dogs, only in this land they existed in the thousands. Same for horses. One day she saw a manada of wild-eyed and hairy-hocked mustangs so massive in number that their thundering passage seemed capable of shaking the sun out of the sky..

When night bathed the land, she would huddle beneath her bower of brush like a prairie hen with the scent of a bobcat on the wind and try not to think about how far she'd come. Not an easy task when all she could think about was how much she wanted to go home.

One morning she found a baby rabbit in her snare. Some predator had taken advantage of the fact that it was trapped and helpless and had chewed the poor thing all to hell.

She couldn't get that rabbit out of her mind. Its plight seemed to have set something in motion in her mind. She started thinking some pretty strange thoughts. Like the idea came to her that maybe her ma hadn't been such a dumb cluck after all. Just look at all the things she'd never had to do. She never had to kill a baby animal caught in a snare. Never had to kill a horse with a knife. Certainly never had to kill a man. Heck fire! She'd never even had to kill a chicken! She simply told Nate Cutter that the blood bothered her and that was all it took.

Why couldn't there have been some middle ground for her? Why'd she have to decide to be like one or the other? Why not a bit of both? It didn't seem that she'd ever had a choice. Not that she could remember. It sort of made her mad when she thought about it.

Good water got scarce. In search of some she was following a course that corkscrewed through a range of low mountains. Finally the barely discernible trail led her to a small clay-colored stream. The water was brackish but drinkable and it was getting late in the day. Normally she would have stopped for the night, but she paused only long enough to water her horse and refill her jug. A mile more and she understood why the place had given her the willies. She had ridden onto another place of death. Ribbed frames of oxen lay in leather traces among burned wagons. Frayed belongings and bones had been scattered hither and yon by the coyotes.

Although exposed to the passage of time, it was easy to reconstruct what had happened. The travelers had eaten, watered and slept and then, as they prepared to leave in the morning, they'd been fallen on by bandits or Indians who killed or carried off everyone.

Off by itself lay a blackened spool doll. She scooped it up and brushed the dirt off its faded smile. Once again her imagination took her and she smelled the smoke and heard the screams and then the terrible eerie silence that followed. A silence that was broken only by the sound of the wind. The panting of a slinking coyote. The flapping of wings.

A quick prayer and she got whacking.

2nd of July—Dawn to dusk riding Has brought me To a more hospitable land that has, as can be expected, a Lot more peple. Hardly does a day go by that I don't see sheep or catle or goats and rare is the nite with out the scent of a meskeet Fire in the air. Yesterday I road through a valey where the grass grew horse-high and where Easy spooked up more Quale than I thought existed in the hole universe.

She sat on a rise, looking at the dished-in place where Magdalena lay deathly still in the midday sun. The only sign of life was an eagle hunting against the treeless slope and a burro that was squeaking its way round and round a flour grind. Then a quick movement caught her eye. Two barefoot boys were running from bush to bush, heading, it appeared, for a clay and stick house with a cowskull nailed above the door. Suddenly they crouched down behind a bush. From the other direction came an old woman with two clay jars suspended from a yoke across her neck. Nessa hoped the boys were patient. The only sign that the woman was moving was the tiny puff of dust that rose with each shuffling step. *Idn't that sweet! Those kids are going to surprise their ol' gran'ma . . .*

When the woman reached the place where the boys hid, they leapt out and chucked rocks at her, crying, "Bruja! Bruja!" A rock struck the woman and she dropped one shoulder. Water splashed out of the clay jar.

Nessa heeled Easy down and hollered, "Hey!" Two heads popped up and turned toward her. Why, the little turds weren't any more than six. "Vamoose!" They took her seriously and took off, their brown feet flying over rocks and thorny clumps of cactus. Whistling and yelling as if she were moving horses she herded them toward the edge of town and then she rode back to the woman who was still down on all fours. "Bien, mamacita?" she asked as she knelt beside her.

The woman touched the bloody spot above her eye and then looked at her fingers. "Sí, está bien."

"Those boys! Más terrible!"

"No, no. Solamente joven."

Nessa helped her to the door of the hut and paused. "Con su permiso?"

"Sí. Venga."

The one-room hut had a clay floor and furnishings of only the barest necessity. A crude table, two chairs, a corn husk mattress against one wall. But it was curiously homey. Broken bits of colored glass were stuck into the walls. Gourds, onions and dried red peppers hung from the ceiling.

She helped the woman to her bed where she sat propped against the wall. While Nessa gathered water and a clean rag the woman took in everything she did with eyes so deep set they might've been doweled.

"Gracias," she said after Nessa bound the gash.

"De nada." Nessa sat back on her heels and looked at the old woman who resembled a living mummy.

The woman pointed to a black kettle above a low fire. "Frijoles?"

"Oh, no, gracias," she said, but the strong smell summoned spit.

"Cómo no? Un poquito. Comida para usted también." Nessa looked outside at her horse who was chomping on some dried bunch grass and at Bite who was taking a rest in the shade. "Well . . ."

"Sí! Sientese."

"No, you sientese. I'll get it."

The steaming pot contained frijoles black with chili peppers. A flat pan contained a stack of corn tortillas. As she knelt to fill the two bowls of unfired clay a horned toad startled her by running across the hearth. Smiling ruefully she said she almost had herself a bean sombrero and the woman replied with a cackle of carefree laughter that bared gums as smooth as a china bowl.

The woman ate very little and then pushed herself up on the bed and rolled herself a corn shuck macuche. At her insistence, Nessa had another helping.

"Cómo se llama?"

"Nessa Cutter Fane," she replied, polishing the sides of the bowl with a rolled tortilla.

The woman pointed at herself. "Consuelo Miranda."

"Mucho gusto."

"Igualmente."

"Donde va?"

"Aquí. Magdalena." She explained that she had traveled very far in order to find someone she believed lived in this town. The woman nodded. She was very cagey looking, as if she knew what Nessa was going to say before she said it.

"Y quién es?" she asked.

"He is called El Ladino."

"Aiii!" The woman jerked upright. "Està muy malo. Es el diablo! Està bárbaro!" El Ladino, she said, had killed her only son, Esteban. "Ah, Esteban! Hijo de mi cara!" The old woman shook her head, muttering about the caprices of life. If only her son had married Carmelita. Such a nice girl. And what a good mother she had proven to be! But no. Esteban must have Paloma Lopez. Paloma Lopez! Bah! The kind of woman who is never happy. Never. It was a terrible misfortune. She had warned him. Her son, her fine son.

Nessa had never been in a situation like this. Fortunately she didn't have to worry about what to say. The old woman continued without pause.

Influenced by the greedy Paloma, her son fell in with a bad crowd. "Pistoleros!" she hissed. "Banditos!"

Even El Ladino. Each time her son rode with him the old woman would pray without ceasing until he returned safely. "Entonces," she said with despair, there came the time when he did not return. She went to El Ladino and asked about her son. He laughed at her. When she refused to leave, he threw rocks at her. Still she would not leave and he beat her gravely.

When she was able, she went again to his house. She waited there until she found his woman alone. She begged her for information about her son. "Ask him about my son and please tell me. Por favor! It is torture not knowing how he died or where he lies. Please. I will pay."

"Did she help?"

She looked at Nessa. "Never. She never told me anything." She touched Nessa's arm. "Why would a girl such as yourself seek El Ladino."

"Because he killed my husband."

"And now you will try to kill him?"

"Yes."

Consuela Miranda could see the girl's determination. Some people, she believed, are not destined to live very long. Esteban had been one. Maybe this girl was another. She studied the girl but it was in vain. Without examining her spit . . . "You are certain you must do this thing?"

"I must," Nessa replied. "Please. Do you know where I can find El Ladino?"

The woman sighed. Qué será, she thought and told the girl that El Ladino drank at La Perra Negra.

"How will I know this place?"

Magdalena is a small village, she said, with only two cantinas. One is on the other side of town and one faces the plaza. It is the latter.

The woman offered her hospitality for the night but Nessa declined thinking that, if she failed to kill Ladino, it wouldn't go well for anyone who'd helped her.

The woman cautioned her that there were scalp hunters between Magdalena and the border. "Los Mataderos," she hissed and crossed herself. Nessa thought: A fitting name, the slaughterers. She told the old woman that she moved very cautiously and very quickly. And that she must now leave. "No hay tiempo que perder."

The old woman lowered her head. "Bien. Cuidado!"

"Mil gracias," Nessa said. *I will need it!* "Adiós!"

* * *

La Perra Negra—The Black Bitch—was one of several grimy adobe buildings that encircled Magdelena's hub, which was a rock fountain with a wooden statue of the Virgin.

For two days Nessa stood in the shadows between the buildings. She saw women with clay urns on their head come for evening water. She counted an amazing number of burros, chickens, hogs and goats that wandered around unfettered. She observed an old leper in rags who sat in front of the church for hours on end holding out his dirt-seamed palm. But she did not see the bandit known as El Ladino.

The third night found her in the same place. She stood with her shoulder against the wall, chewing on a strip of carne seco the old woman had insisted on giving her and watching the plaza. Which was presently only occupied by a scratching dog. Someone down the way was strumming a guitar and singing a ballad which contained a lot of "mi corazóns." From the cantina came the faint sound of conversation and card playing.

A couple of hours before dawn found her sitting in the dirt with her back propped against the wall. Both the carne seco and the dog were gone. The lovesick singer had put a sock in it. Which was good and bad; now she was having trouble keeping her eyes open.

Suddenly two men strolled out of the cantina. Her heart tripped when she saw that one of them was about the right size. But when they paused to share a match she could see right off that neither man was Ladino.

Idly she watched them walk off, her eyes almost

squeezed shut, her mouth stretched into a black maw. Then when she glanced back at the cantina, there was Ladino, backlit in the doorway. A goatskin dangled from one hand. She scrambled to her feet and plastered herself to the wall. He turned and set off, tacking his way down the street. Using the shadows and keeping the buildings between them, she sped down the narrow street that paralleled his path. Here and there she caught glimpses of him, reeling along. She raced ahead and waited. Gun drawn she sighted down the black alley between two buildings. But as El Ladino staggered into view so did a man on the far side of the street. The man sleepwalked a few feet from his front door to relieve himself and El Ladino, like a duck at a carnival shooting gallery, jerked out of her gunsights.

"Balls!" she muttered and ran on, but she couldn't get a clean shot before he reached a small adobe building that was set apart from all others. He stumbled inside. Seconds crept by and then the lantern within was extinguished.

She waited for a long time before she approached and then she did so by zigzagging from bush to bush. Once closer, she dropped to her stomach and crawled. When she reached the wall of the hut she pressed close to it and listened. Loud rhythmic snoring came from within. She crouched, went under the opening to the other side and looked inside. Too dark. She couldn't see anything but the pale square of a pallet. Motionless she waited. One hour. Two. Then she went over the sill.

El Ladino lay spread-eagled on the pallet snoring

deeply. Someone—it looked like a woman—slept on the floor at his feet.

At the same instant that Nessa covered the woman's mouth she stuck her pistol in her ear. The woman's eyes flashed white in the dark but other than a tiny hiss of breath, she made no noise. Leaning close, Nessa whispered, "If you make a sound I'll shoot you in the head. Comprende?" The Indian woman stared back at her, her face like a board with eyes. Nessa was preparing to repeat the words in English when the woman nodded slowly.

Nessa motioned with her gun that the woman should stand. Again the woman nodded submissively but then she jerked like she would make a run for it and Nessa eared back the hammer on her gun. Keeping her hands out like a supplicant, slowly the woman signed: I-am-not-trying-to-run and that was when Nessa saw she was a cripple.

Moving crablike the woman sat in the chair Nessa indicated and folded her hands in her lap. Nessa tied a rag around her eyes then tied her wrists together. Her poor feet, so arched that her toes almost met her heels, Nessa tied to the chair leg. Then she stood. "Do not make a sound." The woman nodded. Nessa walked back into the other room.

I looked down at El Ladino, helpless as a babe in his drunken stoopor but I felt no Pang of conscience. I flashed on Bob on the ground and on El Ladino with his nee on his chest. I remembered how Ladino had laffed

*and went "Aiii!" and jumped back when Bob's blood
spurted.*

*I was going to ask him . . . do you know who I am?
do you know why you are dying today? but I ended up
doing neither. I just shot him.*

Fourteen

In the hushed moments after the gunfire, there came a soft scraping noise and then a complete and eerie silence. El Ladino's slave held very still and prayed. Not for her own life, but for the death of El Ladino.

She used to be known as Rabbit Foot. She was Papago. Her family had been killed in a Comanchero raid. Her mother raped and tortured, her father and two brothers shot and scalped. She had just seen her thirteenth summer.

El Ladino was in the Comanchero camp when the jubilant raiders rode in. Although he said he preferred money for the guns he had for sale, he agreed to accept her as part of his payment. She heard him say that he would sell her to a brothel that serviced the silver mines in Coahuila. She knew now that she'd have been lucky if he had, but he brought her to Magdalena instead.

She scorned him when he took her and at the first opportunity she tried to escape. She succeeded in getting away from the village and for two days she ran. Ceaseless. Tireless as an antelope. Until she thought her legs would fall off. It was the last time she would ever run.

She fought like a cat but he beat her senseless and staked her in the sun for three days. Weakened by the lack of food and water she could not fight when he wedged her mouth open with a stick. Nor when he pulled out her tongue with a blacksmith's iron tongs and cut it off. While she was strangling on her own blood, he held a hot branding iron to the bottom of her feet.

He no longer threatened to sell her south because he had found that he could make a few pesos by giving her to men who did not care if she was a cripple. Or to men for whom a cripple was an amusing diversion. Or to men that even the hardest putas would not accept. Or to men who took pleasure in causing pain. Sometimes he would sell her to two men at once because he enjoyed watching them fight drunkenly over who would have her first. Thus had her life been for over eight years.

Abruptly she ceased her prayers. She'd heard something, a soft sound such as would have been made had the antelope skin moved that hung over the doorway. Her senses strained. Cool night air brushed her cheek and a board creaked and then she heard footsteps. A soft and slow cadenced walk. The killer returns and she thought: Good. For she was prepared to die. Far back in her throat she started to hum. But then her bindings were cut and her eyes uncovered and she choked off her death chant in shock.

"Here's some money. Pack some food an' water an' get on that paint pony out there an' go. Keep a sharp eye out for Comanche now an' don't stop for nothin'. Not until you reach your people. Well? What're you waitin' for, girl? Go on an' git! You're free."

Fifteen

*5th of July—I troted through the shadows to Where
Easy was tyed, scarcely breathing until I cleared the Village and then I road fast. I reloaded in The sadel and
found That there were fore bullets gone. That was the
only Way I knew how many times I'd fired.*

*I am heading north West now on a path that roughly
paralels the Rio Grande. Making For the border and
Caleb Flat.*

It wasn't a full-blown dust storm but it was coming
straight on hard enough for her to cover her mouth and
nose and ride head down. When it finally ended and the
dust settled she was surprised to come upon a wagon
track. Apparently someone else was crazy enough to
travel in that storm! She got off her horse and fingered
some droppings. Mule. And not two hours old either.

She followed the trail and soon came upon a flea-bitten
blue mule pulling a buckboard with at least seventy-leven
tumbleweeds snarled in its wheel spokes. At the reins
was a mound of rags.

She stayed back a ways and followed for a time watching. The wagon rumbled and bounded along, drifting to
the left until the mule reached some impediment and then
heading right for a while. A calliope noise came from

some unrecognizable objects that hung on ropes strung across the flat bed. When she rode closer she could hear thin reedy singing . . .

> Tobacco's but an Indian weed,
> grows green at morn, cut down at eve.
> It shows our decay, we are but cla-a-a-ay,
> think of this when you smoke tobacco-o-o-o-o.

The voice was unmistakably female. Nessa reined in alongside. "Hello there! I sure am surprised to find you clear out here . . ." The mule kept plodding, the wagon kept rolling. Nessa removed her hat and smoothed her wind tossed hair and watched it go. "Well, for pity's sake!" The wagon was a half mile distant before she rode up again. "Ma'am?" Nothing. "Hey!" When she leaned over and snagged the rope halter, she understood why the woman didn't answer her. Clasping her hand was like grabbing onto a hot flatiron.

She tied Easy to the whip stock and climbed on the wagon seat and then circled back to a tiny stream of water.

The woman was all bones and sharp edges, and getting her off the wagon was like wrestling with a big sack of sticks. Steeling herself, for the woman smelled like a billy goat, Nessa examined her for the source of the fever. Finally she removed the woman's mismatched boots and there, on her left foot, was a festering bite.

She built a three-sided wickiup against the bank and rolled the woman into it. Over the next two days she used up her aunt's cure-all and then started treating the woman's foot with prickly pear poultices. During all that time the only thing she found out about the woman was that she could out-cuss a mule skinner. On the third day the woman startled her by abruptly opening her eyes. She was cotton-eyed on the left but her right eye was bottle-glass green and gleamed like a hot ember. It transfixed her for a long minute flickering like a big bird sighting prey.

When the woman started to hum, the hackles on Nessa's neck kept time.

The woman didn't regain consciousness again until late on the third day when she abruptly opened her eyes and moved her head and limbs in an agitated fashion. Nessa sensed her need to speak. These words might very well be her last, she thought. She placed her ear close to the woman's cracked lips.

"Have ya got any 'backy?" she shouted.

Nessa sat back on her heels and augered her ear. "No, I do not!"

"Shit!" she said and floated off again.

Wherever she went, she stayed another two days.

"What do you think bit you?" Nessa asked once when the woman had her senses.

"It weren't a snake. I hit at it an' felt fur."

"What's your name?"

"Janet Moon," she replied.

"Where's your home? What happened to your people?" but the woman lapsed into unconsciousness again.

In the rocks nearby Nessa made a corral of sorts for the woman's mule and for Easy. After concealing the wagon with branches she waited for the woman to die.

11th of July—I am not hartened By Janet Moon's simtoms—pain, burning, muscle jerks and Difficulty swalowing. I am Sure that This is the same disease that killed old Pico.

One of her aunt's vaqueros, a man named Pico Gonzales, had been bitten by a fox one night when he entered an isolated line shack. He fell sick immediately and, in spite of every curative skill her aunt knew, continued to worsen. Under penalty of the worst consequences, Nessa was not allowed anywhere near the cabin where her Aunt Etta was caring for Pico. But being only ten, genuinely worried and hopelessly curious, she simply couldn't resist. Ol' Pico was her friend! The kindly old man had taught her everything there was to know about knot tieing! She couldn't not see him while he was sick! She would just say "hey!" to him from the window. So she defied her aunt and peeped inside the cabin.

Pico was tied hand and ankle, his body a rigid bow. From his mouth came yellow froth and hideous, not human noises. Jerking against his bonds was causing a rhythmic thunk and bump as the cot hit the hard packed dirt. She was backing off when there came the unearthly shriek of a thing tortured past endurance. She took off and ran right up an old oak like a treed coon. When she was as high as she could go she realized that she could see the cabin in the distance. She stayed. The wild noises continued far into the night, but at some point she must've slept.

The sound of a gunshot awakened her. It was near dawn but still dark. She rubbed her eyes and sat up and looked through the leaves to the cabin. Her aunt, tired and messy-looking, stepped into the rectangle of light that came from the shack's open door. She turned her face skyward and shut her eyes and stood there. Sanchez came out a minute later. They spoke softly and then her aunt walked slowly toward the house. Sanchez sat down in a chair in the doorway and buried his face in his hands. They buried Pico that day.

Janet Moon's fever finally broke and she slept. So, at last, did Nessa. As usual, she took her gun to bed with her.

"HAW!"

Nessa leapt up, sleep-drunk. Gun out and blinking like an owl, she chanted, "Where? What?"

"Hold it right there!"

Nessa fanned back the hammer on her gun and skated in place. "Where are they, Janet?"

"I wouldn't try that if I was you!"

A coyote barked. Bite woofed softly in reply and then dropped his head back onto his paws. Nessa came out of her wide-legged crouch and walked over to the mound that was Janet Moon. "This is your last chance!" Janet cried.

Nessa lowered her gun. "Janet?"

"You haven't heard the last of me!"

Truer words were never spoken.

In the morning, Janet exclaimed that that was the best night's sleep she'd had in ages. Nessa glared at her with red-rimmed eyes and thought: If the disease doesn't kill her, I will.

Janet Moon made a remarkable recovery. Nessa watched her like a hawk but she didn't seem to be given to sudden changes of mood. By dusk she apparently felt well enough to sing.

Will you come to the bow'r I have shaded for you?
Our bed shall be roses all spangled with dew
There under the bow'r on roses you'll lie
A blush on your cheek but a smile in your eye.

Janet's taste in music leaned toward trashy. Her favorite tune was a many-versed ditty about a Wyoming woman named Watty Kay who rode a tarantula and made music by flexing certain unspeakable parts of her body.

The Wyoming woman named Watty Ka-a-a-y
Roped a tarantula and tamed it one da-a-a-y
She called her spider Harre-e-e
and her cunny Merre-e-e
and braided them both with garlands of berre-e-e.

The melody was similar to "Sweet Betsy from Pike" and Nessa had to admit that it was sorta of catchy. Particularly the refrain which ended "Yah, Go Yah Yah. Go Yah Yah Go."

17th of July—I've seen no sign of Comanche All though I have Twyce seen smok signals in the distance. I'm as Cautious as I can be and Still take care of a sik woman. I use dry wood and build our Fire under a branch so the Smoke spreads. All though Janet is still singing her heart out, I fear her next tune will be a swan song.

It was late. The wind stirred softly, a whining lament made worse by the doleful *pee-ik pee-ik* of a night hawk. A rind of moon hanging askew in the sky reminded

Nessa of another meager moon on another night. That
was all it took for her to start feeling downright . . .
moony.

"That the last of the coffee?" Janet asked.

"Yes. Unless you want me to make more."

"No. Not for me."

A shooting star pulled Nessa back to the problem at
hand: what the sam hill was she going to do about Janet
Moon? She looked at her, humming and cracking her
knuckles in order. "Well, Janet?"

"Yeah?"

"How do you feel?"

"Jus' like I look," she replied. "Tougher'n a boot."

More like a split rock, Nessa thought, considering her.
She'd heard it was common for the symptoms of hydro-
phobia to disappear for days, maybe even weeks at a
time. How long would it be until she fell ill again?

"I see yer admirin' my hair," said Janet, and tilted her
head coquettishly. "Ain't the color pretty?"

"I'll say." The color was a lot like what's left in a
chamber pot after it's been dumped. Janet fingered the
skinny braids tied under her chin and then, holding
Nessa's eye, she grabbed a handful at the nape of her
neck and yanked.

"Why, you are bald as a coot!"

"Had ya hornswoggled, didn't I?" She gave a phlegmy
laugh, pleased as Punch. "All my hair fell out about five
years back. Luckily I found this wig behind a hurdy-
gurdy house in Matamoras." She patted it and dislodged
a few nits. "Ain't it amazin'?"

"What?"

"What folks'll pitch out." She clucked. "Why, I've

found furniture, nice china pieces, clothes with only a few rips in 'em. All sorts a' stuff."

"Behind hurdy-gurdy houses?"

"Some. I generally check the alley behind them places." She rolled her upper lip, which was big and rubbery-looking. "You know them whores."

"Nuh-uh. I don't know a one. Well, I met one onct . . . no two. I met two onct over in . . ." But Janet Moon never listened to anyone but herself.

"Well, I can tell ya: Whores'll always buy new afore they'll mend."

"Huh," Nessa said. "I may make a sampler like that. Onct I get home."

"Huh?"

"Nothing."

A few minutes later Janet continued, "Ya jus' wouldn't believe some of these people headed west. Why, they'll start out cartin' everythin' but the shit house outa the back yard. Then they find out how hard the travelin' is. When they jus' can't cart it no further, they'll pitch it. That's how come you can find some of your best stuff on the trail."

While she talked, Janet admired her bare foot which Nessa had helped her elevate on her saddle. It was the purple of a wild plum getting ready to go bad. "Can you feel your toes, Janet?"

She wiggled her toes which were trestled by long, yolk-yellow nails. "No, but my foot don't hurt none neither."

It will, Nessa thought. "Were you riding the grub line, Janet?"

"Sure. I'll take a hand out if it's offered. I ain't proud.

But I mostly traded for my needs. A axe head for a bag of beans. A bent pot for a sack of turnips."

"So you just happen on most all your ah . . . inventory?"

"Mostly. Find some here. Find some there. Some times I got real lucky. Like the time a few months back. You know, the Injens won't generally leave a good arrowhead behind, but I come on this burned out place and found enough of 'em to fill a sack. I figure somebody must've come along and run 'em off afore they could collect 'em. Stuff was scattered to kingdom come. Buckles, a whole box of buttons."

"Don't you worry about the Comanch' yourself, Janet?"

"Why? If they're gonna git me, they'll git me."

Nessa thought: maybe the Comanche think she's a pwasa, their version of a crazy person.

"I only hope I git it fast," Janet continued. "Those red devils know every inhuman way there is to kill a person. Why, one time I come upon this ol' boy sittin' all by hisself clear up on the top of a hill. He was wrapped in a blanket and had his hat pulled low. I watched him for a long time but he just sat up there la-dee-da, like he was waitin' on a friend. Bothered me, you know? There weren't a soul but him and me in a hunnerd mile. 'Say!' I hollered, 'Say, feller?' He didn't say a derned thin'. So I crawled clear up there." Janet leaned closer, obviously enjoying herself. "Deader'n a doornail, he was. Those red devils had scalped him an' then stuck his hat back on. There was a sharpened stick up his bunghole to keep him sitting up straight. I could see the point clear up between his shoulder blades."

"Janet!"

"That weren't what killed him though. From the amount of blood, I'd have to guess that that feller had bled to death."

"JANET!"

"What?"

"I wish you wouldn't do that."

"Poor thin'!" Her eagle eye held a self-satisfied gleam. "Got yerself a bum stomach, huh?"

"Me? Heck, no! It's that durn knuckle-crackin' I can't take."

Old Janet Moon thout she had me. I wish I cood make a drawing of the expresshun on her face!

Sixteen

20th of July—Janet's geting a Round with the ayd of a narled Stick, Only now she has reel painful Throat contrakshuns when she tries to drink water and is unable to sleep for more than a few hours at a time.

I don't know what to do. Tye her to a tree and watch her dye like a dog? Or shoot her and get it over with? She knows her number's up. Yesterday she said . . .

"I know I'm gonna die of that thing."

"I doubt it, Janet. You are too derned ornery to die."

"No. It kilt me. Whatever it was."

Nessa knelt and stirred the rabbit stew. "I'm thinking, Janet, that maybe I'd better take you back to my aunt's place."

It was the last thing she wanted to do but she didn't see a ready choice. So she told Janet about her Aunt Etta and her home remedies and about how she could cure people nobody expected to pull through. Then she described the ranch and the river and the rolling grasslands. Janet listened closely as she made her pitch and then said, "No. Thank you kindly but I won't go."

"Janet! You don't exactly have a choice. What if you get that fever again? An' us clear out here in the middle of nowhere?"

She shook her head. "No. If I can't go along with you, then me and Marmaduke'll just head off on our own . . ."

"Hold it."

"Huh?"

"You and who?"

"Him." She pointed at the mule. "Marmaduke."

Nessa was silent, thinking. Well, all right then. Maybe it was the only logical solution. Balls! She hated like hell to do it! She'd be lucky to do three miles a day, trolling Janet and that wagon of hers.

Janet must've read her mind. "Don't worry about ol' Duke. He moves along right smart when I ask him to."

"Janet, it is not 'ol' Duke' I am worried about. It's you. I don't think you're up to traveling."

"Why, sure I am. Git a gander of this." And with that, she leapt up and did a frog-legged cartwheel.

Nessa groaned and buried her face in her hands. Reproduced on her closed eyelids was a rainbow of thick hairy legs and naked buttocks.

Much later, still hoping against hope for a reprieve, she asked, "Janet, you sure there isn't anyone else? Some place you can go to . . . uh . . . heal up?"

"No. No home. No man. No kin. I got no money and no way to get none. Jus' ol' Marmaduke there."

Nessa added a stick to the fire. Poor Janet. Being totally alone in the world must truly be pitiful. "Where do you sleep in the winter, Janet?"

"Why, same place as in the summer. Under my wagon." She cocked her head. "Will ya listen to that mockingbird cuss?"

Nessa stared into the fire. Life's a cruel trick of fate for some. Come to think of it, if it hadn't been for her aunt when her parents died she'd be all alone, too. She looked over. "I'm sure sorry you're all alone, Janet."

"I had somebody onct. Long time ago. You probably won't believe it, seein' me now . . ." She leaned forward, intent. ". . . but I was once married to Newt Moon." She sat back, waiting for Nessa's reaction . . . which was "Oh?"

"Well, you've heard of him, 'course."

"No, can't say as I . . ." Nessa back-pedaled when she saw Janet's eye start to glow.

"You mean t'say you ain't heard a' Newt Moon?"

"Well, now. Wait up a minute. Maybe I have. Newt Moon, you say? Yes, I believe I have. I don't recall where though."

"Big hero at the Alamo."

"The Alamo?"

"Yep. That was my husband, Newt."

"Hold it a minute. Are you saying your husband died at the Alamo?"

"Naw. Newt was the only survivor."

"Janet, there were no survivors of the Battle of the Alamo."

" 'Cept for Newt. There's only a few knows that. He escaped there at the very end and went on to fight Sant'ana at San Jacinto. He was a big hero there too. Swung that whole battle to the Texicans."

Nessa was not going to argue with her but it was well known that every defender of the Alamo had been killed. "How did you happen to meet this . . ." Smirk. ". . . big hero."

"Well, have ya ever been to Clute?" Nessa shook her head. "Nothin' much t'see. Jus' a nice little ol' town. That's where we met." Janet leaned her head back and looked up at the stars. "My parents had come through Clute on their way south. We were afoot as our oxen had up and died on us. That's how come my pa bound me over."

"What's that mean? Bound you over?"

"I did four years labor in exchange for four mules."

"You're joking!"

"Four years ain't nothin' to joke about."

"Your pa did that?"

"Well, we didn't have no money. Had plenty of kids though. They was eleven of us."

"For pity's sake! Your family left you there? All alone?"

"Well, yeah. They went on, you see, to find good river bottom land. That's what my pa was after. River bottom land. They was supposed to write and tell me where they finally settled, but they never did."

"They probably did! Sure they did. Only the letter got lost in the mail. That happens all the time. Even nowadays."

"Mebbe." Janet didn't look convinced. "Well, anyhow, I stayed on when my time was up. I worked in that boardin' house near ten years. I was . . . let's see . . . twenty-six when Newt come along. I was a grateful spinster. Oh, I'd had offers but only from ol' widder men with a passel of kids or some ne'er-do-well, lookin' t'git hisself some slave labor. I turned 'em all down." She huffed. "Thank you, ma'am but I'd done enough slavin' for somebody else.

"But then Newt Moon come along one day. My, he was fine! Well, he brushed the cobwebs offa me and said, 'This here's the gal for me.' Married me right off the bat. Didn't care a bit that I was older'n him and had no kin or money or belongings. Didn't care about this one eye of mine." She pointed. "I got this one eye looks back behind me."

Nessa responded dryly with, "I noticed."

Janet chuckled and shook her head slow. "Ol' Newt used t'say 'Hell, most people got to get a crick in their necks afore they can see behind 'em. Not my Janet. Alls I got to do is say, 'Janet, what's acomin' up behind us? An' blam, she gives me the whole picture.' Naw, Newt didn't care about none of that. 'Course I cain't actually see nothin' back there."

"Really?" Smirk.

"Naw. Just the inside of my head." She looked at Nessa. "You know what the inside of your head looks like?"

"Haven't a clue."

"Did ya ever mix buttermilk and corn bread?"

"Uh, yeah."

"There you go."

"Huh. I'll be."

"Yep. Buttermilk and corn bread. With little teensy red dots like somebody'd ground up some chili peppers in it."

"Yuck."

"Yep."

Janet stared up at the sky for a time. "We were together one hundred and fifty-three months. Newt and me. Same number of fishes Jesus brought out of the Sea of Galilee. We was real happy."

All this Janet said in a very matter-of-fact manner, as if Nessa should know it already. "Did he pass on, Janet?"

"Yes. Him an' Blue, too."

"Who's Blue?"

"Blue was my boy. His real name was Diligence but we called him Blue."

"And he died as well?"

"Yep."

"God, I'm sure sorry, Janet. Real sorry."

"Yeah, well. Right after that was when my house got burned. I lost everythin' I had except for that mule an' the clothes on my back. Every blamed thin'. Gone."

"Aw, that's terrible! I feel awful! Was it Indians?"

"What?"

"Did the Indians burn you out?

"Naw, I did."

"You did. . . . What?"

"Burnt my house down. You see, I killed Newt and Blue with those tomatoes I put up. I didn't eat 'em. They did. They died."

"Oh, God, Janet. I don't know . . . what to say."

"Yeah, well." She took a moment to blow her nose on her dress. "You see, I didn't deserve no nice home to begin with. God never intended I should have all that. Got above myself there for a while. That's how come He called me on it."

She was plenty agitated now, rocking back and forth and crying. Strangely, it looked like only half of her grieved because while tears tunneled pale streaks down one side of her face, the blind side remained curiously dry.

"Don't never want nothin' again. Not never. Nothin'. No how. Nossirreebob. No more."

24th of July—That was awfull. Thank goodness that Janet has not said any more about The death of Her family. I have no idea what to say to some body who claims to have killed the onle people they loved. I did try To tell her that I thought she was being Too hard on herself, that even if the Toematos had gone bad, she didn't make them That way on purpose. All my arguments were futyle. Convinced of her own rong doing she has condemned herself and will not be soothed.

28th of July—The days go by and since Janet Moon continues to defi fate, I have decided to Tote her along with Me. I have no choyce. It'll be slow going but At least I'll be on my way agin.

The moon cast a gun-metal path on the stream. Crickets chirred and bugs buzzed accompanied by the usual chorus of coyotes. Nessa stirred the batch of pinole she'd made, tasted it and then removed it from the fire. "Well, Janet, I've decided that we will take off outa here tomorrow."

"Oh, my," she pumped her hair. "We'll gussy up, ol' Duke and me."

And so they left.

Whenever possible they followed stream beds or stayed close to the cover of trees but most of the time, with that old rattletrap wagon, they had no other option but to follow the rough trail of others. Nessa wrapped, greased and muffled everything before starting out but they still sounded like a herd of buffalos.

A very slo moving herd, she wrote. *Wering a lot of jewellry. The onle positive thing about traveling with*

Janet Moon is I no longer have to be worryed about sparing my horse.

Finding water was simple; the trail generally led straight to the nearest source so Nessa spent her time ranging ahead, on the look out for Indians. Most nights she could scout the area and water Easy and set her snares and make camp—all before Janet Moon's wagon rattled into sight.

Nessa was tired but since she'd seen recent tracks around the rain-filled waterhole she'd circled the area several times. Her wariness was in vain for she saw no one. She returned at dusk, just as Janet drove up.

"Wonder what that is?" Janet said. Nessa followed Janet's finger to a piece of paper tacked to a dead alamo.

"I'd swear that wasn't there before." Nessa crossed to the other side and pulled the paper off a bent nail.

TERN BACK AFORE YER KILED

Nessa snorted and hoped the noise covered the pounding of her heart. "Would you just look at that?"

"I cain't. Not until you stop beatin' your leg with it."

Nessa opened the note and read it again. "That fella's got more gall than a bladder."

Janet was looking over her shoulder. "What's that there drawin' on the bottom?"

"It's a doubletree."

"What's that mean?"

"I don't care to discuss it right now."

"Huh?"

"I said . . ."

"I heerd ya." Janet limped toward the mule, mumbling "Well, la-dee-da dee-da!"

Nessa couldn't think of anything else but that note and what it meant, all through the meal of beans and bacon, all through clean up, even as she lay silently watching the stars come out.

He *had* been back there behind her. All this time! She pulled up the blanket, shivering from sheer excitement. He'd been here! Right here! Maybe he'd stood exactly where she was laying. Something warm and liquid released inside. Oh Gol! She wound herself in her blanket. Rolled around. Stuck the toes of her boots in the dirt. Wiggled her heels.

"Ya on top a ant hill over there?"

She froze. "What?" Muffled by the blanket.

"Ya either got ants or the heebeejeebees."

"Nothing. It's nothing." She sat up. Smoothed her hair. Respread her blanket. She ought to be damned disappointed with herself. She *was* damned disappointed with herself. For, without realizing it, she had come to count on him. In the back of her mind she'd known he was there and she'd relaxed her guard because of it. Boy, that showed damned poor judgment on her part. If there was one thing her father stressed above all else, it was that she learn to rely totally on herself.

Janet cocked her eye at her, unable to contain herself a moment longer. "Well?"

"Well what?"

"Was that note from somebody you know?"

"Sorta."

"Sorta?"

"I've had . . . dealings with him."

"Dealin's?"

"He's a lawman friend of my pa's." *Nosey ol' witch!* "Wonder how he knew we'd end up here?"

"It figures. Anybody traveling this stretch'll end up here. It's about the only reliable water for a hunnerd mile."

The faint breeze stirred the fire. Nessa sniffed. "Can't spell for beans."

"What?"

"I said he can't spell for beans!"

"Lemme tell ya somethin', girley."

Nessa looked over at Janet, surprised at her serious tone.

"Spellin' ain't at all important in a man. Not at all."

"Well . . ." Huffy. "Well, of course it is. It sure is."

Janet shook her head. "No, it ain't. I'll tell ya what's important." Janet looked off somewhere and then down at her hands and her voice went soft, like Nessa'd never heard it before. "Big hands is important. Arms like iron bands. Hairy legs. Yeah. Hairy legs."

After that there stretched a long silence filled only by the noises of the night, the rustle of the wind, the lonely hoot of an owl. Nessa lay back against her saddle. All her bones had turned to mush.

The shadow of something winged sailed past the moon and Easy blew and stamped before Janet added, "Ol' Newt could tie a knot in a string with his tongue." Nessa groaned and plugged her ears.

I turned On my side to diskourage further conversashun. No thing, how ever, relieved the stab of desire in my gut. Before That nite in the adoby ruins I wood have Had to ask Janet to explain that last comment.

Seventeen

Ranger Headquarters
Del Rio, Texas

"Giff."

"Tom."

They shook hands and sat amid the loud creaking of straight-backed chairs with rock-hard wooden seats. Giff Minger took hold of the cuff of his pants, pulled out the bottom desk drawer and laid his bum leg on it. Doubletree rolled a twirly and lit it and then studied the other man through the smoke.

Minger had been commander of the company of rangers headquartered in Del Rio since '48, the same year he'd been hamstrung by a Kiowa knife. Although he was only fifty he appeared older with a face as scarred and worn as the land he used to ride.

Minger nailed the spittoon square before he asked, "What t'hell took ya so long?"

"Shit, I come more'n two hundred mile."

"Hellfire! I sent word three weeks ago. Did ya walk?"

Doubletree stared at his smoking twirly. "I couldn't leave right then."

"How come?" Through the open window came the

shrieks of kids at play, the barking of a dog. "I say, how come?"

"I heard ya."

"Well?"

"Well, it's kinda personal."

"Personal?" Minger dropped his head between yoke-like shoulders, a bull that's had too much pic. "What's that mean?"

Doubletree shrugged. "Just . . . personal I guess."

"Huh." Minger picked up a pencil and frowned at it. There was a minute then he asked, "Is it somethin' you figure you can break yore self of?"

"Mebbe I ain't lookin' to."

Minger rubbed his lantern jaw. It couldn't be female trouble. Tom Doubletree was about the most fiddle-footed fella Minger knew. Why, one time Minger heard him say that the ideal woman would be one that turned into a poker table and five guys soon as a fella finished with her.

"Reason why I didn't hurry was I already knew what you wanted," stated Doubletree.

Minger pulled a bottle from the drawer and elevated it. Doubletree shook his head. Minger took a swig, re-plugged it with a slap and returned it to the drawer. "You tell me what I want then."

"You want somebody to go down to Chihuahua and talk to the Governor."

"Yore damn right."

"Well, I can't."

"Why?" Minger asked but Doubletree ignored him again.

"I saw young Dub outside. Why don't you send him?"

"Because I'd druther send you. Besides, Governor

Pease asked for you in particular. Listen to this." He hooked the wire rims of his spectacles over his ears, unfolded a piece of paper and started tracking the words with the pads of two fingers. "I ask that you send Tom Doubletree . . ."

"How long did it take you to learn to read fast like that?"

Thrown off, Minger looked up at him. "Huh?"

"Read. How long did it take you to read fast like that?"

"Hellfire! I don't know. I cain't remember clear back then."

Doubletree got up and started wandering. Tethered by his bum leg, Minger had to contort his torso in order to follow him around the room. Minger was glad that the man finally lit and planted both hands on the window frame and stared outside. *Suppose it could be sunstroke?*

"You were a kid, huh?" Doubletree asked.

"Well, I . . . yeah. I must've been. I don't remember exactly when learned. I just could." Minger spit, missed, looked at the brown gob on the floor in disbelief and then turned narrowed eyes on Doubletree. "What the hell is this sudden gawddamned interest in readin'? You fixin' t'retire 'n' be a schoolmarm?"

Doubletree stared out at the street. It was Saturday morning. Buckboards rattled by with bare brown legs dangling off their tailgates. Small groups of people were gathered on the corners and in front of the stores. Isaac Solomon, the owner of the Del Rio Bank stood outside his establishment talking to a woman who wore a floral print dress and a man's hat. Doubletree was thinking that men's wear just might become the fashion someday when Minger's voice intruded.

". . . wants the scalp bounty lifted afore every Texan man, woman and child is rubbed out in reprisal. Three days ago the Comanche hit the stage station clear across the Frio . . ."

Doubletree glanced around. "Where?"

"The stage station between the Sabinal and the Frio. Nobody was lost. They fought 'em off with the help of some travelers."

"I met those people a few weeks back," he said softly.

"The Cobbs?"

"Yeah," Doubletree said and looked outside again.

Minger waited. He'd give him some time to think it over. He never doubted Doubletree wouldn't go to Chihuahua. The man had never shirked a duty in his life.

"How's that bank doin' yonder?"

"Bank?" Minger tossed down his pencil again. "What bank?"

"That one di-rek-ly across the street there."

"Hellfire! What's that got t'do with anythin'?"

"Anybody robbed it yet?"

"Robbed it? That bank? Hell, not hardly. Not seein' as how it is directly across the street from this here office."

"Pretty smart of that ol' boy. Openin' up his bank across the street from ranger headquarters."

"Smart? Of course he's smart. Those people are borned smart. Leastwise about things like that."

"What do you mean 'those people'?"

"Jew people."

"Is that what Solomon is? A Jew?"

"Yeah, didn't you know that?"

"If I heard it, I forgot it. Anyhow, what's your point?"

"My point is that a Jew'll have as many as three extra lobes in their brain. Over yore ordinary person."

Doubletree looked around at Minger, interested. "What's a lobe?"

"It's a . . . well, um, a compartment-like thing in the brain. It's what gives 'em their knack for handlin' sums an' their tolerance for desert heat an' their passionate natures. Stuff like that."

"Passionate natures, huh?" Doubletree looked back at Isaac Solomon. Far as the shape of Solomon's head went, he might as well be looking at his own. "I never heard that before."

"Well, it makes plenty of sense to me. You think on it a minute. Isaac Solomon is about the richest man in this here county, he's got seven kids already an' another'n in the hopper an' I ain't never seen him raise a sweat."

Doubletree took his chair again. "I've poured the savings of many hard years into that bank."

Minger snorted. "Poured? Did ya say poured? Haw! Haw! That's a good one!" He shook his head. "Poured!" When he and Doubletree started rangering the pay was $1.25 a day. The increases in twenty years could be counted on one hand. "That reminds me." Minger dug in the drawer. "You'll want to draw yore wages for the month."

"Keep it."

"What?"

"I was gettin' paid for doin' a job. Since I ain't gonna do it no more, I'll take no more pay."

"What's got into ya?"

"I'm fixin' to quit."

"Quit? That'll be the day!"

"You'll live to see it. Old as you are. Once I get Caleb Flatt hung, I'm done."

"Yore serious!"

"Dead." Their eyes locked.

"Are you sure, man?"

"Yeah."

A fly hummed. Minger brushed it aside. He looked sad. "Twenty years. We've been rangerin' together more'n twenty years."

"Yeah, I reckon."

"Well."

"Life's damned unpredictable, ain't it? Well, lemme get ol' Dub in here for you."

Minger watched, puzzled as Doubletree padded catlike to the open door. Outside there was a man slumped in a chair that was precariously balanced back on two legs. Hat down. Legs loose. Sound asleep. Doubletree turned and grinned at Minger and winked. Then he yelled "Hey!" and simultaneously slapped his palm on the wall.

"WAH!" The man croaked. The chair crashed back and flailing legs and vivid curses filled the air.

Hands on his knees, Doubletree bent over. "Hey, Dub!" The young man glared up at him. "How ya doin', Dub?" He helped the man gain his feet.

"Horseshit! Seein' as how I jus' ruint my best pair of pants."

"Aw! Damn! I'm sure sorry!" He clapped him on the shoulder. "I only wanted to tell you that the major wants t'see you."

Dub picked up his hat and beat it against his leg. "Damnit, Doubletree, you coulda jus' said that. You ain't still upset about that ice water?"

"Nope. That whore might be but I ain't."

"God, I hope this makes us even."

"I expect."

"Well, all right then." Dub resettled his hat then shuffled into the office.

"Dub, I'm gonna need you to go down to Chihuahua," said Minger.

Dub looked at Doubletree. "I thought you was goin'."

Minger inserted, "He cain't go 'cause he's got pressin' personal business."

"That so?" said Dub and studied Doubletree with interest.

"Well, Dub," Minger said, "I expect I better ask ya if ya got anythin' that would keep ya from takin' care of this chore?"

Dub thought about that a minute. "Well, Major, there is my shoulder. You know, from that arrow I took last winter? Hell, I can't hardly do this no more . . ." He pinwheeled his arms. ". . . without I get real bad pains right about here . . ."

"Then don't!" Minger advised abruptly.

"Huh?"

"Quit doin' it."

Dub lowered his arms. "Right." His brow furrowed then cleared. "Oh, you mean that dose I had? Nah, Doc fixed me up right good." He frowned again. "Unless last night . . . I suppose I coulda . . ."

Minger grabbed Dub's hand and slapped the letter in it. "Take this damned letter an' go on an' go. Take Clell Adkins with you."

Dub hesitated, shifting his feet and rolling the brim of his hat. "Uh, Major Minger, sir?"

"What?"

"Uh . . . well, it's about Clell, sir."

"What about him?"

"Well, you see. We was havin' a couple last night an'

ol' Clell got pretty well roostered an' . . . well, you know, one thing led to another . . ."

"Good gawd a'mighty!" Minger's pencil pinged off the wall. "Don't tell me he sold his saddle again." Dub said nothing. He didn't have to. "Damnit!" Minger glared a long minute then rooted around in the drawer until he found a coin. He pitched it at the young ranger like he was chucking a rock at a rabid dog.

Dub caught it and slammed on his hat. "We're on our way, Major." With a nod to Doubletree, he left.

"What's that all about?" asked Doubletree.

"Some ol' boys from the Bar X hang around 'til Clell's so drunk he cain't pound sand in a gopher hole. They buy his saddle. I buy it back. They buy his saddle. I buy it back."

"Sounds like a right profitable enterprise," Doubletree said as he picked up his hat. "Well, I can't say that I know Clell Adkins at all, but I was with Dub during that fracas in Llano last year. He has a flash temper when he is drinking but other'n that he's fine. He's just young. Hellfire, Gifford, you was young onct yourself."

"I don't never recall bein' that young."

"Me neither. An' I ain't never gonna be again. That's the whole thing in a nutshell. Well . . ." Doubletree paused, hand on the door knob. "I imagine I'll check back after I take Flatt in."

"You do that."

"Hey, don't forget to write down that ten bucks."

"Right."

Doubletree settled his hat and left. Minger fingered the papers on his desk looking for the tally of expenses he'd been meaning to send to Austin. When he didn't find it right off, he promptly forgot it. It was what happened to a lot of his personal funds.

"I may just quit myself," Minger mumbled to himself. "Hell, why not?" Seemed he spent all his time now filling out forms, adding numbers and writing letters. Far cry from what he'd had planned for his old age. Through the open door he could see Doubletree wheel his mount and head out of town. Dust settled on the street.

Minger liked and admired Doubletree. Trusted him implicitly and respected him too, as he did few others. Yet after all this time he figured he knew the man about as well as he knew President Franklin Pierce. Thing was, Minger knew he wasn't the only one who felt that way. There was a side to Doubletree he didn't think anybody knew, a private aspect that separated him from ordinary men with their ordinary dreams. That's why it surprised him to learn that Doubletree coveted something. Like an ordinary man.

But why should it? Minger thought. Hell, at one time he'd had those dreams himself. Hard to believe it now but it was true. He'd hoped to save up for a modest spread, ultimately marry and have a family, someone to fill the void in his heart. But it seemed that one night he went to bed thirty years old and woke up fifty. He knew that day it would never happen for him. His chance was gone. That's when he'd started trying to fool himself into believing that the life he had was plenty good enough.

He looked at the pile of papers, the thick layer of prairie dust coating every flat surface and thought about the room in the rear of the seedy boarding house down the street.

It wasn't enough. Not by a long shot. But it was too

damn late now. Well, maybe it wasn't for Tom Double-tree. Maybe somebody or something had made him stop and take stock. If that was the case, Minger envied him. He sure wished it had happened to him. Back when it'd've done some good.

Eighteen

12th of August—We've been inching our way along. Poco a poco. Every day was Pretty uneventful until yesterday. We had ourselves a run in with The sort Of person who helps give the Nueces Strip its nasty reputashun. Janet had him pegged rite from The gitgo. She called him "a shifty-eyed four-flushing rannie." He called himself Garrison Feeney. "Gar to his friends."

Bite growled softly and Nessa opened one eye. Across the low fire she saw that Janet was also awake. She laid a finger on her lips, quieted the dog and then slipped out of her bedroll and into the brush. Gun cocked, she crouched and waited. Unfortunately she'd picked a clump of skunkbush to hide behind. It was a long five minutes before the man showed himself.

"Hello, the camp!"

"Step into the light, mister," Janet said.

"I hope I didn't startle you," the man said as he complied.

"Not hardly," Janet replied. "You been crashin' around in those bushes for nigh on an hour."

The man reached for the coffee pot, bold as brass and Janet hollered, "Hold it, mister!" He froze with his arm outstretched. Except for his small dark eyes, which were rolling around like two BB's in a glass. "I wouldn't make any fast moves, mister. My partner Ratigan's got a gun pointed right at your brisket."

Ratigan?

"Please tell your . . . partner that I am an honest traveler who has suffered a terrible misfortune. I've not only lost my horse but find that I am totally lost myself."

"We knowed ya weren't no scout for the army."

He swept off his hat and pointed one foot. "Garrison Feeney, madam. Gar to my friends. At your service."

A fancy dan, Nessa thought, taking in the ferris-wheel-sized spurs, the black weskit with shiny silver threads and shell buttons. Keeping her gun trained, she stepped out of the bushes and into the fire's nimbus.

"Ah! There you are!" he said like he knew her. "Gar Feeney, ma'am." He made his foot again.

"So I heard."

Janet gave him her eye burn and asked, "You got any 'baccy, mister?"

"Yes, madam, it so happens that I do."

"How about handin' it over."

"Glad to share my weed. Say, I wonder . . ." He pointed at Bite who was bristled out like a hedgehog. ". . . if you would mind calling off that wolfhound? I'm afraid to move a muscle." Janet had already tucked half the contents of his pouch in her lower lip.

Nessa pointed at a rock with her gun. "Sit right there, Mister Sweeney."

"Feeney." He looked at the rock. "Why, I'm delighted. And thank you!"

Feeney was a powerful talker. Before five minutes had passed he'd told them his opinion on Texas independence and how to boil coffee properly and had got pretty far along in his life story.

". . . in Baton Rouge. My entire family died in the cholera epidemic of '48. You probably heard about it. Well, I can tell you first hand that it was ghastly, simply ghastly. Hundreds died."

"But not you," Janet remarked with regret.

"Ah, no. Fortunately my body was able to fend off the ravaging disease and though terribly, terribly weakened, I finally revived. That, however, was only the beginning of my trials."

"An' ours," Janet mumbled.

"I was, as I'm sure you can see, born to a life of ease . . ." He studied his hands, turning them this way and that as if they satisfied him greatly. ". . . and I was therefore completely ill-prepared to take on the management of our vast holdings. Alas! I lost it all. But I'm not one to mope. Not me. No, *c'est la vie,* I said and that very day I packed everything I could fit into one small valise and left. Forthwith."

Janet spat before she spoke. "Sounds like a man dodgin' his creditors t'me."

From the slash of color that rose on Feeney's sallow cheeks, Nessa knew that Janet had hit home.

"Ha! You are quite the comedienne, madam! Why, you belong in a minstrel show. Doesn't she?"

He looked at Nessa but she didn't return his smile because she was spellbound by the way his nose moved when he talked. It came to a moist point on the end and then hooked over his itta bitty mustache. When he talked his upper lip jerked it around like something in its death throes. *There it goes again.*

". . . headed for Mexico City and a new start. Have

you ever been there? I've heard that it is the Paris of this hemisphere."

From Janet there was a well-aimed spit and a muttered suggestion that he should strike out that very night.

13th of August—Mr. Feeney has asked To travel south with us but I Am afraid one day Of him is about All I can take. I snuk out of camp While it was still pitch black. I had to backtrak almost three miles but there was Feeney's horse—tyed up with a long rawhide riata and fit as a fiddle.

Now there was no earthle reason for him to hide that Horse unless he Is up To some mischief. But what? For the life of me I can't feature him as a cold blooded murderer. I can't believe that little pisant has the Grit for it.

Upstream from their camp, Nessa was kneeling to get a drink when a boot to her rear plowed her chin across the gritty stream bottom.

"How fortuitous!" crowed Gar Feeney as he pulled her out by her boots and rolled her over and stuck a short-barreled gun in her face.

"What in the hell do you think you are doin', Feeney?"

He drove his hard fist between her breasts then hit her such a stunning blow to the head that a windmill of stars exploded behind her eyes. He pulled her gun out and tossed it aside then stood over her straddle-legged.

"What am I doin'? I'm gettin' ready to take you to Mexico City with me. I'm gonna dress you up in feathers and beads. Push up them little titties. Oh, yeah. I'm gonna get a good buck for you. But first I want to make sure you're worth my time and effort."

She noticed that his fancy dan accent had gone south. He unbuckled his belt and said, "Get ready to spell Ohio for me."

Was he loco? "Spell Ohio?" she gasped. It felt like she'd swallowed a rock.

"Not yet. Not yet."

He got one leg of his trousers off and then the other. His fish white and hairless legs made a triangular frame for a determined-faced Janet Moon who was hobbling up behind him. Nessa laid back and waited and tried not to snicker. *This ought to be good.*

"Oh yes!" he said. "I can hardly . . . WAUZGH!" he screamed as the toe of Janet's boot cleaved into his crotch like an axe. He landed with both hands clapped to his privates. Making a high animal noise, he walked— knock-kneed and pigeon-toed—for about a foot. Then he keeled over and started urping.

Janet adjusted her wig, which had been listing hard right, and offered Nessa a hand. "You all right?" She had to speak up to be heard over Feeney. "Ya look downright pukey yerself."

"Yeah, I'm all right. Just give me a minute. I think my backbone just met my belly button."

"Dirty four-flushin' ranny!" Janet picked up Feeney's gun and pointed it at him.

"No, Janet! Don't shoot!"

"Why not?"

She shook her head. "Comanche." She coughed and rubbed her chest. "We'll tie him up and leave him here. They'll be by sooner or later."

Feeney managed a few tight words between episodes of urping, "Please. You mistook me. I was jus' funnin'."

"Your sense of humor stinks, mister."

When Feeney could stand, Nessa tied a rope around his neck and walked him back to where his horse was tied.

"You can't leave me here to be tortured by the Indians! You wouldn't be that heartless."

"I believe I could. Way I feel."

Janet spied his pouch string dangling out of his coat pocket and commandered the rest of his tobacco. "Feeney," she said, "I suggest that when the Comanch' show up you commence talkin'. You'll bore 'em half-witted for a while 'n' I guarantee ya they'll kill ya outright."

Nessa finished knotting the rope, stood back and surveyed Feeney, who was tied to an alamo so skinny that if all else failed he could pull it out by the roots.

Janet and the wagon were already a half mile gone when she mounted up. "Well, Feeney, as you can see, I've left you your horse. You should be able to work your way free in two or three hours. If I was you I'd waste no time getting at it. You never know who might ride over that rise."

She walked her horse in closer. "I'll warn you now, Gar Feeney. Never let me lay eyes on you again. If I see you," she sliced air with her hand. "I will kill you out of hand."

15th of August—To day Is my birth Day. Whoopeedo

Nessa was awakened by a cry. "Thar goes your horse!" She simply pulled the blanket higher, thinking

Janet was hollering in her sleep again. But then a boot gave her a rude shove on her rear end.

"Thar he goes! I ain't akiddin' ya!"

Nessa heard the swift sound of hoof beats and jumped up but all she could see was a plume of dust. Grabbing up her rifle, she ran to a small hill. An Indian was two hundred yards gone and riding like the wind. On Easy! She knelt and braced her elbow on her knee. Taking a deep breath, she gauged the direction of the wind and the speed of the horse and thought: this'll be some shot. Then she let her brain go dead and squeezed the trigger. The Indian, skylined now against the brightening horizon, kept going. "Damn!"

"Missed 'im?" Janet asked breathlessly.

"Yes. No!" The Indian had slowed. Now he was waving like wheat in the wind. Now he went down. The horse ran a few yards and quit. Nessa sped down the hill with Janet hobbling along behind. She knelt and turned the Indian over. He was a boy only twelve, maybe thirteen, but he'd soon be dead. He'd been hit in the spine, low and dead center. The bullet had exited in front. Blood and worse was everywhere.

Suddenly a bloodcurdling war cry rang out. Grabbing his wrist in both hands was the only thing that kept the Indian's knife from decapitating her. They tumbled down the hill, fighting tooth and nail. He was much stronger than she, even without the use of his legs. *This Indian has been killed and doesn't know it!*

Raw hatred raged in his eyes as he gave a pitiless grin and pressed the knife closer . . . closer. His forearm crushed her windpipe. Her eyes were popping out of their sockets. *He's killing me!*

Suddenly his head jerked back. A stag-handled knife passed across his throat and she was drenched in blood.

The flies and terrible heat spurred them to finish the shallow grave in short order. Nessa folded the boy's arms on his chest.

"What's them markings mean?" Janet asked, pointing.

"Means he's Penaterkuh Comanche. All the bands—Quahidi, Nocona, Kutsukuh, Kwahadie—have different tattoos."

"What do you figure that wristband's made of?"

"Horse toes, Janet. Damnit! I don't care." She was still sick about killing the boy.

"I care. That's how come I ast."

Knowing Janet would not give up on it, Nessa sighed and looked. "Maybe puma."

"It sure is purty." Janet pulled it off and tossed it across the grave. "Take it."

"I don't think I ought to, Janet."

"Aw, go on. It ain't gonna do that boy a bit of good where he's goin'. Besides," she added, "You ain't gonna have it fer long anyway."

Nessa huddled by the fire wearing a blanket, her extra shirt and a Comanche puma claw bracelet. The surrounding bushes were hung with her clothes. She'd buried her blood-soaked shirt. She still felt miserable about the boy.

"I want you to have my wagon and Duke."

Nessa looked up. "You feeling worse?"

"No, I feel about the same. Which is probably as good

as I'm ever gonna feel. What I mean is, if you make it, then you can have my wagon and Duke."

"What do you mean? If I make it?" Janet could be so irritating!

"I figure we're gonna be up to our eyeballs in Injens. Jus' about any minute now."

"Don't start that, Janet. Please." Bite, back from whatever adventure he'd pursued for the past two days, woofed and wagged his tail and Nessa stuck a finger in his face. "I don't want to hear anything from you either. If you'da been here like you're supposed to be, that boy wouldn't have gotten close enough to try and steal my horse."

"Yeah." Janet talked on, in her own world again. "That boy was out to count coup. When he don't come back, his big brothers and ol' uncles are gonna come a lookin'. They gonna find that mound o' dirt an' then they're gonna find us. Shortly thereafter we will be staked to the ground having our skin cut off a inch at a time."

Nessa pulled the blanket closer. "Janet, I just said I don't want to hear it!" She might as well have been talking to herself.

"I expect that by this time tomorrow we'll be roastin' to a turn. I jes' hope they don't scalp my cunny. They probably will though." She sounded mournful. "Especially onct they find out I'm bald. They're prone to do that, you know. Scalp you on both ends."

Nessa pulled her knees to her chest and encircled them. "I never heard of any tribe doing that."

"I expect not. Who'd tell a young girl that kinda thing? Believe me you'da heard that and more. Onct ya spent some time sittin' an' stitchin' with the ol' married biddies."

She was sick to death of Janet Moon. It might be utterly illogical but she believed none of this would have
happened if it weren't for Janet. "You know what I think,
Janet?"

"No." Mildly interested. "What?"

"I think you are prone to make stuff up."

"I am not." She was affronted.

"You know what I said about knowing of Newt Moon?
Well, I lied. I never heard of no Newt Moon. You know
what else? I think you been lying about that too. I think
maybe you never had a husband ever. Maybe you never
had no kid neither. You probably made up that whole
story about the tomatoes." Janet's smile was turning to
tallow, but something pure mean drove her on. "An' even
if there was a Newt Moon, I'll bet he didn't die like you
said. I'll bet you drove him so crazy he just up and left
you. Yeah! High and dry."

*Janet looked like I'd shot her. Of course I imediately
wished I cood take those Words back.*

*I new I wood regret it. I did not no I wood have to
Regret it till my dying day.*

Nineteen

17th of August—I don't no how far we will get today. I suspect that Janet's fever has flared up again but since she is not talking To me there's No way To find out for sure.

It was a bright, clear day and so completely windless that whatever dust the wagon disturbed hung right above it.

They'd been following an old horse trail that twisted through the brush-spotted hills when abruptly the trail became a tunnel-like passage of rocks. Janet gigged the mule forward but Nessa held back and looked up at the rocks rising high on both sides. A feeling of fear feathered up her spine. "Hold up a minute, Janet."

Suddenly hideous cries filled the air as a score of painted Indians sprang out of the rocks. Two Indians leapt down onto the wagon. Nessa fired and hit both. "Make a run for it," she yelled to Janet as she slapped Marmaduke with her hat and spurred her horse. An Indian tried to cut her off. Easy made a quick turn but the Indian raced after her and hit her across the back and knocked her off her horse. Her rifle went galloping away with Easy.

She rolled and fired and killed the Indian who'd unsaddled her. She fired again at an Indian running at Janet with his tomahawk raised and he bowed his back and went down. She caught a glimpse of Bite, snarling and bearing an Indian into the rocks, but it looked bad. There was no place to run and too many to kill.

Janet Moon was down now with an Indian straddling her. Nessa aimed but before she could fire she took an arrow in her arm and it went dead. She tore the arrow out as she ran toward Janet. The Indian pulled Janet's hair up like he would scalp her and it came away in his hand. He looked at the wig and in that second of incredulity, Janet stabbed him in the stomach with that little stag-handled knife. With a cry of outrage, he buried his tomahawk in her forehead.

Nessa turned. There was a tiny lull. She started backing up, moving her knife in a slow arc as ten Indians converged on her. She only had one bullet left. She was boxed.

In a hand-to-hand fight the advantage is to the first move, provided it is sudden and violent!

She would die shortly but, by God, she would not go without a fight! Thrusting her knife above her head and screaming the Cherokee war cry, she charged.

Damn if it didn't stop them in their tracks. She maimed the first Indian without breaking stride. Spinning and leaning away, she delivered a killing thrust to a brave's stomach. An Indian pony stood only a few yards away! As she ran toward it, she stabbed a third Indian, but before she could withdraw her bowie the Indian sat abruptly and trapped her knife between his ribs. Seconds were lost and the others closed in. *This is it!* She tried to turn her gun on herself but that arm was numb and low. She struggled. Panic rose. Her arm wouldn't work!

She was blind-sided with a blow to the head. She tasted blood and then her knees went and the ground rose.

She woke hanging face down, drooling blood. She was on a small Indian pony with her wrists and ankles tied together beneath the horse's belly. Everything hurt, her side, head, arm. Her jaw. God, her jaw hurt! She ran her tongue around her mouth and found a tooth that was hanging by a thread. She worked it free and spat it. A hoof ground it into the dirt then another and another until it disappeared beneath the churning hooves. Her head started swimming. She vomited weakly, then lost consciousness again.

When she woke again, her first thought was, Something has died and needs to be drug off. Then came the sound of barking dogs. She turned her head and saw the Indian encampment. It was a large band and one plainly bent on war; scalp sticks stood in front of most of the lodges.

Someone pulled her hair hard then came a blow to her injured arm and she couldn't keep from crying out. They cut her off the horse. She crumpled and the squaws were at her immediately, kicking and beating her, pricking her skin with red hot sticks. One particularly enthusiastic squaw was pounding her like a tortilla. *That's about enough of that!* She flipped onto her back and planted her feet in the squaw's stomach. Straightening her knees sent the squaw backward into a cook fire. A couple of squaws tittered and held back, looking from Nessa to the downed squaw. The squaw rolled around to get the cinders out, then lowered her head and raised her stick and charged like a bull.

A warrior—probably the to-yop-ke of the raiding party—gave a sharp command that stopped the squaw cold. She looked at him, waiting, so anxious to renew the attack she was quivering like a tuning fork. But he gave another barked command and everyone dispersed except the to-yop-ke.

He stood staring down at her steady, his eyes like the black hollows of a shotgun. Stringy hair parted in the middle hung over his pitted face like a ragged curtain. He was the dirtiest, meanest-looking person she'd ever seen.

Stare for stare, she figured she gave as good as she got. Finally he spoke. She didn't get it all but she understood enough to get his gist. Something on the order of: hope you're this cocky when you are hanging upside down and we are slow roasting your brain. She didn't know any cuss words in Comanch' but those hours spent eavesdropping under the bunkhouse window served her well now. "Chingada! Cabrone!" She sucked up some spit and put it as close to his foot as possible. "Hijo de un puta!"

Nothing! Huh. He must not understand Mex.

Turns out he did. The kick he delivered before he stalked off lifted her off the ground and left her without air for a year.

She must've slept then because the next thing she heard was the beat of throbbing drums and frenzied yelps. She lifted her head. It appeared that everyone was busy preparing for a celebration; one at which she was going to be the main entertainment. Two squaws walked by leading Janet Moon's mule. She hoped she was wrong but sure enough she soon heard the mule's skirling screams. She couldn't stopper her ears against the sound that went on and on and on. *God, aren't they going to kill him before they skin him?* The pitiful noise abruptly ended and she took a long grateful breath.

A glance at the sky revealed that the stars had clustered overhead and that the moon had risen and she knew she had very little time. This night—her last—would be one of unimaginable horror. Unless she could think of something mighty inventive mighty quick. She took stock of her injuries and carefully considered her chances of survival.

She would not die of her injuries and her chances of survival were none. She uttered a low cry of terror.

"A person only dies once," her father once said. "That's why the Indians feel it is so important to make a good job of it."

Well, all right. She straightened her legs as much as the bindings allowed. Her boots and the derringer were gone but by twisting her torso she could feel the sneak knife still under her arm.

At least she had that. She'd have to use it on herself first chance she got. A quick severing slash across the throat. Then let them do what they want. Only she sure hoped they wouldn't do what Janet talked about. *God, please don't let me get to heaven without my scalp or my you-know-what. I'll just die.* She snickered. *Just die! Janet would get a laugh outa that! Poor ol' Janet.*

In a sort of homage—or maybe because she was going crazy—she started humming "Watty Kay." An old brave was walking by right then. He must've thought she was crazy too because he sidestepped and gave her a long, strong look before he went on his way.

More hours passed and still they didn't come for her.

She lay in her own pee and that of a lank brown dog that had trotted by twice and anointed her both times. Huge horseflies droned and dipped to drink their fill. She tried to discourage them by twitching, but the world whirled every time she moved.

In the morning the same squaw she'd kicked into the fire laid a small piece of charred meat in front of her. The aroma was so tantalizing she almost wept. The squaw spoke and toed the meat closer. It looked delicious, charred and juicy. Her throat worked and saliva pooled in her mouth. She looked up at the squaw. Was it Marmaduke? God, she ought to care! She didn't. Ignoring the thin coating of dirt on the meat, she opened her lips and sucked it up. She bit down and gagged on a sudden gush of blood. Tiny knives sliced her gums, lips and the roof of her mouth. She tried to push the chunk free and impaled her tongue. Fresh rivulets of blood bracketed her chin and dripped onto her shirt. The squaw rushed to her in a burst of fury and beat her methodically head to toe. Finished, the woman stood looking at her. Her ebony eyes were cold and cunning and they said: That's just the beginning. With sudden wisdom, Nessa knew who she was.

There were no more offerings of food or water. She lost track of time. Her mouth swelled until her lips stuck out further than her nose. Then her nose started swelling as well. She could barely breathe. If the boy's mother intended to smother her, she would soon succeed.

A hand pressed over her mouth brought her hips off the ground in pain. "Don't make a sound!" Doubletree whispered. "Can you walk?"

She nodded although she really wasn't sure if she could or not. He cut her bonds and helped her stand. Slumped against him, she tried to hug him but her arms had turned into rooster wings. He knelt and rubbed her legs, bringing stinging needles of pain. "All right?" She nodded again, took a step and stumbled. He righted her and gripped her shoulders and stared at her steady. She stared back. *Pieces of the moon are caught in his eyes.* He made a fist. *Strong!* He signed the way, made a fist again. She nodded that she understood. She would do it. She must. She put every shred of strength she had into staying upright. Holding her wrist and crouching low, he pulled her this way and that. Between teepees, around low-banked fires, always toward the perimeter of the camp. Somehow she kept her balance. At the edge of the compound she thought: We're going to make it! The idea that they had a chance brought an energetic outbreak of crow-hopping on her part.

An Indian walked around a teepee, scratching his groin and she froze. So fast she barely saw it, Doubletree drew his knife and threw. The Indian slid silently to his knees, clutching at the hasp in his throat. Before the Indian toppled face down, Doubletree had removed his knife and was silently urging her on.

She soon heard the sound of many horses stirring. At the place where the ponies were kept there was the lifeless form of another Indian. Doubletree hoisted her up onto a roach-maned pony and wrapped her arms around the horse's neck and tied her wrists. He looped a rope around her ankles and tied them under the horse's belly. "I can't take a chance on you falling off," he whispered. She nodded, so grateful just to rest against the horse. Doubletree pulled off the dead Indian's leggings and slung them over his shoulder and mounted and they moved out on deerskin-sacked hoofs. Once across the creek he chucked the horses up to a trot.

She drifted in and out of awareness until they descended a steep clough that led into a twisted tangle of mesquite and she heard other horses making soft whickers of welcome. She looked again, certain she was mistaken. Damn, if that horse doesn't look like Easy!

Doubletree cut her bonds and she laid her palm on the horse's nose. It *was* Easy! Her eyes teared with happiness. She sure never expected to see her horse again! Doubletree sent the Indian ponies packing then went through the process of tying her on again.

"We got t'vamoose outa here. You gonna make it?" Her mind said Yeah but her mouth made a strange muffled noise.

"What the hell is wrong with your mouth?" She smelled sulphur and then felt the warmth of the match on her cheek. "What t'hell is in there? Huh! Well, whatever it is, it's gotta come out. You still got that little sneak knife?" She nodded and moved her arm.

"Well, all right. Maybe I can slip it in there and flip it out. I better see if I can get it now. Your tongue's stickin' out like a hung man!" She nodded. "Hold real still." She nodded again.

She closed her eyes while he dug at the meat and fought a powerful need to clench her teeth. She now knew why a person in pain is always given something to bite on.

When he finally pried the meat free it felt like her face had gone with it. Blood splattered her shirt front, the horse's withers.

"There's thorns embedded in your mouth but there's

no time to mess with them now. You'll have t'hang on a bit longer." She nodded. He mounted and they set off again, at a trot this time.

A long time passed. She looked up once. In the distance were some low foothills strung against the sky like a black cockscomb and she wondered: Is that where we're headed? She tried to sit up but she couldn't get her back to work. She woke to the echo of clattering hooves on rock. They had started climbing a narrow path.

By sunup they arrived at a rock house stuck on the side of the hill like a burl on a tree. Doubletree untied her and carried her inside and laid her on a corn husk mattress. "I'll tend the horses."

The air inside was as cool as an underground cave. She looked at the crudely made table and chairs, the stone walls chinked with mud and chino grass, the puncheon shelves for storing things and the dirt floor but then her head met the bed and she couldn't lift it again. She was weak as a cat.

Doubletree returned, started a fire, took a bucket off a nail and left again. He was soon back with water which he put to heat. He picked her up and set her in the chair and then unrolled his blanket and spread it on the bed. He tucked it under top and bottom then spread her blanket on top. He folded it back invitingly. It seemed odd to see him do such wifely chores. Gently, he laid her on the bed again.

"I'll get those thorns out soon as the water's hot." He unbuttoned her shirt. "Whewee! You stink like you've been dipped in shit."

Close, she thought and wished she could tell him about that dog that peed on her. He'd sure get a laugh out of that!

Bits of her shirt were stuck in her arm wound. He kept wetting it with warm water until it came loose. She looked at the wound with interest. The arrow's path had peeled her skin back on her upper arm. She'd carry a two-inch scar from her run-in with the Comanche. She counted herself damned lucky. It had started bleeding again.

"Let it bleed," he said, as if she had a choice. "The bleedin' will clean it out some. Meanwhile I'll tend to those thorns." He skinned her out of her tattered filthy pants and covered her with the blanket. He looked at her face and her mouth and then away. "You remind me of a puppy I had once. Right after he tangled with a porcupine. I'm gonna need more water'n this . . ." She grabbed his arm. "What?" She pointed at her face. He tossed her pants on the floor and shook his head. "You wanna know what you look like?" She nodded. "A hunka fresh-skinned buffalo meat. With blue eyes. Now lay back there." As he left she heard him mutter, "Wimmin!"

He put on another pot of water and laid his knife on the fire. There was a small clay jug on the shelf. He poured some of its contents on his fingers and then tilted the jug to his lips and took a big swig. He shuddered like a wet bear, said, "Shit!"—made a face like that was what he'd swallowed—and then took another swig!

He washed one side of her face first then turned her head with a light finger on her chin. "You got some blood in your ear." She felt the water, a slight stinging then soothing warmth. He rinsed the rag in one bucket and then dipped it in the one containing clean water. "Well . . ." He cleared his throat. Smiled big. "Let's get started on those thorns. They're probably mesquite.

Dipped in poison, I expect." He was sitting on the edge of the bed. "This one right here'll be easy. I'll jus' . . ."

If she could've she'd've smiled at how determined he looked, with his eyes narrowed and one side of his mustache clamped between his teeth.

He caught the thorn between his thumbnail and his knife and all thought of smiling left her. "That was pretty easy, wasn't it? Now then . . ."

The next one was not easy either. It felt like he was hammering a ten-penny nail through her cheek. Last thing she recalled was noticing the beads of moisture gathered on his brow.

"I doctored your arm while you were out. Feel any more thorns?" She shook her head. "I think I got 'em all. Now don't let that bleedin' bother you. That'll help clean it out." He held up a rusted tin can. "Here. Spit in this."

Spit?! But he was patiently holding out the can so she dutifully dribbled on her chin.

"Good!" he said. "Real good! Now . . ." He blotted her chin gently. "Now sleep. Just sleep." She prevented him from rising. His eyes went from where her hand rested on his arm to the velvety tears shimmering in her eyes. "What is it?" He leaned closer, searching her face. "Does somethin' else hurt, darlin'? Where? Point where."

She'd never wanted to speak more. She gently stroked the back of his hand, touched a place where he'd barked his knuckle, then pulled his hand to her and tried to put her heart in her eyes.

"You'll be fine now, darlin'." His voice sounded like it came from his boots. "Jus' fine." He dipped a rag in cool water and wiped the tears from her cheeks then he folded it and laid it on her forehead. He pulled the blanket up to her chin. She slept like a baby.

* * *

20th of August- A fevre Has laid me so lo that Doubletree's had to do every thing. Fed and doctored me, bathed my body, washed my clothes. He has even—to my mortificashun—Carryed me outside so I can P. (I haven't done the other and won't.) Last nite he washed my hair. He had to kut some snarls out. When he thought I'd gone to sleep I watched him fold some of My hair in a scrap of paper and put in his hip pocket.

21st of August—He made some kind of paste out of The juice of a cactus and smeared it on my lips and gums. Makes me dream of apricots. I am shufling around on my own now. First place I headed was The bushes. Thank you, Lord, for That small favor.

She tore a page out of the back of her journal, wrote and then held the paper up for Doubletree. It was while he was leaning down with a deep line between his brows that she remembered the note he'd left on the tree. She quick crumpled the paper and signed: Never-mind.

"Hey! What'd you go do that for?" He caught her hand and opened it. "I almost had it." He smoothed the paper. Very slowly he read. "Did . . . you . . find . . . Bite?" She nodded, much relieved.

"Yes. He's dead, darlin'. An' I'm sure sorry. He was a damn good ol' dog. What I knew of him."

She nodded sadly. She'd figured as much.

He poured some coffee. "Here's what happened. I saw where you'd been taken and hightailed it after you. I'd made a side trip to ranger headquarters in Del Rio which put me half a day behind you. I caught up with the war party about a mile from the compound. My thought was to try to ransom you but then another band of renegades rode in. They'd been on a raid too. Had a bunch of fresh scalps. I recognized the leader, a fella by the name a' Scar. I knew ol' Scar never ransoms hostages, so I figured I'd have to wait 'till dark and sneak you out. There wasn't a thing I could do in the meantime. I almost went crazy waitin' so finally I decided to backtrack to the ambush site. Buried your friend. Followed a trail of blood to where your dog had crawled off and died." He mopped her eyes with his neck hanky. "He put up one helluva fight. I can tell you that much. May even have taken one of 'em with him. If not, I can guaran-damn-teeya there's one Indian who'll never forget his run-in with that dog." He waited a bit. When he went on, it was with some emotion himself. "Don't cry no more, darlin'. Don't now. You'll stop up your nose holes and smother yourself to death." She nodded—it was true—and choked off her tears. Poor ol' Bite. Poor ol' Janet Moon.

"Say! Bet you were happy to see your horse? That was pure luck."

What-happened?

"Near as I can figure she took a bullet across her withers. Spooked her so bad she lit off an' didn't stop 'till she was a good five miles south. I had her in tow when I spied two braves coming. They were reading sign, obviously looking for her, too. Comanche appreciate a good horse more'n most, you know. Anyway, I decided to send ol' Scar a message. So I left her for bait and laid in wait."

He smiled. It was an evil smile if she ever saw one. She drew a question mark in the air.

"A Comanche is a lot like a kid in some ways. Superstitious, easy to spook. They're kinda mystified by, you know . . ." He twirled one finger at the sky. ". . . supernatural things. So I roped one of the braves to his horse and sent him back toward the compound. They ought to be findin' him right about now."

Nessa made a question mark again.

He took the paper and drew a doubletree and pointed to it. "Carved it on his back." She continued looking at him. He grinned. "Member how they did us in those ruins? Hootin' n' hollerin'?" He tapped the paper and his grin turned mean. "This here's part of *my* show. Let's 'em bastards know they ain't up ag'in no woman." He looked at her. "No offense intended."

She inclined her head solemnly. None taken.

Twenty

24th of August—I woke and found him siting In a chair at The foot of my bed. He was propped aginst The wall, feet vee'ed and head kocked at an imposible angle. His mouth was open and he was snoring softly. There was a dime sized hole in his soc.

I was looking at him, wondering how I had ever thought I had loved before when he woke up and kaut me.

"Hey, big eyes!" Yawn. Smacksmack. Scratch. "How you doin'?" She nodded. She slowly pushed her body up and the blanket down. His eyes dropped. He rubbed his face and muttered an outloud soft "damn!" before he looked at her again.

"Well!" Real hearty. "You all right?" She nodded. "Want some water?" She shook her head. He stood and reached for the ceiling for a long minute then ambled over. He bent down, his attention studiously on her mouth.

When I can speak I'm going to tell him that his eyes are the color of old coins.

"Hey, lookin' a whole lot better. Ain't near so . . ." Something had triggered his Adam's apple. "So . . . swollen."

She looked at him for a long moment before she touched his chest. His skin rippled like pond water. She leaned into him and nuzzled. "Ah," he said when her fingers found his nipple. By the time she reached for his belt buckle he was trembling. "Here now!" She lifted him out and measured him. "Don't, darlin' . . . Mm, better not . . ." He sucked in his breath and gritted, "God, I'm afraid I'll . . . Ah . . Damnit!"

No man was ever so care Full with his caresses but His sweat stung my kuts and his guiding hands hurt. He finally Sat on the edge of the bed and I stradled him like a horse. "Where there's a will," he said and gave a half assed chuckle. His teeth were Bared as if he was in terible payne but when he whispered, "Sweet Jesus!" it sounded To me like he was praying.

Twenty-one

25th of August—Well that was it. No holds barred. We spend Practicaly every waking minute fornycating like rabits. We leave the bed onle To eat and some times not Even then. We don't hardly do inny thing else. Well, once in a while we play some kards.

Table stakes were a hundred dollars, two hundred fifty dollars and five hundred dollars, three raises maximum.

"The game is five-card Doubletree," he said. "Nothing wild but the players." He winked at her and then he dealt a card down and a card up to each of them. "You're high with that jack showin'." She waved her hand over her cards indicating she passed. "Up t'me, eh?" He looked at his hole card. He had a deuce showing. "Aw, hell! I'm paired up already. You're probably gonna wanna jus' toss your hand on in. No? Hell, a person would be crazy to bet into this!" He raised his eyebrows, waiting. "Huh! Well, all right. It's your money. But don't say I didn't warn you. I'll bet five hundred."

She nodded and tossed a matchstick in the center of the table and then added a pinto bean. "Bumpin' me, eh? Jus' like that." He riffed the deck. "Ain't scared you none. Nosiree. Well, I'll bump you right back." He threw in two beans. She matched his bet and waited for him

to deal. She had an ace in the hole and a jack showing.
He dealt them each another card, a jack for her, a five
to his deuce. "Paira jayboys bets four hunnerd, huh?" he
said. "Well, I'll bump you another hunnerd makin' it five
total. Jus' t'keep it interestin'." Nessa put in a matchstick,
took out a bean.

He looked at his hole card again and volunteered, "A
paira ducks an' a pair of jayboys. Your bet, jayboys."

Although she observed him very carefully, it was near
impossible to tell when he was bluffing. She believed,
however, that he was. Yes, she was sure of it. This time,
he was.

He wasn't. Her pair of jacks were beat by his three
"ducks."

"Your deal, Nessa darlin'," he said and pushed the
deck at her.

She shuffled swiftly and expertly, and then dealt five-
card draw. He squeezed his cards into a tight fan and
studied them. She got up and stirred the beans—the ones
that hadn't been consigned to the game. After resuming
her seat she flipped her hair to one side and fingercombed it. It was getting long again. She'd better cut it.
Before she left for sure.

She looked at him. His hair hung now almost to his
shoulders. Smoke dribbled from his nostrils as he scru-
tinized his cards squint-eyed. He looked up and smiled
at her and winked. Damn him! He knew he was annoying
her, taking so long to discard.

She drummed her fingers on the table. Then she
knocked the table leg with her knee. Which gave everything but Doubletree the jitters. She had several ragged
pieces of paper next to her poke. Call! Bet! Play! She

rifled through them, found the one she wanted and held it up. IT'S YOUR BET!

He leaned close as if he'd never seen it before and read: "How . . . about . . . another . . . throw?" He looked at her, drop-jawed, a simpleton in shock. "Another throw? Goodlordamercy, girl!" He shook his head. "I'm sorry but I've got t'turn you down. Hell, you like t'bust it last time you got a holt it. Queen of the May!" He sniffed. "Nuh-uh."

She snickered. He returned to studying his cards. There was dead silence. She was writing . . . "Have you dropped off?" when she felt his gaze. She looked up and lifted her brows . . . What? He pointed at the paper. "That knocks me out."

What? she signed again.

"How you can write like that."

She shrugged . . . no-big-deal.

"Takes me ten times as long to read than it does for you to write." She waited. He looked at his cards then at her. "I wish I'd studied my lessons when I had the chance. Maybe I wouldn't be so damned . . . ignorant."

Nessa began writing. And kept writing. He ran his fingers through his hair. "Hey, give me a break, huh?" She finally held the page up to him. He sighed deeply and said, "Shit!" He leaned forward, stabbing each word with a blunt fingertip. "Readin' is . . . not . . . important . . . in a man. Big . . ." He looked at her. ". . . hands?" Her swollen lips formed a smile. She nodded and motioned . . . yes-go-on. ". . . hands an' . . . an' arms like iron . . ."

"God, woman!" He tossed his cards down, scooped her up and threw her over his shoulder. "Well, all right. But go easy on that Queen of the May stuff."

* * *

. . . The bed—flat raw hyde strips tyed between a Wood frame—makes A reel strange sound when In use. Doubletree, having taken a trip to Denver one time, says it is like the squeal a boot makes on sno. He also says it is musik To his ears.

Later they were again sitting at the table. Flushed. Mussed. Hair every which way. "I'll take three," he said, as if they had not just been doing what they'd just been doing. She dealt but being sort of drowsy she was apparently slow at snaking her second card off the bottom.

"Haugh!" he hollered.

She jumped a foot. What? she signed, holding her heart.

"I accuse you of manipulatin' the cards."

What-Who-Me?

"No use in you puffin' up like a horned toad. You can't deny it."

She nodded emphatically.

"Like hell you can! I've been watchin' you. You've been doin' it since you found out you can't beat me honest. The first time I thought—Ain't that cute? The second time I thought—Well, it's the only game in town. But now I'm startin' to think—Here's a gal with some real serious character flaws."

She tore a fresh piece of paper from the back of her journal. She scratched a note, drew a line through one word and wrote another and drew a line through that one, too. She thought, shrugged and wrote a four-letter word she knew he'd have no trouble making out. She held up the note.

He read: "You have . . . shit? . . . is that word shit?" She nodded. "You have shit on my . . . good name. Step . . . outside?" He looked at her. She pointed at her gun belt hanging on a nail on the back of the door.

"You wanna yank iron again' me?" She nodded. "Awright, by God! I'm pissed now! Git your damned gun an' git it on."

They stood on either side of the table, ritualistic as samurai warriors. He shucked the bullets from both guns. She solemnly strapped on her gun belt and eased her gun in and out of its holster. She rolled her shoulders and then her head. He slung on his gun belt and then tied down the holsters. They looked at each other. "All set?" he asked. She nodded. He adjusted his belt, flexed his hands. "Let's go."

They walked outside. She was barefooted. He was barechested. She stepped to the west, which put the sun square in his eyes.

"All right, Vanessa Cutter Fane. I'm callin' you a cheatin' little rat turd! Go for your gun whenever you're ready."

She set her stance, balanced on the outer rim of her feet. He bent his legs slightly. She waited . . . and . . . went for it. There was the scuff of metal against holster leather, metal on metal as two hammers fell.

Snick click click.

Late. She'd been late! No! He couldn't be that quick! She'd been sick. Her arm was still stiff. She hadn't been set.

He shoved his gun home and straightened. "Don't give me that look! You had your chance." He turned but she ran to him and grabbed his arm. She held up two fingers then three.

"Two out of three?" he asked. She nodded.

They resumed their original positions. There was a long moment when nothing happened. "Tell you what," he said. "Hold your left hand out waist high. That's it. Now drop your arm when you're set. I won't move a muscle till you give the signal."

She let her eyes go heavy lidded to counter that infinitesimal widening that occurs when . . .

"Do I have time to roll a smoke?"

She dropped her arm. His hand flashed and his gun came out. Snick click click.

"You can't claim you still weren't ready?" He looked at her, incredulous. "You can?"

She tried a quick draw, no warning. Snick click click.

"How about I wear a blindfold?"

Snick click click. Dust boiled knee high around her feet.

"Aw hell, honey . . ." Snick click click. "I was jus' teasin'." Snick click click.

"Hellfire! I'll cheat myself. If I get the chance." Snick click click.

She holstered her gun and showed him her back. She whined deep in her throat. Then she unbuckled her gun belt and stood looking off into the distance where a dust devil danced its way across the valley.

Doubletree thought: This is the first time I've beat someone and had to worry about 'em cryin'!

She knew there would never come the day when she could outdraw him and that sure knowledge made her feel lower'n a snake. Empty as a whore's hope chest. Short.

"Now, don't go gettin' yourself all worked up. Only a greenhorn cares about flashy gunplay." He walked toward her, arms out christlike. "Look at what you've gone and done now. Plugged up your nose holes, ain't ya?"

Only his famed chain-lightning reflexes saved him from being coldcocked by a sailing gun.

Twenty-two

28th of August—He says The rangers have been using This little cabin for years as a place to go to ground, lik their wounds and gird up for The next fite. Its main add vantage, he says, is that you can see some body coming from at leest Ten mile off.

They were sitting outside, watching the sun set in a bruised and bloody-looking sky when Nessa pointed at a narrow curlicue of dust rising across the valley.

"I saw 'em," Doubletree said. "Looks like a small band of Kiowas. Following the game higher, I expect."

He went hunting the next day. When he returned he had a dead antelope tied behind his cantle and a spotted puppy under his arm.

What's that? she signed.

"It's a dead antelope. . . . Ow! That hurt! Oh, you mean this thing . . . ?" He held up the dog. Its babyfinger tail was wagging so hard its hind legs jerked.

"Hmm. Looks like some specie a' dog, possibly the very rare spotted variety . . ." He danced just out of reach. "It's yours. If you want him." He set the puppy down and it promptly spread its legs and piddled. "Here! None of that!" He picked it up and deposited it outside the door where the dog raced around in a circle barking.

"What d'you think?" he asked. "You like him okay?"

She nodded . . . very much . . . and started to cry. *Damnit if that's what I don't do all the time now.*

"Aw, don't, darlin' . . ." As he walked toward her the dog charged him, grabbed his pants cuff and growling, hung on through a slew of curses and jerks.

The dog kept them awake that night with its whimpering. Doubletree finally got up, grumbling about scarcely "gettin' any rest in this bed as it is." Nessa woke when he crawled over her. She lifted her head. The dog was curled up on a pile of rags near the fireplace, quiet at last. What-did-you-do?

"I reminded him that come winter Indian dogs are scarce as snake tits."

He had his arm crooked over his eyes. She used her nails softly down his arm. Down his chest. Slowly across his stomach.

"God! Woman!" he said as he took her in his arms.

For a silly little dog it didn't take long for it to worm its way into their hearts. It had an endearing way of cocking its head as if it understood human talk. And, in all things but one, it appeared exceptionally smart. The one thing: Doubletree might've given her the dog but the dog gave himself to Doubletree. She mentioned the dog's apparent lack of character assessment ability.

"I disagree. Seems he's a good judge of character."

He asked later what she wanted to call him. Two Bites, she wrote.

"Two Bites, huh. Sounds Indian."

Well-that's-what-he-is.

"All right. Two Bites, it is."

***

*29th of August—I can speak now all though my tongue
Is still numb and often gets in The way of my teeth. My
arm is heeled, too. There's reely nothing keeping me from
leaving. Except Tom Doubletree.*

*Last nite I dreamt I was a litle kid. My mother was
by the fire. Like always, she sat with the scarred part of
her face to the hearth. Above the squeak of The rocker
I cood hear my lather's voice. He was after me to do
some thing but I cood not make out his words. I tryed
To find him but cood not. Then there he was, standing
at The door. He motioned to me then turned and walked
off. He looked back once To see if I was coming and I
was trying to but my feet were stuk in sand.*

It didn't take a lot of heavy thinking to figure out the
meaning of that dream. She knew exactly what was riling
her pa. And he was right. Her wounds were licked and
she was as girded as she was ever likely to be. She had
to get back at it. She intended to do just that. Soon as
she figured out how to tell Doubletree.

Tonight. She'd tell him tonight for sure.

As was their habit, they'd pulled the two chairs outside
to watch the sun merge with the western horizon. She
had washed clothes earlier and clean laundry now deco-
rated the bunch grass that rimmed the cliff. Doubletree
had shucked out of his shirt so she could wash it too.
She was rubbing grease into her saddle and wondering
how to tell him she was leaving tomorrow.

Doubletree had been carving the dog's name on a flat
piece of wood but now he was watching her. "Does that
rubbin' bother your arm at all?"

"No."

"I'd be glad to do it for you."

"It's all right. I like to do it."

"You do? It's always been a chore to me."

"Not me. My Pa gave me this saddle." Neither said anything for a minute. "He gave me his knife too. And then I went and lost it. God, that really galls me."

"Did you lose it when the Indians got you?"

She nodded. "That's what bothers me the most, knowing some ol' Indian's got Pa's knife."

"He probably traded it for a jug of rotgot by now." They were silent a while. "I'll get you another knife, darlin'."

"Thank you but you see it wasn't just any knife. It was given to Pa by Bowie hisself."

"That is a shame."

"Did you know him? Jim Bowie?"

"No, we never met." He stretched for his pouch of Lone Jack draped over the window ledge and then rested his furry forearms on his knees. She'd started to grease the interior of her holster but her hand slowed and then stopped as she looked at the way the waning sunlight turned his back to burnished brass.

"I never met Bowie. By the time I got to the Alamo it was all over." He tapped tobacco into the paper trough. "About all that was left of Bowie was a big charred place."

"A charred place?"

"Yeah." He licked the twirly into shape. "Where the Mescans set fire to the bodies."

"I never knew they did that."

"They buried their own but they threw ours in a big pile and had a bonfire. Hundred-eighty-some-odd bodies." He spat tobacco. Or maybe it was ire. "They said a person could smell the burnin' flesh for miles."

Neither spoke for a time, Nessa thinking that it was no wonder there was so much ill will along the border.

Something moved in the brush and then a jackrabbit streaked across the clearing. Two Bites gave a sharp bark and lit out in hot pursuit. "I had big plans for that knife" she said, watching the spot where he'd disappeared.

He said nothing.

"I was gonna pass it on to my grandkids."

He looked at her. "You plannin' on a lot of 'em, Nessa darlin'?"

"At least seventy-leven."

"Huh."

"I was gonna say: Lookee here at this here knife."

He glanced around at her again. Staring off, she had her arm up, like she was about to lead a saber charge.

"Notice the blade. Made to stab like a dagger or slice like a razor or chop like a cleaver. Whichever way you want to use it.

"This particular knife was given to the famous Nate Cutter by the almost as famous Jim Bowie. Nate Cutter used it successfully in eleven hand-to-hand fights against the Comanche and Kiowa, during which he dispatched his foes in as humane a manner as possible." As an aside to Doubletree she added, "Considering the circumstances, of course."

"Of course."

"Nate Cutter was a fierce fighter and an uncommon man." She lowered her hands. "That's what I was going to say."

"Whewee!" Doubletree said. "That's quite a speech."

"I was gonna work on it. Over the years."

He continued digging on the collar a minute then tossed it aside and stood and went around the side of the cabin. She retrieved the piece of wood from the dirt. The 2 was finished. The B and I was done, the T roughed in. She looked up to see him hauling his saddle over. From a special leather boot he removed two bayonets which he then laid across her knees. "What are these?"

"Mexican lances. From San Jacinto."

"San Jacinto! You aren't old enough to have been there!"

"Yeah, I'm sorry to say that I am. I was only a jug-eared kid but I was there."

"Think of it." She touched one of the lances. "The Battle of San Jacinto!"

"It was more a massacre than a battle."

"First I heard that."

"Well, it's true."

The puppy returned—rabbitless—and lay down beside Doubletree's foot.

"We'd been retreatin' since Gonzales on the 13th," he said, rubbing the dog's stomach with his bare toes. (He was unconsciously kind to animals; it was something she really loved about him.) "In spite of the fact that it had been rainin' for days, Houston ordered everyone to leave their mounts behind. I was boilin' mad! Leave my horse behind! What kinda army fights on foot in the mud and rain? Practically every man I talked to felt exactly the same as me. We'd all heard what happened at the Alamo and Goliad and we were ready to get at it! But instead we kept retreatin', always retreatin'. It appeared that Houston was avoiding every opportunity to turn and fight. Tempers were gettin' plenty hot. I figured that if he didn't find some Mescans to fight pretty damned quick, he was gonna have a mutiny on his hands.

"Well, we'd established ourselves in a line of trees in the fork of Buffalo Bayou and the river and that's where it finally started. The Mescans never knew what hit 'em. We were sorely outnumbered but every one of us fought like ten. When we'd used up all our ammo we went to clubbin' 'em. My rifle broke off at the breech and I was using my stock when these two fellas come at me from both sides, trying to gig me like a frog. I made a matador-like move and they run each other through." He touched one of the lances remembering the sick sweet smell of blood, the cries of the wounded men and animals.

"I looked around then and I could see it was all over. The only men left standin' were Texans. I took these lances offa those two dead Mescans and I left. Walked back and got my damned horse. I was still mad about that." He knelt in front of her with his hands on her chair. "Well, what do you think, darlin'?"

"If they were mine, I'd be proud as a buck in velvet."

"You mistake my meanin'."

No, I don't, she thought.

"What I meant is: how about you show your grandkids these here lances? Tell 'em their ol' granddad was jus' a common man who was uncommonly lucky. And a damned good fandango dancer. How'd that work?"

Nessa was having a hard time holding onto her feelings. "What are you saying?"

"Nessa, darlin', I'm tryin' to ask you to be my wife. Unless you want to have grandkids together and not get married. 'Course, it's entirely possible the matter's already out of our hands."

"It better not be!" she replied hotly.

"Well, it's what happens, you know." He tried to read her face. "I guess I expected something more than dead silence."

"I'm not free to say anything. Not till I lay Bob to rest."

"Holy shit! You mean that boy's been dead all this time and you ain't buried him yet?"

"I mean in my mind."

"Nessa, darlin', I believe you have buried him in that bed in there. In your mind. An' everywhere else as well."

"What I mean is that I won't be at rest until I fulfill my commitment to him."

"That's uncut bullshit." He rose and took up whittling again.

She could tell he was restraining his temper and was glad of it. Instinct told her he had the sort of temper that flared like a grass fire and was twice as hard to squelch.

After a long minute he said, "Your husband never told you he expected you to track his killers and execute them one by one."

"What would you do? If you were in my place?"

"I am a man."

"That doesn't matter."

"Of course it matters."

"No, it doesn't. It's not like I'm gonna challenge Flatt to a bare-knuckle fight."

"Hell, I don't see why not."

She ignored his mockery. "I'm going to shoot him. For that I need cunning and careful planning and accuracy."

He asked the sky, "Do you believe this bullshit?"

She stood and stomped off to collect the clothes from the bushes. He watched her, moving stiff and jerky. *Shit!*

"Darlin', allow me to take care of Caleb Flatt for you . . ."

"I must kill him myself. Me and no one else." She tapped her chest. "Me."

"You're bound an' determined to get yourself killed!"

"Not if I can help it."

"But that's just it. You won't be able to help it. Nessa, you have shot a shave-tail kid and a man who was passed out in bed, dead drunk. Caleb Flatt is neither. He or one of the men he rides with will kill you. An' by the time they do, you'll be damned glad they did. They will use you and . . ." She was looking at him strange. "What?"

"How did you know the way Ladino died?"

"I know 'cause I was there."

"You were not!"

"You went out the window as I came in the door. It happened just about like that."

"No." She shook her head.

"I've been half a step behind you ever since the adobe ruins. Except for the day I rode to Del Rio."

She snorted.

"Wanna know what you had to eat every night?"

She ignored that. "I suppose somebody could've told you about Ladino."

"God, woman!" He held up a hand. "Well, can see I'll have to prove it. All right, let me think. Ladino's woman had a black eye. Her right eye. She'd got it likely two maybe three days before. She was wearing a ragged piece of buckskin with one arm ripped out. The left. You used a honda knot on her feet and a cow hitch on her wrists. And you shot Ladino four times, two to the head, two to the heart." He looked at her. "Just outa idle curiosity, don't you think you mighta overdone it? Seein' as how you was standin' less'n a foot away?"

"It wasn't my intention to stun him."

He waited, watching her pace. "You got to believe me now!"

"I believe you." She continued pacing.

"What then?"

"That woman. I've been thinking about her for days . . ."

"I let her go. She's probably three hundred miles gone by now."

"She sure was different-looking. I couldn't figure her tribe from looking at her and she never did speak."

"She was Papago and she didn't speak because somebody'd cut out her tongue. Probably the same person who held a branding iron to the soles of her feet."

"God!" She shuddered. "I wondered how come she was crippled up like that."

"A brandin' iron is a favorite Comanche method for keepin' a captive from runnin'. That or hamstringin' 'em. They use one as much as the other."

"I am continually amazed at how cruel human beings can be to each other," she said, staring at the spot where the land met the sky. Full dark had fallen and the night was splattered with stars. She finally looked at him. "It isn't that I don't want to marry you."

He rubbed the puppy's ear. "You could be carryin' a baby."

"I doubt I am."

"Why?"

"Because Bob and I used to do it at least twice a week. For almost two months—except when I had my uh . . . moon time and . . ."

"Couldn't control yourselves, huh?" She glared at him and then stood and started pacing again. "Sorry. All right. Go on. An' . . . ?"

"And I didn't get caught then."

"Well, darlin', I can practically guarantee you that you are caught now."

"Why? Am I holdin' my mouth different?"

"We've been goin' at it at least twelve times a day . . ." She snorted and picked at a place on her thumb. "Twelve times a day . . ."

". . . for over a week and . . ."

". . . and you're such a he-man, I suppose?"

"You complainin'?"

She tossed her head. "You know what I mean."

"All I am sayin', Nessa darlin', is that it sure ain't hard to get caught." He looked at her then away. "An' I'm sayin' that I know I ain't incapable of fatherin' a child."

"What does that mean?"

"It means I have a child."

"You have . . ." She sat. ". . . a child?" He was rolling another smoke. "But you said you'd never married."

"I didn't get married." He raised his hand. "An' before you go all sanctimonious on me, let me say that I couldn't have married the woman if I'da wanted to—which I didn't—because she was already married to somebody else."

She thought about that. "The . . . baby lives with her?"

"Yeah."

"Where?"

"Outside Blue Gap." He lit his smoke.

"You don't ever see it or anything?"

"Hell, I didn't even know the kid existed 'til almost two years after it was borned."

"Why not?"

"She never told me. I mighta never known if I didn't just happen to be in the area . . ."

She looked away, disgusted. "You just happened to be in the area . . . I wonder why?"

"Listen." He jabbed a finger at her. "I wanted a woman and she was willing. There's times when that's all there is to it." She rose and went inside.

Virtuous as a nun, he thought. He looked in at her, stirring the stew then banging the lid back on the pot and shook his head. *Wimmin!* He called, "Vanessa, do you want to hear about it or not?"

Vanessa. He'd never called her that before. Still, it took a while before she returned and resumed her seat. "Go on then."

"Thank you. Well, like I was sayin' . . . I was close to Blue Gap so I moseyed on over to her place. She came out onto the porch. There was a kid, a boy, sittin' in the yard diggin' in the dirt with a spoon. She pointed at him an' said he was mine! Jus' like that."

"Just like that?"

"Jus' like that."

"What if you hadn't . . ." Smirk. ". . . moseyed over? Would you have never known?"

"I might not've. She claimed she'd sent word by way of Smiley Muldane. Unfortunately, Smiley stopped a bullet at a shootout in Texarkana the year before."

She looked away. She looked back. "How do you know it's your kid? It could be her husband's . . ."

"Hell, it coulda been Smiley's for that matter." He saw

her shocked expression and said, "I told you she was willin'."

"But you know for a fact that it's . . . he's . . . yours?"

"I know."

"How?"

"Because the boy looks exactly like me."

"Do you ever see him?"

"No."

"Why?"

"Because the lady told her husband that the boy was his."

He had a child! A son who looked just like him. She'd've rather taken a Kiowa lance in the foot. She was suddenly bone tired. "I'm going to sleep for a while."

"Nessa . . . I'm sorry."

"No, it's not that. It's just that I'm really tired."

"What about something to eat?"

"Later maybe. Not now."

I heard ma screamin' for me to hurry and kill them. Hurry hurry. I was trying to fire my gun but something was wrong with my arm. Vermilion red faces floated over me holding scalps That still dripped blood. I jolted awake choking back a screem.

She'd never known a more vivid nightmare, but she regained reality when Doubletree said, "Ump" and then continued snoring in her ear.

Well, it didn't take much to figure out that dream either. She lay unmoving and watched the firelight flicker against the wall. God, if only she could make him understand! If only he would accept that for her not to go on with it would be like . . . like going against a law of nature. It wasn't what she wanted to do; it was what she must do.

She closed her eyes and tried to go back to sleep but found she couldn't.

30th of August—The honey moon Is over. Since I told him I Am going we've gone From turtle Doves To mexican fiting kocks. He will Not leave it alone. He wants me to tell him: "All rite. You're rite. I'll do what ever you say . . ." We went To bed last nite and did not even touch each other.

They were eating breakfast in silence. Him chewing nails, her with her eyes glued to her plate and trying not to leap out of her skin everytime he thunked his mug down. He was madder'n a jar of bees. He started talking as if they hadn't been ignoring each other since the moment they got up.

"So. Let me get this straight. I'm supposed to jus' sit back an' tend my knittin' while you go after a known murderer who's backed up by ten mebbe twenty guns?"

Silence. Several minutes passed and then he went off again.

"What kinda man lets a woman no bigger'n a mouse fart go off in country where her horse and outfit would feed a family of four for a year?"

Silence.

"Where you're plannin' to ride there are some people who'll slit your throat for your boots."

Doubletree pushed his plate aside and sat watching

her. She was standing at the door looking out. He studied the curve of her cheek, the soft hair tucked behind her ear and was damned confused. They were in love. He was the man and he'd said no. Why were they still talking about it?

It was a difficult situation. He wasn't used to solving complex problems. Now, what to do when someone's trying to lift your hair? Or if somebody's about to stomp you to death? He had those locked. But this? He wished t'hell he knew what she was thinking.

She was thinking about all the brackish water she'd come across in her travels. She'd noticed that there was a thicket of flame-leaf sumac growing down the rocky hill. It seemed she'd heard somewhere that the Indians'll add crushed sumac fruit to water to improve the taste. She made a mental note to pick some before she left. *I'll have to steal one of his handguns. Some money as well. Not much but a little.*

"Whyn't c'mon along with me. When we get him in, you can march him up to the scaffold yourself. How about that?"

The dog was too little to keep up. Besides, he's more Doubletree's than mine— God, I'll sure miss ol' Bite . . .

"Answer me, damn you!" He stood up and flung the chair against the wall.

She turned and looked at his stone face. "Don't make me do something I don't want to."

"What's that supposed t'mean?"

Silence.

"Nessa, it ain't only because you're a woman. It's because you are *my* woman. Now . . ." He pointed his finger at her. "I'll say no more on it."

When he went outside to tend the horses, she tucked

one of his guns into her belt, took two coins from the table by the bed and started tossing her things into the morral.

I turned and There he was leening in the door watching me. We piked it up rite where we left off. I told Him not to try And stop me and he said you'll have To walk threw me. Then I said, don't make me do this and he said that he wasn't making me do inny thing. That old man Cutter was. He wisht he cood get His hands on him, he'd . . . and that's when I shot him.

Twenty-three

31st of August—The bullet went in six inches above the nee, passed threw And hit the rock wall behind him. He bent slightly with one hand To his leg and then he went down. I didn't look at his face. Onle at the black blood that seeped threw his fingers. I waited long enough to make sure it wasn't pulsing And then I road.

She turned north and then west, following the grass to Hermacita. As before, the dark was her enemy. The full force of what she had done was upon her after sundown and its weight was almost unbearable. She lay brokenhearted, thinking about it. Lord, she'd shot the man she loved! But it had happened so fast! The idea to keep him off his horse flashed through her mind and next thing she knew it was done. Just like that. It seemed to her that it had been a purely physical reaction—like a sneeze is to dust.

Her intention had been to render him incapable of following. Not to maim him for life but her vision had been smeared. How bad was he hurt? Had she muffed it? Struck too high? Too deep?

She didn't know what else to do now but pull herself together and go on. Once she accomplished her goal, she'd find Doubletree and make it right with him but for now, she had to take things one at a time. Her primary objective was to get Caleb Flatt. Her problem was eluding the Indians until she could do it. She'd have to put everything else out of her mind.

7th of September—The days have terned into a week. They'll do that I heer. It has been a long Time since I have ritten in This jernal. My hart has not been in inny thing lately. It feels Like it is broke.

Mindlessly, she took to mumbling her father's sayings like a rosary.

"Most encounters are not won by the very smart or very strong but by the fella that jus' keeps a'comin'!"

"Don't let the sun set on a wrong."

"Beat a man soundly lest he work up his grit an' come back at you."

"Never steal a horse unless it's an Indian's an' then be prepared to die for it."

"Never use a whip on a man . . ."

There was one that echoed through her mind more often than most. "More'n any single thing a person ought to do what he sets out to do. Come hell or high water."

She rode over high grass and on stony ground and through flat brush land. Without her foxed denims she rode with saddle-galled legs and got up the next day and rode again. After a while she ceased being able to think clearly. She couldn't picture her aunt's face any more. Couldn't remember if her room was to the right or to the left side of the hall. She grew gaunt and hollow. One day, leaning for a drink, she caught sight of her reflection and scarcely recognized the sharp and hungry person who stared back at her.

She'd been working poor Easy hard and in spite of her precautions—she walked five miles for every ten she rode—she found a place on the mare's side that looked like it could turn into a cinch sore. She treated it with bacon grease for two nights running. It seemed to heal but nonetheless she figured it was either time to buy a mount or hunt up an Indian.

Her chance to get another mount came on the day following. Trotting toward her, maybe a mile off, was a remuda of twenty horses driven by four men. Judging from their wide bear grass hats with the high pointy crowns, they were Mexicans. She rode out into the middle of their path and waited for them. The closer they got the more she realized she might have made a bad mistake. These men were armed. Really armed. Each wore two or three belted pistolos plus double bandoleers plus side knives a yard long. It was a lot of weaponry for ordinary hardworking caballeros.

They stopped. Two of the men circled the horses to keep them roughly together while the other two advanced until they were within a few yards of her. It was obvious that the four men were cut from a common cloth. They all had the same cruel, greedy faces and the same small, secret eyes. The one nearest had a pug nose and a short upper lip that left his teeth showing like a surly dog. "Buenos días," he said.

"Buenos días," she replied, but her eyes were on the fourth man's mount, a gray gelding with a white face, a horse she'd seen sold while three bodies lay garnering as much curiosity as a pile of goat turds. The gelding's rider was a slack-eyed man with a bumpy potato face.

He looked like he hadn't changed his expression or his clothes in years. He tucked a small black cigarillo between his lips and showed his teeth. They were brown. "A donde va?"

"Not far. We're not going very far."

He made a show of looking behind her. "We?"

"Cuanto es caballo?" she asked.

"Caballo?"

"You do have horses for sale?"

"Oh, sí, sí." He pointed at an appaloosa with a spray of red spots on its back. "Este?"

"No," she said, "el rojo." She moved her horse as if to better point out the rangy sorrel, but she was actually trying to keep them all in sight and get upwind. These men had been too close to nature for too long.

It was a hundred degrees at least, but there would be no hurrying this transaction. She made an offer and potato face countered. She restated her offer and he conferred with slack-eyes and then came down slightly. She pretended to examine the horse again. It was getting harder and harder to ignore the sly looks the men exchanged.

They finally agreed on the sorrel's price—"veinticinco dólares" Mex money and they watched her reach in her shirt pocket like it was a hat.

She could read their malicious intent as if it was printed on their foreheads. It was, she figured, only her vigilant attitude that was keeping them from trying something right then. She tied a rope around the sorrel's neck and took off before they acted on their thoughts.

She kept looking behind her as she rode. Sure enough she soon saw coils of dust rising a few miles back. She descended a hill into a swale and then cut a false trail to the north, along a dry creekbed. After hobbling the horses, she backtracked and crouched behind some rocks.

She waited, loaded for bear. Five minutes and she'd worked herself up pretty good. *All right! You want it?* "Yeah!" she gritted. *I'll give it to ya. C'mon and get it then. Right in the brisket!*

Time passed and still they didn't come. They probably figured she'd be a cinch to catch. No need, they probably figured, for them to run their mounts into the ground.

Languishing there in the sun took some of the heat out of her anger and she started to get drowsy. She was always so blamed tired! A few days back she'd awakened and found she'd been sleeping in the saddle.

Suddenly Potato Face and one of the other men rode into view. She sighted down her rifle and waited, her mouth bone dry, her armpits just the opposite, but the two men rode on by, mistakenly confident of their heading. She stayed there for a time but she could see them already far in the distance.

Neither one of them could track for shit, she thought as she headed in the other direction.

By nightfall, far from the place where she'd eluded the men, she felt safe enough to have a small smokeless fire. She spitted a quail on a green stick and laid it over two crotched sticks. Arms around her knees, she sat and turned the quail until it cooked.

Her mind was far from food; it was on the feelings she'd had as she watched those men ride by. She knew she'd fooled them. She'd succeeded in eluding them without bloodshed. Yet she'd actually been disappointed! The thought had crossed her mind: these men deserve to die. I believe I'll kill them either way. She had played with the idea. Why not? she'd thought. Potato face was an obvious no-good, an ally of murderers, horse thieves and rapists.

Now, several hours later she found that that sort of mind-set bothered her. What had she become? A cold-blooded murderer who kills—not for revenge, not in self-defense—but because she decided the person deserved to die? Apparently. Because if they'd given her the least little excuse she would have shot them both.

She had hewed to murder like a pig to mud. It was damned scary if she thought about it.

In the days that followed she was very careful not to.

20th of September—I bought some grain At an estancia And now have bags strapped over both horses' pomels. I fashuned a feed bag out of a piece of tarpaulin That I can secure with a rope. I ride Easy for a while then switch off and ride the sorel.

I was fortunately off my horse and close To cover when I saw two Indians coming my way.

There was no time to conceal her tracks. She hobbled the horses back aways and then hid herself in some rocks. They were approaching a mile apart, each with their eyes on the ground. One soon found her tracks and got off his horse to investigate. Bandy-legged and stocky, he wore bright cloth tied around cropped hair, a muslin breech clout and leggings, and a jacket that had once belonged to a sergeant in the U.S. Army. The jacket had a bad stain and a three-corner tear in the back. She'd never seen an Indian like him before, but she thought he might be an Apache.

He got back on his horse and rode on, but except for

licking the sweat off her lip she didn't move a muscle. Some sixth sense told her the danger wasn't over and she was right. She soon discovered why those scouts weren't interested in a solitary shod horse.

A score of wild-looking men rode into sight. They wore skins and rags smeared with blood and bristled with upright rifles and medieval-like pikes from which fluttered hair and bits of colored cloth. They drove ahead of them horses, cows and two goats. Strung out behind, trotted four mules, each looped with a grisly garland of scalps.

By some silent signal they stopped and—worst luck!—made camp yards from where she hid. Dark descended and the moon rose. They killed and roasted a goat and ate it half raw, wiping their hands on their hair and letting the grease run down their chests like animals. They went to drinking afterward. A man hung some pouch-like things on a stick high above the fire and soon a strange sweet smell came on the air.

Two Indians of the same stamp as the others rode in trailing a riderless horse. They turned over the reins to one of the men and then joined their tribesmen at a much smaller fire. The white men split the contents of the saddlebags and rolled dice for the saddle, the rifle and finally for the horse. A dispute started over the horse and two men rose huge and tattered against the moon, arguing and shouting foul words. One man drew his gun and shot the other. The shot man fell groaning and cried out in a hoarse, strangled voice and the one with the gun stood over him and shot him again. There were two heartbeats of silence, emphasized by the spine-chilling howl of a lobo, and then talk resumed. Soon there came another division of property—the dead man's—and afterward the body was kicked down into the gulley.

She figured she didn't scare as easy as most, what with the survival skills she had and knowing the things she knew, but after one look at those men she was scared to death. They were the ones the old woman told her about. Los Mataderos. The Slaughterers.

She lay cold and unmoving all night, worried about her horses and the wolves she kept hearing, but worried about those men more.

When the men rode out in the morning two of the Indians gigged their horses up to the fore again and two fell behind; the latter, she guessed, riding as insurance against any recriminators who would follow.

She circled south and then rode in the opposite direction, mingling her tracks with those of the scalp hunters.

Midday she found a dead white man who was dressed in skins like the others. The owner, she guessed, of the riderless horse. He had suffered two knife wounds; one in his gut that would have killed him slow and one in his throat that bled him white in about a minute.

On the day following she came to a small creek and rode in it until she came on four women who had been washing clothes. They lay scalped and mostly naked. Hacked to death. Further on in the middle of the road lay an old man and a burro bound with sticks of kindling. Both had been shot. The man had been scalped and ridden boneless.

Less than a mile further on was a village that was little more than a collection of mud huts. If not for the redblack stains in the dirt and smeared mud walls, a person might think the town had been struck by some strange sleeping sickness for all the villagers lay in the

street and in the doorways and propped against the walls.
Young and old, male and female.

She urged Easy into a canter. The air was thick with
flies and the stench of death. Wings at half cock, los
zopilotes, the big black-necked buzzards, grudgingly
moved out of her path. She didn't see them settle back
in behind her after she passed because nothing in the
world could make her look around.

On the outskirts of town she passed a mud hut where
two children stood hand in hand in the yard. They were
ragged and dirty, the boy no more than five, the girl three
or less. She got off her horse and walked toward them
with her arms out, saying soothing, nonsensical things.
She knelt a few feet away.

"Donde está su madre?" *Please God! Please let her
be off visiting somewhere!*

The girl took her thumb from her mouth long enough
to point at the hut. Nessa got up and went inside and
was out again that fast.

"All right." She swallowed convulsively and sat on her
heels and tried to form a convincing smile. "All right,
now. Donde vive su tía? Un otro pueblo? Cerca?"

The boy shook his head. "No tía."

"Abuela? Abuelo?"

The boy nodded and pointed toward the village.

Oh, God! Nessa touched her forehead to the caliche
and wanted to weep. Why me?

The children looked at the norte americana and then
at each other. The boy shrugged. The gringa was face
down, arms out in the attitude of the cross. It sounded
like she was chanting Yme-e-e-e Yme-e-e-e but they did
not understand ingleis.

Truth was, they didn't understand much of anything

any more. Not why their mother sent them to their secret place. Not why they could not return to the house under any circumstance. Not the reason for the loud booms they heard earlier. Not the crying and the screaming. They were hungry and very tired. When the strange girl rode up they had been discussing whether or not they should risk their mother's anger by going inside. But now . . . now they weren't sure what to do.

Nessa went back into that hut twice. Once for a canvas water sack she'd seen hanging from a rafter, once for some corn meal and a sack of beans and a man's serape. She used the serape as a saddle blanket and set the kids on Easy's back. The mare was much gentler than the half-wild sorrel. The little girl looked down at the ground and Nessa could read her thoughts: so far! She looked like she might cry, but then she got a death grip on her brother's shirt and nodded. Nessa took the lead rope and off they went.

Nessa's nerves were rubbed very thin after seeing what had happened in that village. She got as high as she could get to make camp that night and then spent a couple of hours creating some noisy barriers up the trail. Rocks that would clatter. Twigs hidden under grass. God, how she wished ol' Bite were here tonight.

The two children were asleep when she returned but they woke up when they smelled the prairie chicken, and they ate like pigs.

22th of September—I think Someone has it In for me. I am not naiming naims but His initials might be J.C.

*Every time I get set To tear ahead and do my dutey,
something strange happens.*

Nessa smiled sadly to herself and closed her journal.
It was true. Someone had come along to block her at
every turn. First Doubletree, then Janet Moon and then
the Comanche and then Doubletree again and now . . .
now a twist of fate had taken a hold of her undertaking
once again.

She looked at them in the half-moon-lit night, sitting
small and saucer-eyed. Such a solemn pair! (Or were
they just taking their cue from their grim-faced and hard-
bitten traveling companion?) Their names were Julio and
Juanita. They thought their last name was Diaz and they
thought they were cinco and dos respectively. So young!
And yet so remarkably unchild-like. The little girl had
cried for her mother only once. As Nessa knelt to comfort
her, she had looked into the boy's young/old eyes and
saw knowledge there. The boy would not have to ask
what happened to his mother.

As she regarded them, the little girl's eyes started to
well again. She crawled around the fire and gathered
them both in. They slept that night and every night thereafter like three spoons in a drawer.

She tried to be amusing in the days that followed,
pointing out rocks that looked like animals. Then animals
that looked like rocks. She hummed every song she
knew, recited every poem, said every saying. It strained
her Mexican but she told fairy tales and tall tales and
then started making up stuff herself. "Do you know why
horses don't have toes? No, huh? Well, once upon a time
they did but . . ."

She walked a thin line between caring and remaining

detached and uninvolved, and had to keep reminding herself that it would not do to get too close.

23rd of September—I am surprised At how much ground I am covering. Then I recall That I do not have Janet Moon on this leg.

I am beginning to think I am bad luck. Just look At all the people—even The animals—who traveled with me and now are ded. Makes me scart to deth that some thing will happen To these kids before I can get them away From me.

24th of September—I know I have Been darting around Like a grashopper in front of a on coming stampeed but I've decided to turn dew west and head for Lame Deer. It mite be A bit further than the nerest town at least I no some one there.

"Hello, Mrs. Hahn ah . . . Asia. Remember me?"

Asia came closer and looked. "Yeah." She eyed the two children behind Nessa and said, "Why, ain't they cute little kids?"

A boulder-like weight left Nessa's shoulders. "They are, aren't they. And they're just as nice as they can be. Well-mannered and real polite and . . . nice.

Asia handed them a piece of rock candy each. To Nessa she said, "Don't say nothin' to Otto about the candy."

"Oh, I won't." To the children, Nessa said, "Qué dice usted?"

"Gracias," said Julio.

"Gracias," echoed Juanita.

Asia leaned down, palms on her knees. "Well, grassy ass to you too."

The burlap sacking parted and there—it could be no other—stood Otto Hahn. "What t'hell's all this grassy assin' out here?" He was a ruddy man a good head shorter than his wife. He took one look at the two kids and went tight-faced. He waved a bandaged paddle-like hand at them. "I don't allow no Mexes in here."

"They're just kids, Mr. Hahn."

"I don't care if they're babes in arm. They'll rob ya blind."

"Oh, no. These two little sweetie-pies . . ." She smiled at Asia who did not smile back and that weight descended again like a yoke. ". . . are orphans, Mr. Hahn. Their mother and father were brutally killed in the massacre of a small village . . ."

"I don't care who they are. I don't want 'em in the store." He turned to Asia and said, "You get 'em outa here, Asia Minor." And with that he stomped into the back room.

"Otto fought in the independence," Asia said apologetically.

"What the sam hill does that have to do with two little orphans?"

"He hates Mexes real bad." She stuck out her chin. "I ain't partial to 'em myself."

Nessa looked at the kids who stared back at her with their all knowing eyes. They understood what was happening. Kids're smart that way. It was enough to make a person ill. "All right, Mrs. Hahn, we're going. But just tell me this much. Is there an orphanage anywhere around?

"No, there ain't."

"A convent or something like that?"

"No."

Angry now. "Are there any Christians in town, Mrs. Hahn?"

"They's plenty of Christians but most of 'em would sooner kill a Mex as look at one."

"Is there no one in this town who would care for two children temporarily? For money?"

The money part interested her at least. "Well, I would but not Otto. Not for all the money in Texas." Nessa turned to leave and Asia called, "You know, Maud Latimer might take 'em in."

Nessa paused. "Maud Latimer. Is she the schoolteacher then?"

"Not hardly. She's just got big place and no kids of her own. She might take 'em." She was keeping a wary eye on the kids while she spoke, as if any moment they would take a shovel or a bolt of material.

"We'll go see this Maud Latimer then. But first I'll have three more pieces of that rock candy."

Asia opened the jar and pushed it toward her. "Help yourself."

Nessa selected the biggest pieces she could find, dropped some centavos on the counter, got directions to Maude Latimer's house and left.

Before entering the debris-strewn yard, she spit-cleaned the kids' faces with her shirttail, brushed off their clothes and smoothed their hair. She instructed them to wait just inside the gate.

The place was seedy and untended-looking. Rapping

on the flimsy door rattled the hinges and raised a small cloud of dust.

Nothing. She smiled back at the children and nodded encouragingly. She was about to knock again when the door opened a crack and a large redlined eye filled it. It was the color of pond ice and about as warm. "Yeah?"

"Mrs. Latimer?

"Yeah."

"I'm Nessa Cutter Fane, Mrs. Latimer . . ."

"What do you want?"

"Could I speak to you for a minute?"

"What about?"

Apparently an invitation to step out of the hot sun would not be forthcoming. "Well, it's about those two little children there." She pointed behind her. Mrs. Latimer opened the door wider and craned her neck. She was a big woman with untidy gray hair.

"Their parents were killed down in Mexico . . ."

"Mexicans?"

"Yes, but . . ."

From somewhere inside came a howl that ended abruptly followed by a sound not unlike a death rattle. "Gol!" Nessa stood on her toes. "What's going on back there?"

"Back where?"

Nessa pointed.

"Oh." Mrs. Latimer didn't even turn around. "That Buck is at it ag'in. He's the worst bully! I wisht somebody was big enough t'beat the snot outa him. Speakin' of which . . ." She pointed at the kids. "Those two look kinda puny."

"Them?" She chuckled. "Heck, no. Why, they're healthy as little horses."

"Hm. They probably eat like horses, too. Well, they'll have t'work."

"Work?" Nessa looked at them. "They aren't but two and five, Mrs. Latimer."

"Everybody's got to work."

"Uh, startin' when? I think maybe they're only one and four. Yeah, I think so. One and four. No, three. One and three. That's it."

"Don't matter. Everybody's got t'work."

25th of September—Seems everyone along This border fought In the war for independence and hates mexicans worse than snakes. I do Not know what to do now.

She considered returning to Magdalena and asking Consuelo Miranda to take the children. They would be among their own kind and would not, she was sure, want for affection.

But what about food and clothes? Consuelo's one-room hut would barely be a roof over their heads. And Consuelo was old. Those kids could not be on their own for years yet. Who would protect them from bullies and Indian attacks?

All those factors influenced her decision not to return to Magdalena, but she wrote the real reason in her journal entry that night.

I wood rather be stompt To death than go threw that scalp hunter land again.

In the morning she set the two children on Easy, took hold of the lead rope and headed north. Toward the relay station between the Sabinal and the Frio Rivers.

* * *

26th of September—If the Cobbs won't take them, then I don't no what I will do. Go to Aunt Etta's I guess. I don't have To rite here how terrible I feel about this situashun. But I do not have a ready choyce.

She saw the same things the following week that she had seen the weeks before. Only from the south side. Same trees, same gullies and ridges, same gnarled oaks and same scraggly weeds. She paused at the same water holes, hunted at the same spots and skirted the same hills.

There was where she'd hid from that Kiowa war party. Yonder ways was Dodge, where she shot Trey Henry. And there's where that Mexican family was buried and where poor Duchess died. There's the place where she and Bite stood off those javelinas. All of it saddened her but the worst was passing within a mile of the adobe ruins. Memories of that night came at her in a rush and it was all she could do not to cry.

She had to stay sharp-witted in order to do her duty to those children but as far as Tom Doubletree went, she found she had to let her mind go dead or go crazy.

She might've anyway if it hadn't been for those kids. She had to give them credit. There were no complaints, not even from little Juanita.

She started speaking English to them, thinking that maybe people wouldn't be so hard on them if they spoke the language. It was amazing how quickly they picked it up. There was another thing she hoped to change before they got to the Cobbs. For some reason, horses terrified Juanita. She'd cling burrlike to her brother for hours on end and never make a peep, but she was clearly petrified. Nessa saw her one night watching her as she fed and watered Easy. She coaxed her closer and explained that Easy was one of the most gentle horses she'd ever ridden. She carried her—the girl tried to press herself into Nessa's skin—but together they touched the horse's neck and flank and back and she explained that horses don't like some things done to them. Just like humans. It took several nights but Juanita finally allowed Easy to eat grass from her hand. She was a game little girl.

At an abandoned place Nessa found some tarp and from it fashioned chaparejos for the kids' bare legs. The boy, Julio, liked that. He was a silent, somber boy and very protective of his sister. It was touching to see the way he stepped between her and Easy when he thought Juanita might be in danger.

2nd of October—Ezra herd us coming. He was standing in the doorway with his hand shading his eyes. It was almost sunset.

"Howdy, Mr. Cobb. Remember me?"

"Why, it is you. Mother, you better c'mon out here!"

Gert appeared drying her hands on a cloth. "My stars! If you aren't a sight for sore eyes! Climb down! All of you." She came slowly closer. "Who are these two?"

Nessa introduced them. Mrs. Cobb remarked how lovely was the girl and how handsome the boy and never once said anything about them being Mexican. She ushered them inside and Nessa noticed how her hands never left them, smoothing their hair, petting them on their backs. Inside she turned a smiling face to Nessa. "Don't you say one word about anything until I get some food for these children. Venga!" she said to the children. "Dulce para usted!" She left with them happily in tow. They knew a good thing when they saw it.

"Well," Nessa said. "You figure it'd be all right to ask about that burned place on the front door and why you're favoring your left leg?"

"Indians." Cobb said under his breath and glanced toward the kitchen.

"Don't worry about those two kids. They don't speak much English yet. Was it the Comanche?"

"Yes. They hit us right about this time. Coupla dozen at least. Fortunately it was right before the stage was due. They'd about got us whipsawed when it come down the pike." He shook his head. "It was a welcome sight, I'll tell you. If it weren't for the driver and that extra gun on top we'da had trouble for sure. The stage carried two travelers—both men. All together we stood 'em off. I got this little scratch."

"And a singed door."

"An' a singed door."

Gert came back carrying a huge tray of food and trailing two squirrel-cheeked children. Nessa, Julio and Juanita fell on the sliced ham, cold venison and wild berry cobbler like hogs on slop. Finished, Nessa told them about the village and the scalp hunters. She also told them about her fruitless trip to Lame Deer.

"I am hard-pressed to care for the kids myself and cannot find anyone else. So many people still feel animosity about the war . . ."

"Bull!" Ezra said. "How anyone could hold something like that again two little children is beyond me."

Gert asked, "Do you want to leave them here with us?"

"Well, I thought . . . that is, if it's all right."

"All right?" Gert said. "My dear, of course it's all right." She looked at her husband hopefully. "If it's all right with Ezra."

"If Gert wants 'em, we'll take 'em." Gert turned her head into Ezra's shoulder and he held her hard to him.

"They'll be in good hands with Gert," Ezra added gruffly.

As far as Nessa was concerned, that about said it all.

When there wasn't enough food left to interest an ant, Gert suggested a bath and bed to the children. Which sounded mighty fine to Nessa as well. She watched Gert bathe the two children in the laundry tub on the porch, saw the way she brushed their hair and how she touched them. Ezra walked the boy out back to take care of his business and then kindly patted both their heads when it was bedtime.

Well, she'd brought them to the right place. Even if it did cost time, she'd gotten four people together who really needed each other. Made her feel pretty good about herself.

In the morning she knelt to say good-bye but her throat clogged up on her so bad she could scarcely speak. She just kissed them both, hugged the Cobbs, and then hurried to her horses.

"Adiós!" she cried and then she lit a shuck southward. She thought she'd never outride that little girl's wail.

3rd of October—I am so lonele for those kids and for the Cobbs. Even for craze old Janet Moon. And poor old

Bite and Aunt Etta. I am lonele for Doubletree more Than inny one. If I cood have inny thing I want in this world it wood be To be with Doubletree in one place for ever.

Maybe I am jest lonele period, but it seems To me that My life so far is onle a bunch of partings. One after another. If life doesn't get inny better Than this I believe I wood just as soon forgit it.

Twenty-four

*15th of October—I was about to say that I cood not
do one more mile when I reeched Hermosita. Nothing
special about It that I can see. Looks like just another
dirty border town with more dogs than peple.*

For the whereabouts of Caleb Flatt she needed to go
no further than the owner of the dilapidated livery stable,
a knob-nosed man named Boone who appeared to be in
his late nineties or early hundreds.

They took care of business first and agreed on a price
for stabling her horses. Then, standing outside, she noticed a small procession that was winding its way out of
town. The handful of people were led by a woman and
a man who walked behind a plain buckboard containing
a small pine box. The man had his arm around the
woman's shoulder. She had her face buried in her hands,
staggering blindly. They looked like they were barely out
of their teens.

"Is that a funeral?"

"Yeah," Boone answered. "A little girl four years old.
Name a' Amy Tigg."

The buckboard had no black ribbons; the group included no black-frocked figure. "No preacher?"

"Nope. No preacher and no church service."

"How come?"

"What?"

She cupped her mouth and yelled, "How come?" She had to repeat practically everything she said. She said a silent prayer that she never got as old as that.

" 'Cause we ain't got neither. No church. No preacher. I believe her pa'd druther we had a lawman over a holy man anyway."

"A lawman? Why?"

"To get the men who done it."

"She was murdered."

It was a statement, and from the way the girl said it Boone knew that she might be traveling alone but she weren't no hardened worldwise woman. "Ayep. Somebody broke her neck."

"God in Heaven! Will it never end?"

As if she'd asked a real question, Boone replied. "Not in the forseeable future. Good thin' she weren't blackheaded or she'd've been scalpt as well."

"Was it Indians?"

He tapped one side of his head. She supposed he was supposed to look cagey. "That's what they'd like you to think. Truth is, not all scalpers are Indians. There's some'll take any slick black hair they can find. Like yourn, for example." He cocked his head and eyed her hair. "Ayep. That'd be a real prime pelt."

She was reminded of that Mexican village and the memory sickened her. She led her horses inside, removed their saddles and started to rub them down. She was about finished when Boone informed her that a rub-down was included in the price.

"That's all right." Sarcastic. "I'll probably just go on an' finish up."

"Suit yerself."

Best get down to business. "Say, you ever hear of a fella named Caleb Flatt?"

"Ayep. I have. You know him?"

"No. Heard of him is all."

Boone tipped his hat toward the south. "Ol' Caleb can be found yonderways about a mile or so. Right over the river."

"He lives in a cabin over there?"

"No, he lives in a fort over there."

"A fort?"

"Ayep. Him and a buncha others."

"How many others?"

"Varies from time to time. They'll be upwards of thirty sometimes."

"Who are they?"

"Horsethieves, rustlers and murderers. Scalpers now too."

"Sounds like a real blight on your community."

"Hah! That's a good one. Community! Hell, this town ain't worth goat shit no more. Pardon my French. An' we got that 'blight' t'thank for it."

"Huh. Why don't you get rid of them?" He gave her an offended look. "Well, it seems to me that if you had enough men . . ."

"A regiment ain't enough. Gettin' t'somebody holed up in that place is about as easy as milkin' a duck."

That "place" was a compound, he went on to explain, which had been built back in the seventeenth century by some brown robes from Spain. After their prospective converts, the Apaches, burned them out and scalped and tortured them two or three times, the good brothers chucked it and pulled out. The place fell into disrepair until about eight, ten months back. Boone forked some hay into the sorrel's stall while he talked. "We used to have fifty-two souls in this town. Now we ain't got more'n twenty."

"They've all been killed off?"

"Run off mostly. Even the stout-hearted won't put up with the neighbors. Can't say I blame 'em."

She was thinking: What this town needs is somebody like Tom Doubletree. He'd fix their problem. Damn quick, too. "You have no law whatsoever?"

"We got Fritz Mueller. He weren't all bad neither. Till he got his leg busted to bits. I tole him he weren't worth a puke with two but the truth is, he weren't all bad." He looked at her. "Say, there's no need t'tell him I said so. It'd jes' give him ideas. He's my son-in-law, see, an' I got to live with the man. I'm a widower an' he an' my daughter . . ."

Nessa suddenly pined for Janet Moon. This man and Janet would have been perfect together. Boone and Moon, a match made in heaven. When Boone paused for air, she asked, "How did your son-in-law get his leg busted?"

"We weren't always craven cowards. We went over there and tried to run 'em off." He shook his head. "It was like chargin' hell with a bucket of water. Twenty good men crossed the river. Eight bunged-up ones come back. Two days later Inella Dobbs found the little Banks girl hanging from a tree in her backyard. Left a sign on her. Tit for tat, it said." He shifted the cud in his cheek. "Sumbitches! Pardon my . . ."

She waved off his apology. "Any of them ever come to town?"

"Ayep and they can have the whole kit and caboodle

when they do. Everybody holes up inside an' makes themselves scarce 'till they leave."

She decided she wouldn't beard the lion in his den. She asked about lodging and Boone pointed out a weathered building across the street. "That's all we got."

"It'll be enough."

On the first floor there was one large room and four small ones. Out back there were some brush-skirted stairs that led to a small rooftop room which contained only a cot, a chair and a tarnished mirror. The place had no other tenants and no visible hosteler so she helped herself to the rooftop room. Too tired to look for food, she ate the two tomatoes which she'd purchased at the small store next to the livery. She slept that afternoon and was ready to watch for Flatt that night.

She pulled the bed to the window and kept the chair jammed against the poor excuse for a door. Turned out to be a smart move. In the middle of the night someone snuck up the stairs and rattled the doorknob. Which scared her out of a year's growth. She fired a shot into the jamb. Whoever it was beat a hasty retreat and that was the end of that.

When she was in the room, she was at the window watching, but after two diligent nights all she acquired was an education on town living. Cats fought in the alley and dogs bayed beneath her window. Booted feet clomped up and down the hall and slammed doors and knocked things over. From an open window on the first floor came the constant sound of a hacking cough.

Sometime between four and five o'clock on the second night she made herself a promise: She would never live in a town. Not ever.

The third day she visited her horses—and her friend

Boone—again. She found him sitting on a bale of hay outside his establishment. Business was bad, he said. There were still only two horses inside.

She put her hands in her hip pockets and looked around. There wasn't another soul in sight. "It's sure quiet around here."

"Ayep," he replied and spat.

"I thought you said those fellas from across the border come in here regularly, raising hell and running folks off."

"They do. You can count on 'em at least four five times a month."

Balls! "Only four or five times a month?"

"What?"

"Never mind," she shouted and handed him a coin to pay for Easy and the sorrel.

She rode over the river that night to have a look-see at this fort first hand. One person, small and very quiet might do what twenty good men could not.

She tethered her horse and walked the last mile to the compound. No way a person could miss it, even in the dark. It was as big as a mountain with thick twenty-foot-high walls and two massive wooden gates. From the twisted limb of an old live oak she saw that there were three sentries stationed on the compound wall. Their presence showed that somebody was on their toes. The compound might have little to fear from the town people but the Indians were another matter, especially now that the scalp hunters had established themselves within.

The second night a new moon and a layer of clouds rendered the sky skillet black but the third night was clear. She was on her perch in the oak by midnight.

The sentry who was supposed to be watching the river

appeared to be doing just that. He was leaning against a
wall and smoke was curling around the side of his sombrero. A second sentry sat with his arms folded across
his chest and his hat tipped low. Probably sleeping. As
she watched, the third sentry and a woman slipped down
the ladder. From the ensuing sounds she figured they'd
be down there for a while. Well, she thought, it's root
hog or die. She tied a rope on her rifle and slung it on
her back then she pulled off her boots and gingerly made
her way to the wall.

At a spot opposite the alert sentry, she threw her rope
over the sharpened end of a post sunk into the adobe.
Then she braced her feet on the wall and started walking
herself upward. Afraid of what she might see, she looked
nowhere but at her toes, splayed lizard-like against the
pitted wall.

Hunkered on top she brought her rifle around and
waited. Then she silently duckwalked through the shadows to the edge. After looking both ways, she let one
eye peer over the top.

The compound enclosed what used to be the church
and several long barracks-like buildings, all laid out
around a well-packed patch of dirt.

She hadn't been crouched there five minutes when two
men came out of a low-slung building and crossed the
square. She couldn't make out either man's face but, hoping for moonlight, she brought up her rifle and sighted.
A third man appeared in the doorway, indolently scratching his belly. "Hey, Flatt!" he called.

One man turned. "Yeah?"

"You comin' back?"

"Naw. Deal me . . ." She fired twice. The first bullet
was high and hit Flatt in the shoulder but the second

bullet in the chest put him down like a sack of grain. His companion had thrown himself behind a water trough and was now firing wild and crazy. The sentry who'd appeared to be sleeping earlier was returning his fire. Across the way a door opened a crack and the barrel of a gun spat flame. There was the sound of glass shattering and then firing from yet another gun. The vigilant sentry ran toward her but she shot him and he disappeared over the side.

She dropped her rifle to the ground below and went down the rope fast enough to burn her hands. Someone with a gun stuck his head over the edge of the wall just as she dropped the last couple of feet to the ground. She scooped up her rifle and then ran for the shadows cat-quick. There was the plunk plunk of bullets hitting all around her but she snagged her boots on the fly and kept going.

From inside the compound she heard another scatter of gunfire and a yell of pain. It sounded like they were killing each other off!

19th of October—Back at The bording house I oyled and cleaned my guns then I filled the basin and washed carefully. I stared at my reflecshun for a time. I had done it. It was finished! Just like That. I felt a strong feeling of triumf and releef. I thought—Now I can Finaly go on With my life. I went upstairs To bed And slept dreamless.

Twenty-five

20th of October—I packed up early And headed downstairs. My onle thought was—find Doubletree. I planned To dog him like bad luck. If he wood not forgive me then I wood tell him I was with child (although I new I was not). Sad To say, but I was prepared to do what ever It wood take to bind him to me.

In the front room of the boardinghouse was a long table where two men sat smoking. "So there was four shot, you say?" A short wavy-haired man asked as he dropped a sizzling match into his mug.

"Yeah. Wish it was more."

"Sure be nice." He spotted Nessa and then the morral in her hand. "Mornin', ma'am. Help yourself to any room that suits you. The owner has departed for parts north of here."

"Thanks but I'm just leavin'."

"A wise move. We were just discussin' doin' the same."

"Yeah, before all hell breaks loose," the other man added dolefully.

She couldn't resist walking closer and asking, "Something up?"

"Some sharpshooter killed a man name a' Dobie Flatt last night."

"Dobie Flatt? Did you say Dobie Flatt?"

"Yes, ma'am." She put a hand on the table to support knees that had gone goosey. "Chet here was jus' tellin' me all about it."

"That's right, ma'am." He was a thin man with black crescents under his eyes and black garters on his sleeves. "Fella came into my saloon late last night. Said a lone gunman shot ol' Dobie and then took off thisaway."

She found her voice. "Would that be Caleb Flatt's brother?"

"Could be. Dobie gambled at my place once or twice but I didn't never learn his last name 'till just now."

There was more said but Nessa didn't hear it. Stunned, she walked outside and across the street. She collected her horses and saddled Easy. Boone was nowhere to be seen so she left a coin on his favorite bale of hay and left. A lifeless thing now, she was moving entirely out of habit.

Without slowing, she dropped the pistol she'd stolen from Doubletree a mile out of town and rode on to the bottom of a low range of hills. There she stopped and got off her horse and sat and put her head on her knees.

She'd killed an innocent man. A human being who'd walked, talked, loved and laughed would do so no more. Because of her. Her triumph became ruin; her relief despair. She didn't see how she could go on living. Well, she couldn't because the long and the short of it was: she didn't deserve to.

She stripped both the horses and slapped them on their rears with her hat. The sorrel, not so long removed from the wild, ran and kept running but Easy only went a little ways before she turned and trotted back.

"Git! Go on! Git!" She pitched a rock but the horse dodged it.

"All right, damn it." She picked up her rifle and sighted between the horse's eyes. It got real quiet then, quiet enough to hear a small animal running through the brush. Quiet enough to hear the whistle of a quail in the sage. Quiet enough even to hear the inner voice that asked her if she hadn't done enough killing yet. The gun wavered and dropped. "Starve to death then, damnit."

Among some tumbled boulders she found a small flat place beneath the rim of a bedrock ledge. She looked around at the brush-spotted valley, at the hills in the distance and thought: this is a fine place to die. She lay down and prepared to do just that but then she felt the hideout knife beneath her arm. She cut the thin rawhide strip and pitched the knife down into some creosote bushes and lay down again. She would will herself to die. Animals did it. Indians. Hell, even her own mother . . .

Suddenly she remembered the journal. She went down the hill and got it out of the morral and made her final entry . . .

20th of October—I have merdered a man naimed Doby Flat, a man inocent of inny rong doing To me. I do not deserve To live. These are my last riten words.

She looked at what she'd written for a while—it struck her as sounding sort of mushy—but she didn't know how to fix it. Besides, it did say it all. She shrugged and returned the journal to the morral and crawled back to the ledge.

An hour or so later she got to thinking that she might ought to leave some words for her aunt. Poor Etta Cutter. Poor Cutter family, period. What Indians and bandits and renegades had not been able to end, she would end now, with her death.

She scrabbled back down the hill. She was tearing a piece of paper out of the journal when a flitting movement distracted her. A cowbird had lit on her saddle, attracted, she supposed, by the grease she used to prevent cracking. Soon another bird joined the first, pocking the leather, tearing at the seams.

It took all she had to turn her back on those sharp, busy beaks. Doggedly she began to write.

But then Easy put her wet nose on her neck. "Quit it! Git! Go on, Git! Just git!" She smacked the horse hard on the rump with the flat of her hand and the mare went far enough off for her to set down the following words:

> *Dear Aunt Etta. I am shamed that you shood read*
> *All that is Riten here but At least you will no what*
> *has hapened to me. I hope by the time you get to*
> *this part you will no why I have had to end my life.*
> *I cood not bare to look myself in the eye Inny more.*
> *I love you very much.*
>
> > *Yer loving neece,*
> > *Vanessa Cutter Fane*

Twenty-six

Time moves like a caterpillar on a mirror when all a person has to do is look at the clouds and wait to die. And think. That's what she did most of the time. And what things she thought about! Stuff she never would have conceived of thinking about before. Sin, for example. Would she go to heaven when she died? Or to the other? Or to purgatory?

Maybe that's where she'd end up. Purgatory. Well, at least a person had a shot there. If that person had remorse for their sins.

She didn't have to do any soul searching about that. She had remorse all right. Oh, yeah. Deep and torturing remorse.

Funny but she never once considered killing Trey and Flatt and Ladino a sin before. The sin, it had seemed to her at the time, would have been if she did nothing.

But that was then and this was now. Now, strangely, there was no question in her mind.

She imagined she'd get asked some pretty touchy questions in purgatory—like why—and as she lay there waiting to die she considered and discarded arguments until she finally hit on one that just might work. In her behalf she might honestly say that she had not been able to help herself. Yeah. That ought to work. She would liken herself to a sweet pea on a trellis that once established knew what to do every spring. She'd been trained and given the right conditions, she did what she was supposed to. Yeah. That's good. Real good.

Then she got to thinking that maybe she hadn't been in her right mind. Maybe she'd been insane. Hey, better yet!

Oh, if only she had been crazy! It would take such a load off her mind.

The more she thought about it, the more logical it was. She must've been. Thing was, was she still? How did a crazy person know? It made her head pound. Apparently all this deep thinking called for conclusions that were beyond her ability, because that's how most of her thinking sessions ended . . . with a pounding head. Why it should surprise her she didn't know. She'd never been particularly good at reasoning out things systematically. Just not smart enough, that's all.

One day passed. Then another. Determined, she ignored thirst, hunger, the terrible heat and the pain of remaining in the same position for so long. Several times, in spite of her discomfort she dozed and sometimes she dreamt. Her dreams triggered memories most of which had to do with her mother. When she closed her eyes she could see her mother as she'd once looked: young and comely and so . . . soft. She remembered a time when they were collecting eggs. One of the hens had a new brood of chicks. Her mother picked one up and held it to her face. It poo'ed in her hand but she just laughed. She said to Nessa that she hoped her father got that fox that had been eating the chicks. "There ought to be a place for the gentle things in this world. Someplace where they can feel safe and unafraid."

At the time Nessa had thought that there might be a place in this world for someone like her ma, but it sure wasn't Texas.

She hadn't held her mother in very high regard because she'd considered her to be weak. That had seemed an unforgivable flaw back then. She realized now that she hadn't been at all fair to her mother. Circumstances beyond her control had shaped her until she could not change how she was. Same as herself.

She spent three days up on that ledge. She got hungry and thirsty and hot and dirty but she didn't believe she got any closer to dying than when she started out.

Obviously she was doing something wrong. She tried to remember all she'd ever heard about the Indians. It wasn't much. They just went off by themselves and set their minds on dying. Unfortunately her mind wouldn't stay set.

Part of the problem was that damned horse chomping on grass and nickering. She'd tried pitching rocks at her, but the mare would stand and look at her. Just out of range. Oh, that horse was smart! She supposed she could take her back to town and sell her. And then what? Walk clear back out there? It was all getting so . . . complicated.

She must've got the Indian dying ceremony confused with the vision ceremony because she got a vision early on the fourth day. But there was no hawk or puma or fiery fantasy for her. No, her vision came out of the scattered sunlight leading its horse and dragging one leg.

It had taken a human form, that of Ranger Tom Doubletree.

"Nessa Cutter!"

Shit! She flattened herself against the ground. She
could hear him down there, stomping around. No bones
about it, he was plenty mad.

"I know you're up there in 'em rocks. I see your horse
an' all this stuff here. Now don't make me come up there
an' git ya! Nessa!"

She watched him walk around collecting the things
she'd discarded. Her knife, her rifle, her saddle. Making
a pile. Now he was looking her way and she knew those
bullet eyes were covering every square inch of the rise.
Suddenly he pointed a gloved finger right at her. "I see
you up there, making like a 'gater."

He picked up her saddle and whistled Easy over and
started saddling her. "Come down here, damn it! I do
not want to have to crawl up there!"

"Who ast you to anyway?"

"Don't give me any shit! Jus' git down here an' git
on your horse."

"I ain't going nowhere."

"You're goin' into town."

"No! I ain't."

A long minute went by and then she could hear him
climbing up the ledge. She rolled over and flattened her
back against a rock. Pretty soon a pistol was stuck butt-
first in her face. "Did you throw this gun away?" Silence.
"You got no right to pitch this gun in the bushes back
there. This here is *my* gun 'n' I am very partial to it . . .
Quit it, damnit!" He was trying to haul her up and she
was making herself into a log. "Git! Git up!"

"No!"

"I don't have time to argue with you. That gang across the river is stirred up an' fixin' to ride this way an' you're layin' right in their path."

"Good. It's my fault they're coming. I killed Dobie Flatt. I killed an innocent man."

"You killed an outlaw. A man who needed killin'. Hell, he's killed three men that I know of."

"I'm done with guns."

"Fine. That's the best news I've heard in a long time."

She made her legs mush but he hauled her up by the collar and dragged her down the hill like a dead deer. "You're gonna ride, Nessa Fane. Head up or head down. Makes me no never-mind. But you're ride."

He lifted her onto her horse. She slid to the other side and lay there, a crumpled thing.

"All right, damnit. That does it." He flipped her over and hog-tied her onto her horse. "I'm done messin' with ya!"

"Chingada! Cabrone! Hijo de una puta!" He gave her a stinging slap to her butt and then led her off.

It was a long silent trip. Not that she didn't have some things to say, but it's hard to talk belly-down on a trotting horse. In town he untrussed her and handed her a canteen. She took a long swig and then passed her shirt-sleeve across her mouth. He waited, silent. She walked a few feet to a water trough and splashed the tepid water over her face. She could see his shadow a few feet back and to the left. Suddenly she bolted for her horse, but she didn't get midway across the street before he'd collared her. "Ow!"

"Stand still then."

He clamped her arm to his side. "Where are you takin' me?"

"Into that saloon yonder. . . ."

Saloon! She quit fighting him at that and he walked her inside her first saloon!

It was a narrow room with nothing on the walls. The bar was a short plank of wood laid over two barrels. It looked like an outhouse. Smelled like one too. What, she wondered, is the big to-do about?

Three men stood talking to a meaty bartender with a back that was the span of an axe handle. Two of them were the men from the boardinghouse. The ones who'd told her about Dobie Flatt's death.

All heads turned toward them and the conversation ceased like it had been cut with a knife. She adjusted her hat and retrieved her buckskin jacket, which had been coquettishly hanging off one shoulder.

"Hey, Stash," Doubletree said.

"Well, I'll be damned." The bartender shifted the toothpick in his mouth and smiled, splitting the red hair that covered his face from his eyes to his jaw.

"Hell boys, it's Tom Doubletree! How the hell did you hear about this mess, Cap'n?"

"What mess? I've just rode by to see the elephant."

Elephant! Huh! Is that what stinks? She looked around with rekindled interest, but didn't spot anything strange-looking. She was sorely disappointed; she'd never even seen a picture of one.

"I'm damned glad to see ya." Stash offered his left hand.

Doubletree took it and asked, "What happened to your arm?" It was then that Nessa saw that one of his hairy forearms was so lifeless it could've been wood.

"About got it shot off. Don't know if it'll ever be any

good or not. Either way, I won't be doing any more smithin'."

"That's a damned shame. I don't know of anyone who was better at it." Both men were thinking about the last time they'd seen each other, over in Lampassas.

After Stash reset the shoes on Doubletree's horse, they'd sat outside and shared a hip flask. Stash had had a narrow miss the month before in Dallas when a bank robber put a bullet into a tree about an inch from his head. He said he decided right then that he was going to find some other way to make a living. Doubletree commented that he knew more than most about horses and Stash agreed. "Yeah, a smithy livery combination'd be a real sweet deal," he said. "About the only thing a man'd have to be concerned about was singed eyebrows and an occasional flying hoof."

Now he was pouring drinks for board and a room in the back of a saloon. A bad end, thought Doubletree, for a good man.

Stash made the introductions. "Cap'n Tom Doubletree, say hey to Chet Dobbs. Chet's the owner of this here establishment an' the store next door."

Dobbs was the natty dresser who looked like a tinhorn. He and Doubletree nodded at each other.

"This here's Fritz Mueller, our local law."

Boone's son-in-law was a lean, chinless man with a horseshoe-shaped mustache and a humped nose. He offered Doubletree his free hand as he maintained a death grip on a cane with the other.

Then Stash pointed at a weather-burned man with a young face but white hair. "This here's Vegard from Norway. Got a farm five miles north of here. I still can't pronounce your last name, Vegard."

The man said, "Bjornfeldt. Iss Vegard Bjornfeldt." The Norwegian removed one ham-hand from the front pocket of his bib overalls and shook with Doubletree. "Ve never figure tew hav tur-ble trouble lik dis in Amerika, Lena und me."

"Yeah. Well, we're uh . . . gonna get the trouble handled, mister . . . uh . . . Bjorfeldt."

"Vegard iss gut enuf."

"Vegard, it is."

Everyone finished concentrating on the conversation at the same moment and all eyes turned to her with the sort of scrutiny they'd give something that had just arrived from the moon.

"Oh, yeah." Doubletree pulled her forward. "Boys, this here's my new partner, Fane."

Stash nodded at her but addressed his remark to Doubletree. "Never featured you with no partner."

"New regulation. Austin figured two men're better'n one." To her he said, "Stash here used t'ranger some."

Stash leaned close. "Ah, Cap'n? Maybe you didn't notice but . . . he's a girl!"

"Naw!" Doubletree gave her that simpleton look. "Well, dang me if he isn't! An' here I thought he liked standin' in holes!"

They all got a good laugh outa that. "Har! Har! Har!" She answered his grin with a glare and pulled her arm out of his grasp. Which didn't even slow him down. "Give us a couple to wet our whistles, Stash, an' we'll talk this problem over." Stash filled two shot glasses and Doubletree knuckled one toward her. "Bottom's up, uh . . . Fane." He showed his teeth. She showed hers back and grabbed the glass and threw down . . . hot ground glass, nails and live cinders. Her mouth opened and squared. Her nose and eyes ran and her ears plugged. Doubletree clapped her on the back hard enough to raise dust. That unplugged one ear in time for her to hear Mueller say . . .

". . . damned place attracts scum like stagnant water. Drifters, scalpers, horsethieves, cattle rustlers, part bloods . . ." He looked at Doubletree and his face went white as rice. Its expression said: Shit!

"Go on, Fritz," Stash grinned. "Ol' Doubletree here's been called a lot worse'n a half breed."

"That's a fact." Doubletree allowed. "Go on with it, Mueller."

"Uh, well anyway, it started a couple of months back. Two or three fellas'd come into town, get drunk and raise a moderate amount of hell, shootin' off their guns an' their mouths, terrorizin' the women folk. Stuff like that. We knew they was coming from that ol' abandoned mission across the river but nobody wanted to start anythin' with 'em. Live 'n' let live's the code along the border here."

"Not sayin' that it was the right decision on our part, but we figured as long as it was them ag'in them, what t'hell."

"Then an argument turned into a knifin'. An' then one of their men was found dead back behind the old boardin' house.

"Ol' Miz Turner got her arm broke when two of 'em got in a gunfight right in the middle of the street on a Saturday mornin'."

"Innocent people were gettin' hurt."

Dobbs said, "They've been growin' an' the town's been shrinkin' till now there's a lot more of them than there is of us."

"Yeah," Stash added. "Unfortunately we didn't know that when we got fed up an' rode over there to flush 'em out. That's how Fritz got his leg shot up an' I got my arm busted."

Mueller added, "They're armed an' mean an' have a lot more practice killin' than we do. It's more'n I can handle."

"You can see why they like it here. We're pretty isolated," Chet Dobbs said.

"Any trouble since you made your play?" Doubletree asked.

"They've come over once since the night we crossed the river. They obviously didn't expect much out of us an' they didn't get it," said Stash. "We hid what we didn't want ruint an' waited 'till they left. Shames me t'say it, but it's true."

"That might work our way," Doubletree said. "Maybe they'll ride right in, confident-like and we can take some of the fight out of 'em before they know they're in one." To her, he said, "You want another, Fane? I'm buyin'." She tried to say I'll pass and blew a spit bubble. "Guess not. I believe I'll have one more, Stash."

Boone gimped into the bar then, out of breath and holding his side. "Thar's more'n twenty men ridin' this way. Comin' slow, like they're on their way to a picanik but totin' plenty of fire power . . ."

"We best get ready then." Doubletree tossed off his drink. "How many men here can shoot?"

"Hvat?" Vegard asked Stash.

"Vegard here don't understand English so good."

"I don't care if he speaks Tasmanian. Question is, can he shoot?" He made a pistol with his hand and Vegard understood that. "Ya! Shoot! Ya can shoot! Yew bet!"

"All right. So it looks like we got six countin' . . ."
He looked at Boone. "Uh, what's your name again?"

"Boone," Boone said. "Dan'l Boone."

"Any relation to . . . ?"

"I'm him. That other fella was a dadblamed imposter.
Say, mister? I might jus' mention somethin' about that
thing you left with me."

"My horse?"

"Naw, I'm talkin' about the thing that looks like a dog
but is really a locust."

Two Bites, Nessa thought. He's carted that puppy with
him here.

"Danged thing's chewed through every bit of leather
I got."

"Remind me to make that up to you."

"What about takin' care of it right now? Jus' in case."

Doubletree shook his head and tossed him a coin.
Nessa nudged him and cocked her head toward Boone.
"You aren't gonna include him, are you?"

Doubletree looked at Boone then at her. "Why not?"

"Well, look at him."

Boone realized that he was the object of their attention
and gave a snaggled grin that turned his face into a dried
creek bed. "Yeah! Why not? Hell, I ain't used up yet.
Nosiree. Not by a long shot! Point me at 'em 'n' look
out . . ."

Six against twenty, she thought. Remembering those
scalp hunters she shivered and then looked around at the
men one by one. Stash the one armed ex-ranger. Chet
Dobbs the tinhorn. A one-legged sheriff, Vegard the Vi-
king. Boone, a man in his late nineties and early hundreds—still going on about being half alligator and half
bull. And then there's Doubletree. Bunged up as well.

But, she allowed, worth four men even if cut off at the knees.

"We'll be buckin' the odds," Stash said.

"It won't be the first time," Doubletree replied.

Stash shrugged and nodded, "So, what's the plan, Cap'n?"

"Fire from concealment when they're right about there." He pointed at the street. "If you can't hit the man, hit his horse an' don't quit till it's done."

"Simple enough. Well, put me someplace where I can prop my gun," Stash said.

"Where would you recommend?"

"Top of the saloon'd be good, I guess."

"All right. Boone, you go up with him. Rig somethin' so he can fire his gun without showin' himself."

The batwing doors separated with a bang and admitted a young man. He had an Adam's apple the size of a duck egg and wore a battered hat that was screwed down to his eyes. Nessa knew who he was before Stash said, "That there's John Tigg, Cap'n. The father of a little girl got killed."

"Dat vas a tur-ble ting," Vegard said to no one.

Tigg stepped up and Nessa looked away from his red-lined eyes and determined jaw. In a voice years older than his age, he said, "I want in on whatever you got planned."

Doubletree nodded. "Do you have a rifle?" Yes, he replied and then held up an ancient gun the likes of which Nessa'd never seen.

"I've got some better guns next door," offered Dobbs.

Doubletree turned to the Norwegian. "Vegard?" He stepped up militarily. "Hvat ar yew vuntin' me tew dew?"

"Go with Dobbs. The two of you can hand out guns an' bullets all around."

"Yew bet."

"There's a buckboard down the street. One of you swing it around to the end of town. When the shootin' starts, drive it out into the street to block 'em off. Then get behind it an' fire from there."

"I'll do it," said Tigg.

"All right then." Doubletree put on his hat and ran his fingers down the curl of its brim. "You men'll have to show no mercy. It's brutal and cruel but if you don't nip 'em now, they'll likely come back at you again." He thumb snapped a match. "A lot of men'll most likely meet their fate today. Don't think on that. Just make sure you ain't one of 'em."

Vegard nudged Dobbs and leaned close, "Hvat did he say?"

Dobbs ushered him toward the door. "I'll tell you while we get the guns."

"Should we scatter out on both sides of the street?" Tigg asked.

"No. We'll all find spots on the west side of town. That'll put the sun at our backs and keep us from killin' each other in a cross fire. 'Member t'wait 'till they get beyond Stash up there on the roof before you commence firin'."

Nessa walked to the window and watched everyone hurry into position down the street. After a bit she felt Doubletree's gaze. She imagined that he was thinking about offering her a gun. She faced him. "I don't have it in me any more."

"What?"

A burro brayed at the other end of town. Tigg, trying

to get the buckboard into position. "This . . ." She shook her head and looked at her boots. "I just can't any more."

He stared at her then looked outside. "Listen . . ." His voice was softer. "This fight has to be finished before I can deal with you."

"I understand that you'll have to do your duty. I'm ready."

He took her arm. "Good. In the meantime . . ." He pointed at the boardinghouse. "We'll go make us a little nest over there."

Twenty-seven

They did just that, but first they stopped at the store where he selected a rifle, a carbine and a Paterson Colt. At the boardinghouse he turned a table on end and used it to block the bottom half of the window. Then he pulled another table over and arranged his weaponry on it. Then he loaded his guns and filled his belt loops. And then they waited. He sat on the floor with one arm on his raised knee. She stood at the door and looked out into the shimmering heat. A weed rolled slowly by and from across the way came the creak of the saloon's wind swung sign. "The wind's come up," she said. He grunted a reply. She looked back at him, a shadowy hulk after the glare outside and saw his twirly glow briefly before he flicked it away. Without the right words, she looked outside again.

A droning blow fly thudded on a pane of glass and from somewhere came the faint tinkling of a bell. Soon she saw a goat, slowly walking down the far side of the street. Doubletree saw it, too. He straightened and muttered a curse. At that moment a boy—five, maybe six— tore out of nowhere and grabbed the goat's rope. The goat set its hind legs and Doubletree cursed again but the boy tugged the goat down the alley and disappeared. Doubletree settled back and the silence descended again.

After a few minutes, he spoke. "You sure you want to stick around for this?" She shrugged. "Ain't gonna be pretty." She shrugged again. "Well, suit yourself. Once it starts I want you to stand over there . . ." He pointed. ". . . behind that door."

"What am I supposed to do there?"

"I don't care. Stand there and look mean if you want. Play pat-a-cake. Whatever. Unless you've changed your mind?"

She walked to the door and turned to face him and her hands hung big and empty on the ends of her arms.

He took off his hat and fingercombed his hair then rocked his hat to reseat it. "Should something untoward occur here I know you'll have the good sense to get out of town. Your horse is hobbled about one half mile east along the river." She didn't respond. "Well," Leather creaked as he stood. "I guess they're comin'."

She went rigid, listening, and soon she heard the sound of hoofs thudding on hard ground. A minute more and she saw them. They rode in two and three abreast, carelessly holding their carbines across the bows of their saddles. Los Mataderos. Foul. Ragged. Hairy. Mean eyes looking everywhere, but seeing only the empty street, the locked doors and the boarded windows.

She spotted Flatt, riding round-shouldered in the middle of the crowd and looking smaller and older than she remembered. Or was that her imagination?

The last of them were even with the window—and Stash on the roof—when the universe exploded.

The noise must've knocked her to her knees because that's how she found herself, on her knees, holding her ears. The air was filled with gunfire as rifles cracked and bullets whistled and whined. She crawled to the window and peered over the ledge. Men yelled and horses screamed and milled around throwing dust everywhere. Boone tumbled out of the hayloft but then she saw him move and next time she looked he was crawling off amid tiny puffs of dust. She ducked as wood splintered above her head. In spite of trying to die for three days she did not put herself in the path of a bullet, a telling thing when she thought about it later.

Tigg's wagon blocked one end of the road. Downed men and horses obstructed the other end and like they'd been told, the townsmen were making every shot count. One by one the renegades were going down. A bearded man tried to ride his horse into the boardinghouse but Doubletree took dead aim and the man pitched head first onto the boardwalk.

She was so taken with what was happening on the street that she didn't see the two men who'd come in from the back until they were level with her. But with their narrowed eyes glued on Doubletree, they apparently hadn't seen her either! As one, they raised their pistols and she launched herself at them. Though she ruined one's aim and threw the other one off as well she heard Doubletree grunt in pain. Then she saw that he was on one knee with his gun raised and realized that he was worried about hitting her. She threw herself aside and he fired and the man was dead before he hit the floor. She scooped up the dead man's gun and as the other man tried to rise she jammed the barrel into his neck and pulled the trigger. Then she ran to Doubletree. A dribble of blood stained one side of his face. "All right?"

He was tying his neck hanky around an inch-long graze on his left temple. "Yeah. Get back over there." But she'd already moved to the window and was firing into the mass out on the street. Soon he was kneeling beside her, firing as well.

The whole thing didn't last more than two minutes, probably the longest two minutes in the history of mankind. Only about a handful of men survived and they hightailed it out of town, riding hell-bent and firing wild over their shoulders.

Tigg and Mueller ran into the street and one of them caught the last renegade in the back. He wallowed on his horse but did not fall and the horse kept up with the pack.

Doubletree was hard-eyeing her as he walked toward her. She lifted her arms. "I'm not hit."

"Don't press your luck, lady. The day's still young."

Shaken as she was, he could still rankle her. Especially when he didn't care if he did. She followed him outside.

Men lay in the street moaning or unmoving. Powder smoke and dust hung over everything. After reloading, Doubletree walked around all the downed men putting a bullet into those that moved when kicked. One of the men he rolled over was Caleb Flatt. A worm of blood ran out of the side of his mouth and when Nessa came closer she saw that he'd caught a bullet square between the brows.

Dobbs, Vegard and Mueller were unscathed. Tigg had a flesh wound on his leg. Boone had a new part in his hair—of which he was very proud. The only one unaccounted for was Stash, who had not come down from the saloon roof. Vegard crawled up and then called down that Stash was dead. Dobbs went up to help bring him down and then he was laid in the street and covered with a blanket.

Mueller and Vegard stood looking at the jumble of

bodies and dead horses. "Vat a mess!" Mueller sucked his eye tooth and shook his head, apparently struck speechless.

"We could move the town easier'n we can bury all them," said Dobbs.

"Hvat dew yew tink ve should dew?" Vegard asked Doubletree.

"Tie a rope and drag 'em off a ways," said Doubletree, reloading once again. "That's about all the choice you got."

"What about that gulley north of town? asked Tigg. "Maybe we could roll 'em in there and then cover 'em up."

"The wind comes from that direction," Mueller commented.

"You got a better idea?"

The four men stood there a minute. "No. Guess not."

"I go get my big horses," Vegard said. "Und I tink I vil tell Lena ta kum tew."

"You figure the rest of 'em will come back?" Mueller asked Doubletree.

"I don't reckon they will, but I'll send word to Del Rio. The major'll send some boys over to tidy up whoever's left."

"Thank you, Cap'n." Tigg offered his hand. "We . . . my wife an' me're . . . much obliged."

"C'mon, Tigg," said Boone kindly. "We best get busy."

Nessa and Doubletree were suddenly left standing alone. She'd been dreading this moment, not because she might have to go to jail but because she might lose him. The thought made her skin clammy. Sorrowfully she thought of her aunt and how she'd been alone all her life because she'd loved and lost the only man for her. What happened next meant the difference between having a happy life and living a lonely existence. If only he would forgive her . . .

She held out crossed wrists but he ignored them and took out his makings. He rolled a twirly, licked it into shape and struck a match on his boot and lit it, all without saying a word to her. Just that quick she knew that he still loved her. That he was always going to love her. He wanted her, too. Real bad and right now. Oh, yeah. Desire was rolling off him like heat off a wood stove. She lowered her arms and tried not to smirk. "You forgive me then?"

"Forgive you for what?"

"For tryin' to keep you from ridin'."

"What?" She pointed at his leg. "Oh, that!" He snorted. "Hell, I've had worse scars on my eyeball. However, I will say this . . ." He pointed his smoke at her. "If I ever find myself on the wrong end of your gun ag'in, I'll . . ."

"I wouldn't say nothing if you was to whip the livin' daylights outa me."

"Huh? Oh. Well. That might not be necessary . . ." Vegard and a rawboned woman had arrived at the end of the road. Vegard jumped down and the woman neatly maneuvered the team until the wagon was next to two dead bodies. Doubletree ground out his smoke. ". . . if you're willin' t'pay a fine."

"Fine?" She couldn't help smirking then. She knew his mind. She dirty-walked a bit closer. "What kinda fine?"

He nodded in the general direction of Caleb Flatt's body. "You owe me one ranch, lady."

* * *

"Follow me," I said, "and I'll show you the prettiest ranch in Texas." "If I'm followin' you," he said, "it ain't likely That I'll be lookin' at no ranch," With that he grabbed my but with both hands. I kist him then and I gave it all I had. Nocked his hat off, hooked my leg around his, rubbed him like he was tarnished silver. "Well?" I said, "You gonna follow me or not?"

"Lady," he whispered, "I wood follow you t'hellan-gone."

Epilogue

Becky Doubletree stood on the front porch watering the honeysuckle bush. She glanced toward the river and then stepped out from behind the bush. Shoot! She'd forgot about Gran'ma! She walked to the screen and shaded her eyes. "That you, Wind?"

"Sí?"

"Is there any lemonade left?"

"Sí."

"Can I get a glass for Gran'ma?"

"Sí! 'Momento."

Becky planted her hands on the rail and looked toward the river. Strange that Gran'ma wanted to go through her things today. She generally shied away from reminders of the past. Wind said it was because it saddened her so. Poor Gran'ma. Alone all these years.

Becky'd never known her Great-Gran'pa Doubletree. Kyle said he remembered him but just barely. He'd been a Texas Ranger before they married. There was an old tintype of him somewhere—she hadn't seen it for years— in which he looked more like a desperado than a lawman. Glaring out of the picture with bore-a-hole-through-a-rock eyes, he'd been leaning slightly forward as if facing a strong wind. Wind said he was holding their son, the one that had died before he walked.

Becky had asked Gran'ma about him once. It was for Heritage Day at school. Their assignment was to pick a relation and recount a short story about their life. Gran'ma got an odd look on her face and then she'd started to chuckle! Pretty soon she was laughing so hard Becky thought she'd split her dress! It went on for a time. Finally she said, "Why, Becky, your great-gran'pa was just a common man who was uncommonly lucky. An' . . . an' . . . a helluva good fandango dancer." And there she went. Off again.

A serious child at the time, Becky had turned an unsympathetic back to her great grandmother's frivolity, gathered her notebook and left in a huff. Gran'ma sought her out later. Apologetically she asked if she wanted her to continue telling her about her great-gran'pa. Becky said, "No, thank you kindly." She'd decided to write about her father—who had been a member of the governor's cabinet and who had helped establish the regulatory board for Texas banking statewide.

Wind came out with the glass. "Thanks, Wind." She pointed. "Look at Gran'ma. All scrunched up."

"Poor ol' thing. She's dropped off again. She does that all the time now."

Becky sighed. "I don't see how she can sleep like that. Oh, Wind, what are we going to do?"

"I don't know." Sadly. "I don't."

"She was crying again last night. I tapped on the door and asked if she was all right. She said she was but her voice was all wet and strangled."

"It's so sad!"

"The other day I caught her clear over there." Becky pointed again, now toward the barn. "She had found some ol' bucket and was hot-footin' it toward the south

pasture. I said, 'Gran'ma! Where on earth are you going?' She looked at me—I could tell she didn't know me
from the way she was cutting her eyes this way and
that—and she says, 'Why, I'm goin' t'milk Jude.'

" 'Jude?' I said. 'Who's Jude?'

" 'The cow' ," she answers. 'She ought to be in that
pasture right there.'

" 'Gran'ma, you've got about seventy-leven cows in
that pasture.'

" 'Huh!' she says and shuffles her feet a minute. 'Seventy-leven, you say?'

" 'Yep,' I said.

"Well, then!' she says, 'I expect I better get at it!' "
They laughed together and something white—a bit of
paper maybe—skittered across the grass then rolled to a
stop against the gallery steps.

"What's that, Wind?"

"No sé."

Another piece of paper had just reached the river and
set sail like a child's toy boat. Becky glanced around.
"Why, look! They're everywhere!" Stuck in the mock
orange, clinging to the day lilies, decorating the del-
phinums.

"Who threw trash in the yard?" Wind asked angrily.
Bent on interception, she scurried down the stairs, stepped
on a ragged bit of paper, picked it up, read a minute and
then cried, "Aiii! Señorita! Mira!"

Becky hurried down the stairs. Wind thrust the paper
at her. It was a page torn out of something. Weather-
spotted and ragged.

. . . *sweat stung my kuts* . . . Becky recognized the
cramped writing. "It's Gran'ma's writin'." She ran across
the lawn, picking up bits of paper as she went. "My

stars! She's gone and lost all her papers! Why, way the wind's kicked up these papers will be in Chihuahua by sundown."

A loud boom stopped them both. They looked at each other. Becky said, "I thought that stump remover was finished."

"Sí. He is long gone."

And as one they looked at the small figure facing the river. The thin gray hair hanging in a fall . . . "Oh, God, Wind, you don't suppose . . ." They picked up their skirts and ran, Becky in the lead. Suddenly she grabbed Wind's arm. "Wind!"

Froze statue-like, "Sí?"

"Run back quick and call Doc Lockert!"

Becky ran on, praying she wasn't too late.

Almost there she saw a rawhide vest slip to the ground. From within its fold fell an old gun. Smoke rose straight from its barrel, as if it were a windless day.

If you liked *While the Rivers Run,* turn the page for a taste of Wynema McGowan's next thrilling Western— *Beyond the River,* coming in July 1997 from Pinnacle Books.

It was murder out there. . . .

A wave of Indians came toward them. Suddenly a horseman spurted out of the throng and into the lead. A.A. Bickman pressed his cheek to his rifle, but then he held up. "Hell, that's a white man!"

Bullets and arrows hummed uncomfortably close as Amy Kay crouched behind Mr. Bickman and watched the man ride toward the station. Ten or fifteen Comanches were right behind him.

Mr. Bickman and Mr. Hudman moved from behind cover and stood side by side and fearlessly fired on the Indians that were hot on the man's trail. Mud clots flew as the rider raced under a hail of bullets and arrows. Suddenly the man slued around in the saddle, firing his sidearm and hanging by his thigh. To Amy Kay it was amazing that he could ride like that, much less fire.

"Rides like a damn Comanch'!" A. A. no sooner finished saying that than the man's horse was shot out from under him. Somehow he hit the ground running and had freed his rifle from its scabbard. He spun, went to one knee and shot two Indians just that fast. Then he was up, running again, this way and that. Water and dirt jumped all around him.

"I'll be damned!" Lame Dick stopped shooting to stare narrowed eyed at the man. "That there's Nate Doubletree, A. A." He pointed. "Get ready to open that door, girl."

Amy Kay assumed that meant her since she was closest. Setting Jeremy on his feet, she hastened to do as Mr. Hudman commanded. A. A. and Lame Dick were steadily firing again.

Footsteps hit the porch on a run and Amy Kay threw the door open. Two pursuing Indians went down within yards of the building. One rose again only to be shot by A. A. The others were divided by the continued firing of Julio and Lame Dick and soon retreated. Bodies of dead men and ponies dotted the ground behind them.

The man leaned back against the door, breathing hard but grinning. "Hell of a welcoming party, you all!"

Be sure to watch for, Beyond the River, *by Wynema McGowan, arriving in stores everywhere in July, 1997.*

About the Author

The author is a native Texan, born in San Angelo, and raised in Waco and Forth Worth. Her paternal great grandmother was Cherokee Indian.

**If you liked this book, be sure to look for others
in the *Denise Little Presents* line:**